DEATH DRIVES A SEMI

DEATH DRIVES A SEMI

25TH ANNIVERSARY EDITION

EDO VAN BELKOM

STARK

PUBLISHING

Stark Publishing
October 2023

The original version of *Death Drives a Semi* was published in
1998 by Quarry Press.

Death Drives a Semi / Edo van Belkom – 1st ed
Casebound Hardcover ISBN: 978-1-7390474-1-2
Trade Paperback ISBN: 978-1-7390474-0-5
eBook ISBN: 978-1-989351-99-4

Contents

Acknowledgements

I am deeply indebted to Robert J. Sawyer for writing the introduction to this book and more importantly, for being a friend that I could always count on.

I owe thanks to Judith Merril for giving me a tough, honest assessment of my work (the first person to do so) and for pointing me in the direction of people I could learn from.

Thanks to Peter Straub, Ed Gorman, Joe R. Lansdale, Andrew Weiner, Terence M. Green, and Matthew J. Costello for saying kind things about my work and for treating me as a peer, even though I feel I have no right to be one.

And thanks to Bob Hilderley and Susan Hannah at Quarry Press for taking a chance on publishing something, "commercial," and to Mark Lefebvre of Stark Publishing for believing in the book enough to give it a second chance at life after 25 years.

And thanks too, to Jeff Davis, who said yes to another teen werewolf novel and who has been nothing but a gentleman and friend from the start.

"The Rug," copyright 1997 by Edo van Belkom, first appeared in *Robert Bloch's Psychos*. It was reprinted in *Crossing the Line* edited by Robert J. Sawyer and David Skene Melvin. It also appeared in the audio CD *Fears for Ears: Anthology of Horror Fiction* produced by Aida Memisevic, and produced by Positive Living Productions, 1999.

"But Somebody's Got to Do it" copyright 2023 by Edo van Belkom is original to this collection, first appearing in the 1997 original edition of *Death Drives a Semi*.

"Death Drives a Semi," copyright 1995 by Edo van Belkom, first appeared in *RPM Magazine*, Volume 4, No. 7.

"The Basement," copyright 1990 by Edo van Belkom, first appeared in *On Spec*, Volume 2, No. 2.

"Mother and Child," copyright 1994 by Edo van Belkom, first appeared in *Gathering Darkness*, March/April 1994.

"Mark of the Beast," copyright 1992 by Edo van Belkom, first appeared in *Northern Frights*.

"Scream String," copyright 1994 by Edo van Belkom, first appeared in *Shock Rock 2*.

"SPS," copyright 1993 by Edo van Belkom, first appeared in *Tails of Wonder*, Issue No. 1.

"The Cold," copyright 1994 by Edo van Belkom, first appeared in *Northern Frights 2*.

"Blood Count," copyright 1996 by Edo van Belkom, first appeared in *Storyteller: Canada's Short Story Magazine*, Volume 3, Issue 3.

"Ice Bridge," copyright 1997 by Edo van Belkom, first appeared in *Northern Frights 4*.

"The Piano Player Has No Fingers," copyright 1996 by Edo van Belkom, first appeared in *Palace Corbie #7 (The Piano Player Has No Fingers)*.

"And Injustice for Some" and "On the writing of And Injustice for Some," copyright 1995 by Edo van Belkom, first appeared in *The Iguana Informer*, Issue No. 21. They were reprinted in *Alouette: The Newsletter of the Canadian Region of SFWA*, Issue No. 10, *Midnight Journeys*, and *Northwords*, Spring 1996 issue.

For my wife, Roberta

About This 25th Anniversary Edition

The original version of *Death Drives a Semi* was published in 1998 by Quarry Press from Kingston, Ontario.

This special 25th Anniversary edition from Stark Publishing, released October 2023 contains all the original content of that volume, plus an updated introduction from Robert J. Sawyer, acknowledgements, behind-the-scenes story notes from the author written specifically for this edition, and an additional short story.

Introduction

First, the name: Edo. It rhymes with Laredo (or, as he has recently taken to telling people, since apparently that Texas city is unfamiliar to many of his fellow Canadians, it rhymes with potato).

#

Second, the man: he's sixty-one, bearded, a Torontonian by birth, of mixed Dutch and Italian descent.

He grew up in a blue-collar family in an ethnically mixed suburb—a crucible that's given him an excellent ear for accents. When he met science-fiction author George Zebrowski for the first time, he made a friend for life by pronouncing his name correctly—"Hor-gay Zhebrovskee." Edo's also a devastating mimic, doing impressions of not just TV and movie stars, but writers and other publishing types, as well.

Edo's degree is in Creative Writing from Toronto's York University, and there's an irony in that: he is the most practical, down-to-earth wordsmith I've ever met. His constant challenging of classmates' opinions in his final workshop course (most often by exclaiming, "That's not the way it works in the real world!") made him less than popular.

But it's an attitude that's served him well. Although he's worked as a police and sports reporter, Edo made the leap from first sale to full-time fiction writer in less than two years, and he continued in that role for a couple of decades. In many ways, he was the ideal of what used

11

to be called, back when the term wasn't disparaging, a pulp writer—he wrote stories quickly, often to a given editor's specification, always producing a quality, salable product on time.

And, of course, it came full circle. Edo taught many different writing courses in and around Toronto, has done online tutoring in fiction writing, and has lectured on writing at the University of Toronto and Toronto Metropolitan University. What distinguished Edo's writing courses from most others (including the ones he himself once took) was his no-bull, sales-oriented approach.

What else can we say about Edo? Well, even as the years pile up, he's stayed far thinner than a man who refers to eating as "snarfling" has any right to be. He collects beer cans. When eating at home, his favorite meal is spaghetti; when eating out it's a burger and fries—which he'll try to order, no matter how classy the restaurant is. Edo is husband to Roberta and father to a grown son named Luke.

#

Third, the career: Edo van Belkom's fiction career started with "Baseball Memories" in 1991. Its initial publication venue was about as obscure as it gets: *Aethlon: The Journal of Sports Literature*, put out by East Tennessee State University. But Edo wasn't to dwell in obscurity for long. Karl Edward Wagner picked up "Baseball Memories" for the twentieth annual *Year's Best Horror Stories* collection.

After that, honors seemed to come Edo's way on an almost daily basis. "Baseball Memories" was shortlisted for the Aurora Award, Canada's top honor in science fiction and fantasy writing. Another story, "The Piano Player Has No Fingers" was shortlisted not just for the Aurora but also for the Crime Writers of Canada's Arthur Ellis Award for Best Short Story of the Year. And his "The Rug" was also an Arthur Ellis Award finalist.

And then the biggie: in June 1998, Edo van Belkom and his collaborator Dave Nickle won the Horror Writers Association's Bram Stoker Award, the world's top honor in the dark-fantasy field. Edo was no longer and up-and-comer; he was, overnight, one of his chosen field's top, bankable names.

We all knew that such stature was inevitable. Back in 1992, when Don Hutchison was launching his prestigious hardcover line of Canadian dark-fantasy anthologies, *Northern Frights*, he came to Edo to produce a story to go with the cover painting he'd already bought ("Mark of the Beast").

And early on, Edo was quickly made a contributing editor of the *Bulletin* of the Science Fiction and Fantasy Writers of America, and Canadian membership representative for the Horror Writers Association.

For many years, Edo kept selling stories at a fantastic rate, to markets big and small—stories that were tight and polished and rang true even when they were about incredible things, stories that sent shivers down the reader's spine, or outraged us, or sometimes made us laugh. Stories that were real stories, old-fashioned stories, stories with beginnings and middles and ends ("plot-optional" is Edo's favorite derisive adjective for certain writers' output). Stories with characters we care about and points to make and language used so elegantly as to be all but invisible.

Still, despite all the fun he was having as a horror writer, being a full-time wordsmith has always been financially dicey. Although Edo's wife Roberta had a good job as a librarian, they both decided some years back that it was time for a change: he joined the Peel Regional Police as a prisoner escort officer, and Robi became a bylaw-enforcement officer with the city of Brampton (which is where they live, northwest of Toronto). Shortly, they'll each have put in their time and will retire from their demanding jobs with good pensions.

Will Edo return to full-time fiction writing then? He says no, but I have my doubts. Despite the standard horror-story template being that bad things happen to good people, sometimes the real world is much kinder, and in 2022 a miracle occurred: out of the blue, Paramount Plus bought television rights to Edo's 2004 young-adult novel *Wolf Pack* (which had previously won both Canada's Aurora Award and the Ontario Library Association's Silver Birch Award) and turned it into a hit TV series starring Sarah Michelle Geller. Although always a bit curmudgeonly, and perhaps even a tad more so as the years have gone by, suddenly our man whose name rhymes with both Laredo and Potato is back in the spotlight, and, as one who has known and loved him for a third of a century now, I can say I've never seen him be happier. I don't think it'll be long before he feels the urge to pound the keyboard again.

#

Edo's stories are always good reading, but classifying them is hard. Is he an SF writer? Sometimes. A horror writer? Often. Fantasy? When the mood struck him. Erotica? Yes, that too! Amongst the pieces in this collection, his "Baseball Memories" and "S.P.S." are science fiction, of the *Twilight Zone* sort. "Mark of the Beast" and "Blood Count" are werewolf and vampire tales respectively—each with a new twist, of course. And the "Ice Bridge" and "The Piano Player Has No Fingers" have no fantastic elements at all, which makes their horrors all the more chilling.

Edo's work reminds one of Ray Bradbury, of Dennis Etchison, of Richard Matheson, of Stephen King, of Rod Serling. He takes on writing voices and genres with the same facility with which he adopts accents or does impressions. He has tried his hand at everything, failed at nothing, and always delighted his readers, of which you are now one! Buckle up! You're in for a hell of a ride!

—Robert J. Sawyer

Robert J. Sawyer's *Hominids* won the Hugo Award for Best Novel of the Year; his latest novel is *The Oppenheimer Alternative.*

Note from the Author

From a very early age I knew I wanted to be a writer. I'm not sure why that is exactly, but there was always something about the way others put words together that fascinated me and made me want to try it too.

The trouble in those early years was that I didn't know what kind of writer I wanted to be. I tried a serial story in the high school newspaper about a fictional Grade 9 student, did a kind of screenplay for the film club, and also hosted my high school's Variety Night, writing a skit and the bits I would perform in between acts. Later on I tried poetry, which was terrible, and then rock and roll songs. Trouble with those were, we liked the word, Baby... a lot and it wound up being half the song. Baby! Baby! Baby!

So, while I wanted to be a writer, I hadn't found my way.

That all changed on a rainy day at the family cottage. I spent the day indoors on the bottom bunk reading *The October Country*, by Ray Bradbury. Every story excited me in a way nothing had before. After reading one story and exclaiming, "Wow!" I moved onto the next hoping to be similarly satisfied. And I was. Every story in there made me want to read the next, and more importantly, made me want to write the same kind of stories for others where the reader would end up thrilled and amazed.

Such a tall order for a teenager. But plenty of people had written these kinds of stories, why couldn't I be one of them?

There were plenty of reasons... First of all, I had never really been a good student. Sure, I'd passed all my courses and done enough to get a middling C throughout my academic career, but I'd never applied myself and strived for more. (I will note that my teachers always told my parents I was capable of more if I applied myself. I denied it was possible every time, but maybe they'd been right.)

Anyway, the problem with wanting to write stories like Ray Bradbury is that there were likely hundreds, if not thousands of people who wanted that very same thing for themselves. That meant that if I wanted to succeed, I would have to work harder at it than anything else I'd ever tried in my life. So, while I took a degree in Creative Writing from York University in Toronto, I also began to work for the school's newspaper, first as a reporter, and later as the sports editor, filling numerous pages every week with copy on a deadline.

And I began reading. I was always a pretty good reader, but now I was voracious, always walking around with books in my pants pockets so I could do some reading whenever there was a spare moment. I read in the genres I wanted to write in, and both great books and bad books. My thought was that if I could recognize what bad writing looked like, I might be able to avoid committing it myself. I also read non-fiction and newspapers and magazines as a writer shouldn't just be well-read in genre, but have a good general knowledge of other people's lives and how the world works around them. I even read books about the art and process of writing in the hopes I could learn technique as well.

I also wrote. Of course, I wrote stories, but I continued my journey as a newspaper reporter and began to write copy at a tremendous rate. Most by now have heard of Malcolm Gladwell's theory of 10,000 hours which states that it takes roughly 10,000 hours of deliberate practice to become world class in any field of endeavor. Now, one can argue whether or not I achieved world class level of expertise in the writing field, but I can assure you that I did well over 10,000 hours of writing practice while working at the small newspapers, The Brampton Times, The North York Mirror and The Cambridge Reporter.

Small newspapers are voracious, and I wrote dozens of stories per week for the newspaper while simultaneously writing short stories and novels of my own. In fact, my very first short story publication, "Baseball Memories" was written on the computers at *The Brampton Times* newspaper. (Interesting note: These were first generation computers and had a switch underneath the keyboard that when turned on, would simulate the sound of a typewriter, as the theory was that people needed to hear the *clickety clack* of the keys while typing or they wouldn't be able to cope.)

That story was eventually printed in a literary magazine, *Aethlon: the Journal of Sports Literature*, at East Tennessee State University. From there it was reprinted in *Year's Best Horror Stories XX*, edited by Karl Edward Wagner.

So, my first story made it into a Year's Best anthology.

It's like hitting a homerun at your very first major league at bat. The problem is that hitting a homerun is a very difficult thing to do, and so is getting a story into a Year's Best collection. Never mind that, it's hard just to get another story published. And so I began to get rejected and accepted at a ratio that was hard to take. I remember giving talks about "Thriving on Rejection" in which I would talk about getting rejected fifty times in a year and selling two stories.

But I kept working at it with laser focus.

In my talks to aspiring writers I would often talk about the three ingredients necessary for eventual success. They are talent, luck and perseverance. The truth is, you can often succeed with just two of the three, which means if you lack talent, you can persevere and get lucky, and if you're never lucky you can continue to persevere and your talent will get you there eventually. Obviously, the most important element of the three is perseverance because it's the only one you have control over.

And so I continued to work hard at my writing and things eventually happened.

I wrote a bunch of novels that never went anywhere, but because of my strong short story work I was asked by a role-playing game company to write a novel based on one of their games. And so I wrote and published my first novel *Wyrm Wolf*, which turned into three more RPG based novels.

And because of the stories I wrote, my agent, Joshua Bilmes contacted me to ask if I was being represented by anyone. I wasn't, but rather than just agree to be represented by his agency, I asked him to read my novel *Teeth* and if he agreed to represent it then yes, he could be my agent. He took on *Teeth*, and began to negotiate the RPG novels and some five years later managed to get *Teeth* published.

So, yeah, hard work and perseverance.

But back to *Death Drives a Semi*.

It took about ten years to publish enough quality stories to make a book like this, but once I had the stories, I couldn't have been prouder to put them all together in one place.

This is my *October Country*, the book I am most proud of and the book I most wanted to write when I decided on that career path so many years ago.

And now, in 2023, the book is being reprinted in a 25th anniversary edition, with all the bells and whistles a milestone like this should have to adorn it: updated cover art and introduction, an author's introduction, story notes, and a bonus story that I think is one of my best.

If the original publication of *Death Drives a Semi* was a benchmark moment in my career as a writer, then this edition feels like being inducted into the Hall of Fame.

I only hope that in reading this book, you experience some of the joy I felt in writing it.

All the best,
Edo van Belkom

The Original Cover

EDO VAN BELKOM

Bram Stoker Award Winner

"An entirely nasty book"
— Peter Straub

"This is one hell of a good book"
— Ed Gorman

"Worthy of the young Stephen King"
— The Magazine of Fantasy and Science Fiction

DEATH DRIVES A SEMI

Introduction by Robert J. Sawyer

Original Author Photo – 1998

Updated Author Photo - 2023

Photos by Roberta DiMaio.

DEATH
DRIVES
A SEMI

The Rug

Edna Dowell swept the floor, resting on the end of her broom almost as often as she passed its bristles over the shiny wooden floorboards. She was an old woman on the downside of seventy and more than a little senile, but still sprightly enough to clean the house by herself. It took her longer to do the job than it used to, but by stringing together enough spurts of energy she could usually get it all done in a day.

After a short break she swept the remaining corners of the living room and then passed the broom around the legs of the couch and end table, bringing a small pile of dirt and dust toward the much larger pile in the middle of the floor. That done, she took another moment to catch her breath.

The house was run-down, but clean. Old, mended and recovered furniture was scattered about the room—as mismatched a collection as you might expect from someone who did much of her shopping on garbage day. Each piece had a character all its own, from the chesterfield she'd picked up behind the bowling alley to the chairs in the hall that used to sit in the laundromat, from the pictures of other people's families hanging on the wall to the bookcases full of books she'd never read.

And then there was the big oval rug she'd found behind the funeral parlor two blocks over. The design on it was quite faded, but there wasn't a hole or worn spot to look at. A true wonder of a find, in more ways than one.

Edna's breathing finally eased into a regular rhythm and she knelt down on the floor. Then, lifting up the edge of the rug, she swept the dirt underneath it. The dust swirled toward the rug as if being sucked in by an unseen wind and settled onto the floorboards in a scattered pile. With a satisfied nod, Edna lowered the edge of the rug back onto the floor. There was a slight bulge in it now, but she paid it no mind. In a week or two, when she felt up to cleaning again, the bulge would be gone . . . as would the dirt beneath it.

The first time she'd swept the dirt under the rug was on the day she'd first brought the rug home two years ago. Just as she was finishing up her cleaning there'd been a knock at the door. With nowhere else to sweep the dirt she quickly swept it under the rug and tossed the broom in the closet.

Her guests that day had stayed for hours, and it was a whole week before she remembered what she'd done with the dirt. But, when she pulled back the rug to sweep it up and take it out to the trash she was surprised to find it gone. Not just spread around or absorbed by the rug's fibers, but gone without a trace. After that she swept dirt under different parts of the rug to see if it would happen again—and it did. In time she learned to sweep everything under the rug, and it eventually became as much a part of her cleaning routine as Misters Murphy and Clean.

Unfortunately, not all of her little problems could be handled so easily. The current problem, or perhaps just the latest incarnation of a constant problem, had to do with money, or lack thereof.

Three years ago her pension had been de indexed and no longer kept pace with the cost of living. Then, last year, her rent had gone up three percent, the maximum amount allowed by the government's rent control board. She'd made up the difference with what little savings she'd squirreled away over the years, but that was all but gone now. She wasn't sure if she was one month behind in her rent or two, but what did it matter? She only had enough money for groceries and she'd be damned if she'd go hungry while giving that do-nothing slumlord another red cent.

He'll be coming around soon enough asking for his money, she thought. He can ask all he wants, but I can't give him what I don't have. He can threaten to throw me out too, but I won't move. He might own this house, but this is my *home*.

She patted the bulge in the rug; it shifted slightly under her touch.

#

The knock on the door didn't surprise her; she'd been expecting it for some time. She hadn't paid her rent in months and her landlord was anything but patient. As if on cue, the knocking grew louder and more frantic as the man on the other side pounded harder on the old wooden door.

Edna slowly got up from her chair in the living room and began shuffling her way to the door. "I'm coming, I'm coming," she said in a voice that was barely a whisper.

"I know you're in there Dowell," the man shouted. "I seen you pick up your mail."

When she reached the door she paused for a moment's rest, then unlocked and pulled the door open.

Marty Genetti was a squat Italian man with a full head of black hair that was always blow dried straight back in the shape of a cycling helmet. Although he was probably in his fifties, he still looked like the teenage hoodlum he'd been over thirty years ago. "I come for the rent," he said.

"And a good morning to you too, Mr. Genetti," said Edna. "Yeah, it's a great morning, but it would be even better if you had the rent money you owe me."

"I haven't got it."

Marty just shook his head. "That's crap. I know for a fact that the pension checks went out today and you already took in your mail."

"Well, the check wasn't in the mail," she lied. She couldn't possibly turn over her pension check. There'd be nothing left for her to live on.

"Nice try, Dowell. But never bullshit a bullshitter. You got your check today and you're going to give it to me or I'll boot you out. I got six families practically begging me to live here."

"I don't have it," she said, her voice beginning to crack.

"Fuck this," Marty muttered, barging his way into the house. "Where did you put the mail? In the living room?" He walked into the large room off the hallway and began to look for envelopes. There were a few Christmas cards on the window sills, but they'd been there for years. "What about the kitchen?"

"No!" Edna cried. She'd put the mail in the pantry, but it wasn't very well hidden and he'd find it there as soon as he looked.

He went into the kitchen, Edna following as fast as her feet could take her.

"What's with all the cookie tins? That where you keep your stash?" He started taking the tins off the shelf and opening them one by one.

Edna did keep some bills and a few coins in a couple of the tins, but that was emergency money for doctor's visits and medicine. If he took that she'd literally be without a penny to her name.

"Stop it!" she shouted. "Stop!"

"Oh, am I getting warm?" he laughed, almost as if he was enjoying his little act of terrorism.

"Please, stop!" she pleaded again, but her words only spurred him on.

He found a Christie's tin with some money in it. "All right," he said. "This is a start . . . Let's see what else we can find."

Edna began trembling in frustration and anger. If he kept on like this he was bound to find her pension check and then she'd be left with nothing. She had to do something, but what?

"Heh hey! Here's a twenty," he said, looking more and more like a neighborhood bully shaking down kids for candies.

Edna glanced at the kitchen counter. Her rolling pin was there, a chipped and cracked rolling pin made out of marble she'd found years ago in a dumpster behind the Commisso Brothers Italian Brobert Bloakery. She stared at the rolling pin for what seemed like forever, then finally picked it up . . .

"You gotta have a piggy bank here somewhere."

. . . raised it over her head . . .

"Or maybe a roll of pennies—"
. . . and let it fall.

#

Marty Genetti stared up at Edna, his green eyes bulging out of their sockets in a look of surprise and one side of his head crumpled up like a squashed paper bag. His fingers were closed tight around the money—Edna's money—but that didn't stop her from cracking his fingers open and prying the bills from his fists. After she'd picked the loose change off the floor, she counted all the money and put it in neat little stacks on the kitchen table. It wasn't much, but it was more than she'd thought she'd had stashed away.

She looked down at the corpse in her kitchen and was struck by a thought. With some effort, she got down onto the floor, turned him on his side and pulled the billfold from his back pocket. It was made of black leather, as soft as baby's skin. She opened it up and a smile broke over her face. The wallet was stuffed with bills, the smallest of which were twenties. She took out the money and placed it on the table, marveling at how springy the stacks of paper were.

She replaced the wallet and patted his pockets for any loose change. She found a few more bills—mostly ones and fives—and a bunch of quarters. She considered taking his rings, but figured they'd probably be more trouble than they were worth, and picked herself up off the floor. Then she sat down at the table and counted the money. There was over a thousand dollars there, more than enough to pay the back rent *and* stock up on food.

As she sat filled with joy over the windfall, she began to think about her situation. If the landlord was dead, who do I pay the rent money to? Oh well, not to worry, somebody will be by asking for it sooner or later.

She was about to get up to put the money in a safe place when her foot kicked against the dead body on the floor. "Oh dear," she said, realizing she had a bit of problem on her hands. Killing Genetti had been easy —he was a nasty, dirty little man who'd gotten what he deserved. However, getting rid of his body, now that would be tricky.

Edna sat down and thought about it.

When it came to her, it was like a new day dawning in her life, as if somebody-up-there was telling her she'd done a good thing.

If Marty Genetti was dirt, the only place for him was under the rug with the rest of it.

Edna got up from the table and made herself a tea. When she'd finished the cup of orange pekoe and was sufficiently rested, she began dragging the corpse into the living room. It wasn't an easy task, but by nightfall she'd pushed, pulled, kicked and rolled the body into the middle of the living room. Then with little ceremony she raised the edge of the rug, gave the body one last roll, and lowered the rug over top of it. The rug barely covered it, and the hands and feet stuck out from the corners, but at least the face, with those bulging eyes and lolling tongue, was hidden from view.

Out of sight, out of mind, she thought.

And went upstairs to bed.

#

In the morning Edna came downstairs rested and chipper, having had the best night's sleep in ages. Outside the sun was shining, the air was fresh and it was a beautiful, beautiful day.

As she entered the living room, the first thing she noticed was the bulge in the rug. It was quite lumpy, but considerably smaller than it had been the night before. The second thing she noticed was the curled pair of hands lying just beyond the near edge of the rug, and the pair of black shoes soles up on the floor at the other end. The hands ended at the wrists and the exposed flesh and bone was smooth, as if it had melted away like candle wax rather than cut by a knife. The feet were similarly disembodied—socks, skin, muscle and bone melted away at a slight angle.

Unsightly mess, that, thought Edna, picking up the edge of the rug and quickly kicking the hands underneath with a flick of her fluffy pink slippers. Then she walked around to the other end of the rug and swept the shoes underneath it, too.

"There," she said aloud, noticing there was a bit of color to the rug now. "Much better."

She went into the kitchen, humming a tune.

#

The lump in the rug took about a week to go away. Each day Edna would come down the stairs to see it smaller by half. The last few days she heard a sort of slurping sound coming from the rug—and every once in a while a crack!—but then that eventually stopped and the rug lay flat again, not a lump to be seen.

Sipping her morning tea by the front window, Edna took a moment to look at the rug more closely. If she wasn't mistaken, it looked newer somehow, the design on it brighter and more colorful. It looked like two bright red pools surrounded by some darker colors, but other than that she couldn't make out what it was.

She finished her tea, went upstairs and got dressed. She hadn't been shopping in weeks and the cupboards were practically bare. Now that she had money in hand, it might be a good idea to stock up on groceries.

She was just about ready to leave the house when there was a knock on the door.

"Now who could that be?" Edna said aloud.

She went to the door and opened it to find a middle-aged woman standing on her front porch. She had coal black hair, dark tanned skin and wore a large round pair of dark sunglasses. Although it was quite mild out she had on a big fur coat made from dozens of tiny pelts. Edna thought of the poor hamsters that had died in the creation of that coat and disliked the woman immediately.

"Edna Dowell?"

"Yes!"

"I'm Maria Genetti, my father owns this building."

"Isn't that wonderful," she said warmly.

The woman took off her sunglasses, revealing small brown eyes that were covered by far too much make up. Her painted eyes narrowed into slits as she looked at Edna. "So, he left the house a week ago to collect overdue rent and he hasn't been seen since. And since you're one of the two tenants of his that are overdue, I was wondering if he came here?"

Edna was silent a moment thinking what she should do. If she said he'd been there and then left, the police would surely come asking questions. If she said he'd never been there, then this woman—this evil, evil woman—might go away, but she'd end up leaving with all the overdue rent money. That would never do!

She looked up at the woman. "Maria?"

"Yes."

"He was here, Maria."

"Really? When?"

"This morning."

"That's wonderful," she said with sigh of relief.

Edna nodded. "He came in here looking for rent money." She paused a moment, as if trying to remember. "And then he went into that closet over there and never came out."

The look on the woman's face soured. "What are you talking about?" But, then, ever-so-slowly, a look of terror crept over her features as Edna's words played on her mind.

"Let me see!" she said, barging past Edna toward the closet at the end of the hall.

No manners, thought Edna. Just like her father.

The young woman opened the closet door and peered inside.

Edna went silently into the kitchen, knowing the woman would stand there in front of the closet for a few moments unable to see anything in its shadowy depths.

"There's nobody in here," she said, her head still buried deep in the darkness. "Where did he go?"

She pulled back from the closet and turned around.

Only to get a good look at the rolling pin . . .

"What happened to my—"
Up close.

#

Maria Genetti had had some money on her, but not much. She certainly wasn't as well off as her father had been. After Edna had gone through her purse and pockets she barely had two-hundred dollars to show for it.

"Oh well," she thought. "Better than nothing." She put the money in her own purse, stepped over the body in the hallway and left the house to do the shopping.

When she returned an hour later with her wheeled wire cart laden with groceries, she was surprised to find the dead woman's body lying face down in the hallway. Standing over the corpse, she tried to recall what had happened, then began nodding.

"Yes, yes," she said. "Of course. Mustn't leave people lying around in hallways. What would the neighbors think?"

And with that, she took off her coat, brought the grocery bags into the kitchen, then dragged the body into the living room. As she moved the body closer to the rug she noticed something strange about the floor covering. The edge of the rug was trembling slightly, like the upper lip of a starving man who'd just caught the scent of fresh-baked bread.

"Patience," she told the rug in a tone of voice more suited to house pets than home furnishings.

With one last push she managed to move the body into position. She raised the edge of the rug, gave the body a kick and watched as the rug curled around the corpse, pulling it under.

"Thank you," she said to the rug. "Now, where was I?" She saw the empty wire cart standing at the front door. "Just about to go shopping."

She put her dirty tan coat back on and left the house, headed for the market.

#

The lump in the rug was gone in just under three days. Edna spent nights sitting in her rocker watching the rug slowly getting smaller, shrinking like a block of ice on a warm spring day. There were still the same slurping sounds coming from it, but only for a little while and only near the end.

After the lump was gone, things settled down and Edna was at peace knowing she had more than enough money to live on and that any further problems could be easily swept under the rug.

She was happy for the first time in years.

About a week later there was another knock at the door. "Who is it?"

"Police ma'am."

Edna glanced through the peep hole and saw the uniformed policeman. "What do you want?"

"I'd like to ask you a few questions, Mrs. Dowell. We're looking for two missing persons, Marty Genetti and his daughter, Maria."

Edna was silent. If she didn't let the policeman in he might get suspicious, thinking she had something to hide. Better to let him in, answer his questions and send him on his way. "Just a minute," she said, opening the door.

The police officer was young and handsome, with short blond hair, a bushy blond mustache and pale blue eyes.

"Come in."

"Thank you, ma'am."

"Now, how can I help you?"

"Well, I've been going through the neighborhood asking everyone if they've seen either of the two people. Marty Genetti owned a lot of property on this block."

"Is that so?"

"Yes, and he was known to make visits around the first of each month to collect rent from problem tenants."

"Problem tenants?" she asked with a smile. "Well, that must be why I never saw much of him."

The police officer gave her a polite smile. Edna looked shyly away and noticed the rug.

It was moving.

The policeman kept talking. "That might be so, but some of the people on the street said they saw him knocking at your door a few weeks ago."

Edna suddenly felt warm all over. From what the policeman had said she couldn't deny Genetti had been here. Perhaps it would be better to play along. She took her eyes off the rug for a moment and looked up at the policeman. "Oh yes, that's right," she said, feigning recollection. "You'll have to excuse me, my memory isn't what it used to be."

"That's all right," the policeman nodded. "My mother's like that sometimes."

"He was here. Came to check on a leaky tap in the bathroom, but I'd fixed it the day before, so we sat and had tea in the kitchen. Ate two-and-a-half of my biscuits, and then he left."

The policeman scribbled some notes in his book, asking Edna further questions about when Marty Genetti arrived and how long he had stayed.

"I can't recall such things very well. It might have been ten minutes, it might have been an hour."

As the policeman continued making notes, Edna took the opportunity to glance back at the rug. It was less than a foot away from the policeman's big black boot, inching closer.

"Perhaps you'd like to join me for tea as well?" she asked, walking across the living room and placing both feet on the edge of the rug to hold it in place. "I brew the best on the block."

"I'd love to ma'am, but I've got fourteen more apartments to check out and the captain doesn't like approving overtime."

"Another time, perhaps?"

"Maybe."

"Oh, that would be wonderful."

The policeman took a few tentative steps to the door, waiting for Edna to escort him out. When he finally realized she intended to remain standing in place on the edge of the rug he said, "Well, goodbye."

"Goodbye," chimed Edna. "And good luck."

When the man was gone and the door closed, Edna stepped away and pointed an admonishing finger at the rug. "Naughty rug!"

A ripple coursed over the edge of the rug, and then it was still.

\#

Ten days later, there was yet another knock on the door. "Who is it?" Edna asked.

"Health Department."

Edna said nothing. Why would the health department be knocking on her door. "There's nothing wrong with my health," she said. "Thanks just the same."

"No ma'am. Some people on the block have been complaining of a bad smell these last few days. I need to take a look around, see if it's coming from your apartment."

"I don't smell."

"No one's saying you do ma'am. But there were several complaints and I've got to check out the entire block."

Edna thought it over. If there was a smell (which there was not!) the man wouldn't be easily shooed away. Better to let him in to take a look around, satisfy his curiosity.

"All right," she said at last opening the door.

He was a middle-aged man with a mustache and graying black hair. The name over his pocket read "Dave." As he stepped inside, he began sniffing. "Something die in here?"

Edna sniffed too, smelling nothing. "You watch it, sonny. I might be old, but . . ."

He stepped further into the house, sniffing like a bloodhound.

It was obvious to Edna he was looking for something and wouldn't stop until he found it. Best to stop him first.

"Oh, I know," she said. "Maybe it has something to do with the hole in the wall inside the pantry."

Dave looked at her curiously. "What hole in the wall?"

"Come and I'll show you." She led him into the kitchen and opened the door to the large walk-in pantry filled with canned food, the steering wheel from a 1972 Maverick and two department store mannequins. "See that hole there?" Edna pointed inside the pantry and stepped back to let the man by.

"I don't see anything."

"Maybe it's behind Dolly."

Dave shifted one of the mannequins, then tried the other. "Nope."

He began easing himself out of the pantry when the back of his head was bashed in by Edna's rolling pin. He let out a cry and slumped forward. After a moment, he put a hand over the back of his crushed skull and moaned in terrible pain. His foot slipped on the kitchen floor and he fell backwards, hitting his head again.

As blood pooled on the floor around his skull he looked up at Edna, his eyes blinking as if to ask "Why?"

In answer to the question, the rolling pin came down again, sending his forehead deep into his brain.

#

It took Edna the rest of the day to drag the body into the living room, and the rest of the night to clean up the blood.

By the time Edna dragged herself upstairs to bed, the lump under the rug had shrunk by half; and the rug itself was colored with deep black and purple swirls that circled the two crimson pools like hurricanes around an eye.

The next morning, the lump was gone.

#

It had been two days since Dave had visited and Edna wondered why more Daves hadn't stopped by—or even a Bill or Bob. But while it was a concern, future visits from the health department wasn't what worried her most. It was the rug. It had started getting unruly.

Ever since the policeman's visit, the rug had begun to move. Not much at first, mind you, just a few inches here or there, but enough that Edna was forever setting it right. Over time, it began roaming the room, its bright red circles looking more like angry eyes with each passing day.

Now, every time she walked through the living room it moved toward her, its edges rippling and undulating as if in a wave. At first she thought it was cute that the rug followed her around like a cat wanting milk, but as the days wore on and there were no more visitors, the rug had gotten downright feisty.

This morning after breakfast when she walked past it on her way upstairs, it had nipped at her feet, taking one of her pink slippers from her foot in the process.

"Bad rug," Edna scolded, kicking it with her other slippered foot. "Bad."

And then the rug lurched forward, pulling the second slipper off her foot, leaving her foot scratched and red with blood, as if it had been rubbed with sandpaper.

Edna ran from the living room and hurried up half a dozen steps before turning back around. The rug was there on the landing, trying to flow up the first step but unable to pull itself off the floor.

Edna sat for a long time, catching her breath and watching the rug with a mix of fear and fascination. Finally, it glided back into its familiar spot in the middle of the living room floor and lay still except for a wave that undulated around its edge every few minutes.

After watching the rug for a while, Edna took a few tentative steps toward the landing. With each step the rug became more restless, almost like a dog growling at the approach of a stranger. As she set her foot on the landing, the rug slid across the floor, its leading edge curled back in a sneer.

Edna turned around, ran up the stairs into her room and slammed the door behind her.

#

Edna spent the next day in her room. Twice she ventured out trying the steps only to find the rug waiting for her at the bottom of the stairs.

It had managed to curl over the first step and was inching up the second. Seeing that, she went back into her room and crawled back into bed.

But as the day wore on, the first pangs of hunger began to gnaw at her belly. It had been more than twenty-four hours since she'd had a bite to eat and with each further hour that passed she grew more acutely aware of how hungry she really was.

It almost made her laugh. The kitchen was full of food and her purse was full of money, but the thing that helped her to get those things was the same thing that was going to deny her their pleasures.

It was almost better to be penniless and starving.

Almost, but not quite.

She pondered her situation well into the evening, and was finally struck by a thought, a way to satisfy both hungers—hers as well as the rug's.

She picked up the phone.

And ordered a pizza.

This story was first published in the Horror Writer's Association anthology *Robert Bloch's Psychos.* The book was to have been edited by Robert Bloch, but he passed away before it was completed. I eagerly took up the challenge for this anthology because I am a huge fan of Robert Bloch and the way he was able to meld humor and horror together so seamlessly. So, I began writing "The Rug," but stopped halfway through because I thought the story was just plain silly. Then, as if the ghost of Mr. Bloch was at work behind the scene, HWA issued a call for the anthology that basically said, "We're short on submissions, so if you're working on something finish it up and send it in." Well, how could I not complete the story after that? So I completed the tale best I could, and not only was it accepted, it ended up on a "Best of Year" list as well as being a Bram Stoker Award nominee. My only regret is that Robert Bloch didn't live long enough to read the story.

But Somebody's Got To Do It

It's a shitty job, but somebody's got to do it.
    You hear a lot of that around here, and for the most part it's true.

The shitty job in question is Fireman at one of the biggest crematoriums in the country. The bodies come in at a rate of about thirty an hour and they go out just as fast, or perhaps I should say they go *up* just as fast . . . *up*, as in smoke.

It's a bad joke, I know, but bad jokes are a reality here; they help you get through the day, through the weeks, months, and years. The bodies became a blur a long time ago and they aren't really human to me anymore. Meat, that's how I look at them, or at least that's how I think of them. I don't like to look at them too much, because I like to keep my lunch off my shirt and down in my stomach where it belongs.

The fresh ones aren't so bad—the ones they rush over after car crashes and heart attacks. Sure they're bloody and all, but they don't look or smell too bad. The ones they find in the bush that have been seasoned a week or two in the sun, or at the bottom of a lake, are the ones that make my skin crawl. They're the most dangerous, too, the ones most likely to cause trouble.

Of course there aren't too many zombies around any more, not like in '98 and '99 when the plague swept across the country and infected three quarters of the population with the virus. Back then the Zed Squad was a million strong, and heavily armed. It was war in those days, war on the unarmed masses of walking deadheads. Okay, so maybe it was more like a crap shoot, but the papers and television made it sound like a war. One thing was for sure, you definitely got the sense of it being us against them.

That was then.

It's all changed now. Ever since they banned cemetery burials in '01 the Zed Squad has been able to keep the zombie problem pretty much in check. Sure, there's still the odd one that gets loose, but the Zeds usually make short work of them.

The Zed Squad, The Zeds, Zedders. Their official name is The Zombie Squad, but how many people call the cops the Police Force. The Zeds got a whole set of nicknames and slogans, probably make all kinds of bad jokes, too, just like us. I guess it's all the same, whether you work with dead people or living dead people, you gotta have fun with it or you might stop for a minute and think about what's really going on.

Like I said, it's a shitty job, but somebody's got to do it.

I didn't grow up wanting to be a Fireman, at least not the kind that burns dead people in ovens. I went to college, even graduated with honors. But what do you do with a B.A. in geography besides teach high school?

So, I applied for a job at the government offices and waddyaknow, got offered a job at the province's new creamery. That's one of the nicknames we have for the place. It's another bad joke, but what else can you do?

I don't say much on the job. I don't like to come off sounding conceited or full of myself, but I'm the only guy in the place with any sort of education, and the conversation here isn't what I'd call stimulating.

(Correction! The conversation *is* stimulating, it just doesn't stimulate any part of the body remotely connected to the brain.)

Anyway, Fernando says more than enough for both of us. He's my partner. Don Montalban Fernando. He's part Mexican, part Spanish, part Irish, part Navajo, part Canadian. At least he says he is. I've never challenged him on anything he says because that would mean speaking to him like I was interested in his personal life. Anyway, I'm not sure if he'd know how to handle a regular conversation.

Check it out.

"Hey, man," he says as a fresh corpse comes down the chute. (He usually prefaces his words with those two, or a subtle variation on them. "Hey, hey, hey, man . . . ")

I look down at the body. It's a woman. She looks like she died on the delivery table because she's naked with a long straight incision across her belly. My guess is she was having a baby by Cesarian and something went wrong. I don't like to speculate on these kinds of things, but Fernando does.

"Hey man, I think I slept with this chick last week," he says. "Yeah, I remember riding the hump with this bitch." He cups one of the corpse's large, milk-filled breasts in his hand and squeezes. He's gentle at first, but then his grip gets tighter.

I wait patiently til he's done. He doesn't play with each body for very long because he knows there'll be another one along in a minute or so.

Shit happens and people die. Another of our slogans. It's not as good as *Life's a bitch and then you burn*, but you get the idea.

When Fernando finishes fondling the corpse, I undo the straps holding it onto its transport slab and send the slab down the rollers. When it hits the fortified frame around the furnace entrance, the body slides off the slab and shoots right into the fire.

Fernando hits the button that controls the gas and the flames burn orange-white for a moment, then die down. The heat inside our little hell machine tops off at around five thousand degrees Fahrenheit and the body is gone in less than a minute. It gets burned so clean that the residue only has to be scraped off the inside of the furnace once a month or so.

They say that in another few months the creameries will have put more bodies through the ovens than the Nazis did more than sixty years ago. I don't like to think about that much either, but when I do I console myself by thinking there's a big difference between Firemen and the Nazis — at least our customers are dead before they arrive.

Fernando and I take the slab off the rollers and put it on the hoist that takes it back upstairs.

Another body comes down the chute.

"Oh shit, man," Fernando says. "This one's tender."

By *tender*, he means it's one of those bodies that's been sitting in the sun. It's grey and blue and there's some sort of green-yellow pus oozing out of a hole in its chest. And maggots, lot and lots of maggots.

We both put our masks on in a hurry and take plenty of care unstrapping this one. The grey ones with maggots are the ones you've got to worry about.

I remember one time, about a week after I started, a corpse came down the chute looking a lot like this one. Harrison, the guy I was working with at the time, didn't seem to be too concerned. He put his mask on, but didn't bother being too careful about the rest of it. And wouldn't you know it, once he had the straps off, the grey-green corpse rose up off the slab and took a bite out of his neck. I can still remember the sound made by the zombie's bite — like someone biting into a crisp green apple.

I watched Harrison grab his neck and then I screamed for help and Carbonneau came running out of his office with the standard issue sawed-off and blew that zombie's head clean off its shoulders. I sent the slab down the rollers as quick as I could and then I dared to take a look at Harrison. He was writhing around on the floor like a worm that's just been cut in half. Wet, gurgling sounds were popping up out of the bloody red hole in his neck. A few maggots had made the jump from dead to living flesh and were crawling all over the gaping wound.

Harrison reached out like a drowning man, but nobody moved to help him.

"Turn around if you don't want to see this," Carbonneau said as he pumped a shell into the gun's chamber.

Everyone else turned around but me. I stayed put and watched Carbonneau point the gun down onto Harrison's head and close his eyes. "Forgive me, Harry," he whispered, then pulled the trigger.

The meaty pulp that was left steamed on the floor for a few minutes before it cooled. I helped Carbonneau get the pieces of Harrison up onto a slab and we both made the sign of the cross as we slid him down the rollers.

"One strap left," Fernando says, bringing my head back to the job at hand.

I nod numbly and tense my muscles.

He unsnaps the final strap, and we begin to push the slab toward the fire.

Suddenly, the maggoty green head turns in my direction.

Pieces of grey skin fall away from its face as its mouth opens and black rotting teeth snap dangerously close to my hand.

The head prepares for another bite. Already Fernando has a length of pipe in his hand. He is swinging. The zombie's mouth is open, then closed. I feel something hot on my fingers. The pipe glances off my arm and connects with the hellish green head, splitting it in two.

"Hey man! Are you all right?" Fernando says. He swings the pipe again and smashes the zombie's head into road kill.

"I'm okay," I say. "I'm all right. Just nipped my glove, that's all."

The pain in the end of my finger is incredible. There is a slight tear on the outside of the glove and I know the bastard got me. The skin on the tip of my finger has been broken and there's no doubt that I'm infected with the virus.

Fuck! I scream inside my head. *Shit! Damn! Fuck!*

"I don't feel so good, though," I say a moment later. "I got quite a scare. I think I'll go home, if it's okay with you."

"Hey, man, sure," Fernando says. "Take it easy. I'll cover for you."

I nod thanks and leave.

In the change room I remove the glove slowly because A) it hurts and B) I'm afraid of what I'll find.

I drop the glove on the floor and try to hold my infected hand to stop it from shaking. Already the tip of my finger has turned green. And already, it's starting to smell—bad!

I walk home with my hands in my pocket, deep inside my pocket. The night is cool, but I'm sweating like a cold beer on a hot day and I'm freezing.

I don't look up, don't want to risk looking anyone in the eye, in case they notice something . . . different about me.

I remember one time I was walking home from work when I turned down Main Street. I was nearly blinded by the Zed Squad's spotlights. They'd set up barricades at both ends of the block and in the middle of the street was this grey and magotty zombie stumbling around in circles. There were plenty of film crews and newspaper men— zombies making it that far into town is always big news.

After they let the zombie walk in circles for a bit for the benefit of the cameras, the Zeds at one end of the street took cover and a guy said over a loudspeaker: "Prepare for termination!"

Everyone ran for cover, but there was just this little *Kirack!* of a gunshot. That's all it took, one shot, and this zombie's head exploded like an overripe melon stuffed with explosive charges instead of seeds.

I hung around to watch them scrape body parts off the pavement. The Zeds didn't take too much care while they bagged the zombie, they just shoveled it up and put it into a bag like dog shit off a sidewalk.

My stomach spasms at the thought as I walk along Main Street. I lean against a building and retch. My stomach is empty and all I can manage are a couple of dry heaves.

At last I'm home. My finger doesn't hurt anymore. The pain has moved up my arm and now it's my wrist that feels like it's on fire. I look at my hand under the light of a desk lamp. It's stone grey in places, green like moss in others. The tip of my finger where the infection started is dripping some kind of green liquid. It drips onto the scattered papers on my desk and splatters in uneven splotches like a Rorschach test.

One blot looks like a dog, another like a cat, yet another like a close play at the plate. I squeeze the tip of my finger and the green stuff flows out like sludge. I look down at the paper and think, a broad and two guys fucking their brains out.

I laugh.

I wrap my finger in a towel and walk over to the bed. I lie down. I expect the room to spin, but it doesn't. Instead the walls and ceiling bend and curve as if the room is turning itself inside out. I think I see a light open up above me, but I fall asleep before I can be sure.

#

I wake up and roll over onto my side. It's three in the afternoon—time for work. I feel hungry, but I can wait til lunch break. I walk into the bathroom and look in the mirror. I don't look too bad really, a little pale is all. My finger is healed over now with a hard, green-black scab. I tap it against the rim of the sink and feel no pain.

I look myself over and see that I'm already dressed. I leave the house for work. I walk slowly, like I'm dragging my feet. I try to walk faster but I can't.

Because I can't walk so good, I get to work late. Everyone looks at me strangely—I guess I'm paler than I thought.

"Hey, man," says a voice. "You look like shit!"

"Where you been the last two days?" another voice says. "We've already been interviewing for your job."

I try to answer. My jawbone works but I can't move my tongue well enough to form a word. I try to say "I'm back" but it ends up sounding like "Ugh huh."

"You back to stay?" a voice asks.

I nod, yes.

"All right, then. Get back to work."

I nod.

"Hey, man, we thought you were a goner. We thought we'd hear about you getting' offed by the Zeds. I'm glad you're back. My wife will be glad to hear it, too. When I told her what happened to you, she started getting' all worried about the same shit happenin' to me . . ."

I nod when I think I'm supposed to. This seems to be enough.

". . . Hey, man, not talkin' too much today? Must be feelin' just like your old self again, huh?"

The first body comes down the chute. Its clothes are torn in places and the bits of exposed meat smell delicious. I put a hand on its chest. It's still warm. I want nothing more than to sink my teeth into that soft pink flesh, but something at the base of my skull tells me *Not yet. Wait!*

We unstrap the body and I send it into the furnace. Pangs of hunger begin to rip through me. I want meat, I *need* meat.

"Hey, man, I'm goin' for a coffee. Want one?"

No, I shake my head.

"Okay. I'll be back in a few minutes. I got to take a crap too."

I nod.

A body comes down the chute. It's black and blue and bruised and rotten. Bad meat. I unstrap it and send it quickly into the fire.

Another body. An old man. Heart attack, maybe. He is lukewarm. I bend over him. My teeth open wide and dig deeply into his belly. Delicious. I take three more bites before I send the body down the track.

Another body is before me. A young woman. Half of her head is missing. Car crash. Her blood-blackened blouse is open. A tittie is exposed. Peekaboo! I chomp down on the breast. It is soft and warm in my mouth. Good meat. I quickly eat the other breast and parts of her neck.

I hunger for more, but I unstrap the body and send it into the flames.

"I'm back."

I nod. I continue working.

"Hey, man. Getting' back to work is doin' you good. You already got some color in your cheeks," the voice says. "You'll be your old self again in no time."

A body slides down the chute. A woman. Another car crash, or perhaps the same one.

"Hey, man. I know this bitch," the voice says. "She gave me the best blowjob of my life a couple years back."

I nod.

"Oh, shit," the voice says. "I forgot to take a crap. You don't mind if I take off for a second, do ya?"

No, I shake my head.

I am alone again. A warm tender meal lies before me. I remember something . . . words, a phrase.

It's a shitty job, but somebody's got to do it.

Yes, I think. And thank God it's me.

This one, like "Roadkill," which is also in this collection, are my best post-apocalypse zombie stories from a time before *The Walking Dead* when zombie fiction was all the rage. My thought on this tale was basically -- What would a story be like told from the point-of-view of a zombie? Tricky thing that, because it would have to be in the first-person and the present tense because zombies wouldn't have any memory and the story would have to be told as it happens. That was the thought process, so what better story to tell the story than from the point-of-view of someone who gets turned into a zombie and gets to experience the hunger for flesh first-hand. I also did a zombie novel, *Kilgore and Co.*, which was published some 25 years after it was written. When I told people about it, they always answered, "It sounds like *The Walking Dead*," at which point I assured them it was written long before that show was even a twinkle in *Walking Dead* creator Frank Darabont's eye. An interesting note is that this story was rejected 24 times in eight years before I put it out of its misery and published it as the only original story in the collection.

Death Drives a Semi

Don Moore glanced down at the fuel gauge as he waited for the light to turn green. He'd just finished the late shift at *The Cambridge Reporter*, writing headlines and laying out tomorrow's City Page, but he still had an hour's drive to his home in Brampton before he could call it a night. The fuel gauge read a little less than one quarter full.

Should be enough to get me home, he thought. As long as I take it easy.

The light changed and he eased his foot down onto the gas pedal of his seven-year-old Ford Fairmont. A red Firebird behind him honked its horn and then quickly passed on the left.

"It doesn't get any greener, grampa," one of the teenagers shouted as the Firebird roared by.

"To hell with you," Don muttered back through his open window. He kept even pressure on the gas pedal and the Ford slowly accelerated to thirty-kilometers-per-hour.

I've made it to sixty-five obeying the speed limit, he thought. And I ain't about to go changing. Not now.

Don had worked for *The Cambridge Reporter* for twenty-nine years, starting as a cub court reporter in 1964 and working his way up to managing editor in 1985. He'd spent the last eight years as night wire editor, taking the demotion just to keep his job and preserve his pension.

Now he had two more weeks to go before his retirement and nothing was going to spoil it for him, least of all a bunch of teenage punks in some hopped-up car.

He turned onto the eastbound on-ramp of Highway 401 and pushed slightly harder on the gas until the car crept up to eighty-five-kilometers-per-hour. Seeing no oncoming headlights, he signaled and slowly eased the Ford onto the highway. He set the cruise control at ninety, took his foot off the gas pedal, leaned back and tried to relax.

Five kilometers down the highway, Don passed the Petro Canada filling station without stopping to gas up. There wasn't another gas station along his route, but it was late, he was tired, and he was sure he had enough gas to make it home.

As he passed the gas station and its adjoining McDonald's, he took a good long look at it. Bill Doucet, a features writer at *The Reporter* had a story about the station in tomorrow's paper. It was all about the people who haunt it in the wee hours between midnight and four a.m. It was a good piece and Don had spent precious extra minutes before deadline trying to give the story a headline that would do it justice. He finally decided on an eighteen-point italicized kicker that read:

While the rest of the world sleeps . . .

above a forty-eight-point bold headline that read:

The Truck Stops Here!

Not bad, Don thought. Not great, but not bad.

A pair of headlights appeared in the Ford's rearview mirror. Don tried not to look directly into the reflection, but as he drove he found it difficult to stop himself from taking frequent glances at the blazing lights.

He forced himself to look away long enough to tilt the mirror up towards the headliner. Then, with the distracting lights out of his field of vision, he was easily able to focus his eyes back on the road.

He drove on for a few minutes before the lights began bothering him again. From years of daily driving on the 401, he could easily tell they belonged to a truck, an eighteen-wheel semi-trailer. As the truck approached, the cry of its tires grew louder in his ears until it seemed like the rig was about to drive right over top of him. He glanced to his left and saw the front wheels of the tractor less than a meter away, chrome lug nuts spinning like steel blades in the moonlight. A moment later the tractor's rear wheels came up beside him and the awful noise of rubber screaming down upon the asphalt grew even louder. Don struggled to keep his car headed straight down the highway.

At last he'd had enough. He stepped lightly on the brake and the truck's long dark trailer passed quickly, the dreadful noise of tires and spinning metal rapidly diminishing until it was little more than a dull whine in the distance.

Don wiped a sleeve across his forehead and put both of his hands firmly on the wheel.

What was it I read in that story? he asked himself.

An hour earlier he'd read through the Doucet article fascinated by the lore of the road.

According to one old trucker's legend, the Grim Reaper drove a long, black eighteen-wheeler across Canada's highways stalking weary drivers and snatching their souls.

"Pass you three times and you're a goner," Doucet had quoted one veteran long hauler as saying.

Don had found the legend particularly amusing and had highlighted it within the body of the story with a boldface callout:

Death Drives a Semi.

Now, Don saw the dark trailer growing smaller on the highway in front of him and amused himself with the thought that Death had just passed him by.

"Nah," he said aloud, turning on the radio. He opened up a vent. Although it was hot, the blowing air felt good against his sweat-dampened skin.

A little later, just outside Guelph, Don came upon some traffic. A few rigs were in convoy, and another truck was passing the others in the left-hand lane, clogging up all the car traffic behind it.

Don pulled into the left lane and followed the line of cars until the truck at the head of the line passed the lead truck in the right-hand lane and pulled over ahead of it. The line of cars quickly began passing the trucks. As Don passed the lead truck, he carefully pulled into the right-hand lane and allowed the other faster cars behind him to pass.

The highway was soon free of lights in front of him and he decided things were clear enough to light up a cigarette. Don was quite a bit overweight and had a long history of heart and respiratory problems. He'd always meant to quit smoking, even tried it a couple of times, but he'd been at it too long and enjoyed it too much to stop. Besides, there was something about being a grizzled old chain-smoking newspaper veteran that appealed to him. Anyway, he'd lasted this long smoking a pack a day, why quit now?

He pulled the cigarette lighter from the dashboard and held the glowing coil up to the end of his cigarette and puffed. With the cigarette tipped with a fiery red glow, Don knocked the ashes off the lighter by rapping it against the car's outside rearview mirror.

As he did, a pair of lights appeared in the mirror.

He returned the lighter to its socket and looked back into the mirror. The lights had grown in size and intensity. They were high off the road and bright, stinging Don's eyes like lasers each time he glanced into the mirror. Another truck, he thought. Don't these guys ever sleep?

It wasn't long before the lights filled the inside of the Ford with a soft white glow. As the truck inched closer, shadows crept around the car's interior like spiders.

He could hear the truck approaching, its deep throaty exhaust growling angrily in the night.

Don turned up the volume on the radio and pressed harder on the gas pedal. The old Ford labored up past ninety-five kilometers per hour.

The truck continued gaining on him, the noise growing louder in his ears until the radio had been completely drowned out.

He was up to one-hundred when he decided to abandon the idea of outrunning the truck. He took his foot off the gas and let the cruise control take over, allowing the car to slowly return to ninety.

The truck's roar strengthened. One moment he was even with the truck's front wheels, the next moment he was door to door with the truck's cab.

He glanced up into the open window.

The interior of the truck was filled with a bright red glow. The driver looked down at him, cracking a wide smile that seemed to stretch almost from ear-to-ear. The man had slicked back hair that shone crimson in the light inside the cab. And there was something else . . . The man was wearing dark sunglasses.

Who the hell drives in the middle of the night wearing sunglasses? Don thought.

Don's eyes shifted back onto the highway and he realized that he'd been drifting left towards the truck. He jerked the steering wheel to avoid a collision and darted across the highway onto the gravel shoulder. For several tense seconds he wrestled with the steering wheel trying to get the car's two right wheels back onto the highway. Once he was back in control with smooth asphalt running beneath all four wheels, he stepped on the brake and let the truck pass.

His breath was rapid and shallow. There was a slight feeling of constriction in his chest. His body was damp with sweat. A dull stab of pain ran the length of his left arm.

He let out a scream.

Don's cigarette had burned down to his fingers and he was forced to drop the burning butt onto the floor and try to stamp it out with his shoe.

Taking frequent glances at the highway, he finally smothered the burning embers. The pungent stink of burnt carpet fibers wafted up from the floor.

With the crisis over, Don took a few deep breaths and tried to relax. He was just outside Milton now, twenty minutes from home.

Up ahead, on the right, he saw the flashing hazard lights of a vehicle off on the shoulder.

In the early morning, truck and car drivers alike often pulled over to catch a few hours sleep before continuing on, so Don thought nothing of the truck as he casually pulled wide to the left to pass it.

But as he passed, he saw that the long black truck was the same one that had passed him twice already. He glanced into the cab of the huge black tractor. The light inside was even more brilliant than before and flickered orange and red behind the blacked-out silhouette of the driver.

Just past the truck, Don heard the hiss of its parking brake being released. He turned around to look over his shoulder and saw the flashing hazard lights being replaced by the single flash of a left turn signal. The truck was getting back onto the highway.

Don tried to tell himself he was crazy to think what he was thinking, that the whole thing was just a series of bizarre coincidences that were giving an old man a really good scare.

But what if it wasn't? What if his time had come?

What if Death did indeed drive a semi?

He'd been passed twice already. He'd make sure he wouldn't be passed again, just to be on the safe side.

He took the Ford off cruise-control and pressed firmly on the gas. The Ford's speedometer slowly climbed past the speed limit to one-hundred-and-five . . . one hundred-and-ten-kilometers per hour.

He was through Milton now where the 401 expanded into three lanes to handle the heavy rush hour traffic into Toronto.

At three in the morning, however, there wasn't a soul on the highway except for him.

Him and Death.

Don readjusted the inside rearview mirror so he could see directly behind him. The truck was just a pair of pin prick stars in the distance that appeared to be growing smaller every minute. He looked ahead and pushed the gas pedal further towards the floor. The speedometer crept up to one-hundred-and-twelve.

On the right, Don saw the sign for the Mississauga City Limits. He was less than five miles from home.

And then the truck was upon him, appearing without warning in an explosion of light and thunder.

High-beams flashed like lightning; smoke blacker than night belched up from the truck's twin chrome exhaust pipe. A gas horn's blast cut through the darkness like a dull, broad knife.

Don felt a sharp stab of pain in the center of his chest.

He grabbed the wheel firmly and put his foot to the floor.

The Ford's engine whined in protest and the entire car began to shudder and shake.

As it approached, the truck's diesel engine roared like an angry beast, its tires screaming against the pavement with the cries of a thousand anguished souls.

Don took a hand from the steering wheel and clutched his heart as if to keep it from exploding from his chest. As he did, the Ford swerved to the left and collided with the truck's right-front fender.

The jolt of the collision forced Don to grab the wheel with both hands. He pulled the car back into the right-hand lane and pushed the gas pedal down as far as it would go.

He pulled ahead of the truck and crossed over in front of it to prevent it from passing him.

The lights of the truck slowly edged right as it moved into an open lane. The roar of the truck's engine rose in pitch, becoming a howling demon scream as it accelerated to pass him. A broken piece of metal from the truck's front end hung down and scraped against the highway, trailing a shower of sparks behind it.

The Ford suddenly lost power.

Don pumped the gas pedal and the car shot forward for a moment, then died. He glanced at the fuel gauge. The needle was well to the left of the *E*.

The truck pulled even with him, then slowly began passing him for the third and final time.

The pain in Don's chest intensified as flickering life images flashed through the mind.

Work late on nights and weekends. A sixty-hour week here. A fifty-hour week there. A wife he hardly saw. A family he hardly knew.

And now it was over, two weeks before he'd have the chance to make up for all his lost time.

"Not if I can help it," he cried.

He turned the wheel hard to the right.

The Ford cut almost diagonally across the truck's path.

Sparks flew as metal scraped against metal. The truck popped up off the highway and into the air, driving over the Ford's hood and crumpling the tiny car beneath it like paper. The rear wheels of the tractor bounced off the Ford's ruined hood and the entire semi-trailer lurched to the right, its fifth wheel twisting like a broken spine as it plowed into a clearing off the edge of the highway.

The Ford's tires bit into the road and the car was sent rolling down the highway . . . four . . . five . . . six times before coming to a stop in the same clearing as the truck.

#

Tap. Tap. Tap.
"Hey, buddy!"
Tap. Tap.
"Are you all right?"

A young blond-haired man was rapping his knuckles on the front windshield of the Ford.

"I beat him," Don said in a labored voice. It hurt him to talk but he didn't care. "I beat Death."

"He's still alive," the blond-haired man shouted. "He's delirious, but he's okay."

In the distance, through the upside down and shattered windshield, Don saw a line of flashing red lights approaching. Help was on its way.

Much closer, he could see flares burning on the edge of the highway near the overturned truck. People were crawling up the roof of the tractor to get to the driver inside the cab.

"There's nobody in here!" a man called down to the others gathered around the accident scene.

"Did you see where he went?"

"Where did he go?"

"Maybe he was thrown clear."

Don watched as they began to search the ditch at the edge of the clearing. He managed a little laugh before the pain in his ribs and shoulders forced him to content himself with a smile.

They'd never find the driver.

The driver would find them.

When I was working as a sports reporter for *The Cambridge Reporter*, my daily commute included an hour-long drive in the morning and another at night, mostly along Canada's largest and busiest highway, Highway 401. One thing I hated about the drive was the rain. While it might not be raining very hard outside, the water that was thrown up by other traffic, semi-trailers in particular, made the drive so much worse. And, if you found yourself tired or distracted and falling behind in speed, there was never any shortage of truck drivers who thought nothing of passing you with their semi-trailers, even if their speed was only marginally better than your own and it took them three to five minutes to actually get past you. This was the background for the story "Death Drives a Semi." On one trip I just thought, "What if" (the genesis of most fantasy stories) "Death was behind the wheel of one of those things—not hard to imagine—and if he passed you three times on the highway, he could collect your soul?" Premise in place and paranoia allowed to run wild, the result was the title story of the collection, which, by the way, was first published in a trucking magazine called, RPM For Truckers.

The Basement

Mrs. Caputo walked by the basement doorway and made the sign of the cross.

It was a smooth movement, so practiced over the years that it hardly interfered with the rhythm of her limping gait as she carried on into the kitchen.

Five years had passed since she'd found her husband's body, bent and broken at the bottom of the stairs, his mouth open, his eyes shut and his face covered in blood. Five years had passed since she'd been down there, five years since she had even opened the door.

The basement was an evil place. It had taken Mario from her and left her to live out her life in an empty and lifeless house.

The basement was evil, too . . . because of the noises.

The noises had started a week after Mario died. They were soft slithering sounds at first—the kind of sound you can hear a snake make if you put your ear close enough to the grass. Later, the noises changed, became more of a skittering sound, like rats crawling over dried and crinkled newsprint. In the last six months, however, the noises had gotten worse, especially when the sun set and the streets were quiet. She could hear the creaking weeping of the steps, as if someone were pacing up and down, looking for a way out. Or waiting for someone to come in.

She heard the noises wafting up from the basement, but always shook her head and told herself that the house was still settling down on its foundation. She told herself that, and then she prayed.

Standing in front of the stove, Mrs. Caputo spooned a single scoop of sugar into her espresso. As she stirred the coffee, the big black cat—her only comfort the last five years—rubbed itself against a wrinkled stocking.

"Micio," said Mrs. Caputo, looking down at the cat. "Some milk for my friend?"

The cat was already standing on its hind legs, stretching its paws up against the edge of the counter in anticipation. *"Corri giu,"* Mrs. Caputo scolded. A second later the cat was back with four paws on the floor and its tail wrapped around a table leg.

She poured some milk into a saucer and placed it at her feet.

The cat scurried across the floor, its old and unretractable claws clicking a frantic rhythm on the ceramic tiles. It skidded to a stop in front of the saucer and quickly began lapping up the milk. Flying droplets splashed up and landed like snow on the black fur of the cat's face.

Mrs. Caputo limped a few feet and took a seat at the kitchen table. The bottle of Vecchia Romagna rested in its usual spot in the middle of the table. She looked at it for several moments and with an old and tired breath blew a spot of dust off it. The brandy bottle had been half full the last five years, waiting patiently for someone to visit the old woman, for someone to come by to talk and have a shot. But no one came.

Without Mario why would anyone want to visit?

Even the children didn't come around much anymore. They were grown now with children of their own, had moved to smaller towns outside Toronto where house prices were cheaper. They called once a week, visited every month or so, but they never stayed long.

She took her first sip of coffee.

The taste of the strong black liquid reminded her of the times when she made coffee for Mario and his friends as they played *briscola* or just talked of the old country on long summer Sundays. In those days there had been a new bottle of brandy on the table every second week.

She finished her coffee and squinted through her thick horn-rimmed glasses at the calendar on the wall by the refrigerator.

It was Thursday. The man would be coming to look at the furnace at ten. Margarita would be by early in the afternoon to take Mrs. Caputo first to the bank, then to the supermarket. Margarita lived on the next street over and took Mrs. Caputo shopping every Thursday. Mrs. Caputo suspected she did it out of respect for Mario's memory, either that or Mario had left her some money and asked her to do it for him. Whatever the reason, Margarita never really seemed to enjoy it. Dinner would be at six and at eight, on Channel forty-seven, she would watch *Music of your life Italian Style con Nico Navarro* . . .

There was a knock at the door.

The cat cut short its post milk lip smacking and darted off towards the sound, ears upright and curious. With some effort, Mrs. Caputo got up from her chair, placed her coffee cup in the sink and limped down the hall, making the sign of the cross as she passed the basement doorway. There was a second knock on the front door before she could open it.

"Mrs. Caputo? I'm here to check your furnace," said a handsome young man on the other side of the screen door.

"Hallo, come, come," Mrs. Caputo said, opening the door and taking tiny steps backward to allow the man room to pass.

"So what's wrong with your furnace? All it says here is that it doesn't work," he said, looking at a slip of paper stapled to a work order. "When was the last time someone had a look at it?"

Mrs. Caputo smiled back at the man. "I me sorry, I no good English, *parli l italiano*?"

"Uh?" the man paused. "No ma am, I'm afraid I don't speak Italian. But if you like we could send another guy who does. Might take a week or so."

"No, no, today please," Mrs. Caputo said, thinking he'd said he'd be back next week.

"All right ma am, but I'd still like to know how long it's been."

"Huh."

"How long. How. Long. Since. Your. Furnace . . ."

Mrs. Caputo understood a few of the words, "five," she said holding up her hand, fingers pointing in five different directions.

"Five years! You know you should get it checked a little more often than that. It might just need a good cleaning, but you never know." He paused for a moment as Mrs. Caputo stared at him, a blank look on her face. "Well, we'll soon find out. Where's the basement?"

Mrs. Caputo understood the word "basement" and the image of Mario's body lying bent and broken at the bottom of the stairs was brought back sharply in her mind.

"*La,*" she said pointing down the hall at the tiny door tucked beneath the stairs that led up to the second floor.

"Thank you. I won't be too long."

The young man walked down the hall and as he opened the door, Mrs. Caputo turned her eyes away and stared out into the empty street. After a few moments she turned around and saw the door to the basement was wide open and blocking her route back to the kitchen.

"*Chiudi la porta!* Close door," she said as loud as she could. "Close door. The cat!" If the cat got into the basement, she would have to chase after it, down to the place where she found Mario's body bent and broken at the bottom of the stairs.

Several seconds passed before the young man clumped his way back up the stairs and poked his head out into the hall. "Pardon me."

"Close door, close door, the cat, the cat."

"Oh I'm sorry," the young man said and closed the door. Mrs. Caputo could hear him whistling as he clumped back down the steps into the basement.

Two hours passed.

Mrs. Caputo helped nudge the time along by baking some cakes for the young man in the basement. He was a little skinny, probably not eating right, probably needed a good woman to look after him.

Margarita came before the young man had finished. Mrs. Caputo heard the old Dodge Dart rattle up the driveway and knew Margarita would be in a hurry. She wouldn't want to wait for the young man to finish. Margarita's son would be coming home from the university at four and she didn't like his supper to be late.

"Tell him I'll be leaving, tell him to take the cakes by the door and lock up when he leaves," she told Margarita in the Emilia Romagna dialect she and Mario had used all their lives, even after they had come to Canada.

Margarita went down into the basement to speak to the young man while Mrs. Caputo wrapped the cakes in a paper towel and placed them in a plastic bag.

Margarita and the young man came up the stairs together.

They stood in the hall for a few seconds before Mrs. Caputo called out from the kitchen, "close door, close door."

The young man closed the door. "Uh, I'm almost finished for today, Mrs. Caputo. Your furnace was pretty dirty, I gave it a good cleaning, but the motor was burned out. Strange thing that . . . looked like a screwdriver or something had been wedged into it." He held up the heavy electric motor for her to see; a section of the outer casing was bent and twisted. "I ll have to come back tomorrow with a new one. Will you be home around ten?"

"Huh," Mrs. Caputo said.

Margarita translated. When she came to the part about the motor, she gestured to the man to hold up the motor. Mrs. Caputo looked at it for a few moments before lifting her head. "*Oh Dio, oh dio,*" she said softly, making the sign of the cross three times across her chest.

"What? What's wrong?" the young man asked. Margarita gently took the young man by the arm.

"Everything's fine," she said. "She's old and she's alone. She worries about the house, that's all."

"I didn't mean to upset her," the young man said, his face knotted in concern.

Seeing that she had upset the young man, Mrs. Caputo pulled herself together as best she could. "Is O.K., is O.K.," she said, her breath still a little labored. "Here, take." She thrust the bag of cakes toward the young man and then spoke in her Italian dialect. "You need to marry a woman who can take care of you, you're too skinny, need someone to make you fat."

"I don't understand," the young man said, a nervous smile on his face.

Margarita translated.

The young man smiled. "Thank you very much," he said.

Mrs. Caputo nodded back at him as he disappeared into the basement.

"A nice boy," Mrs. Caputo said, "but he needs a woman."

"Yes, a very nice boy," Margarita said trying to get Mrs. Caputo to move along. "Now let's get going. I have a nice boy of my own to think about and I don't want his supper to be late."

#

The house was silent as Mrs. Caputo opened the front door and entered. She placed her shopping bags on the floor, put her keys back into her purse and hung up her coat on the rack by the door.

She looked down the hall. Her stomach and heart seemed to jump up into her throat and for a moment it was hard to breathe.

The basement door was wide open.

Mrs. Caputo made the sign of the cross seven times and began whispering a prayer under her breath. The open hole of the doorway gaped at her. It seemed huge, as if it led not down into the basement but into some other world far, far away.

She called for her cat. "Micio? Micio? Cicci."

From somewhere deep down in the basement came a response. It was a faint meow, unlike any she'd ever heard before. It seemed to float on the air to her. She called again, "Micio, Micio, *vienni qui.*"

There was a second meow. Like the first, it was peaceful, contented.

Mrs. Caputo picked out a box of dried cat food from one of the shopping bags at her feet and shook it. The sound of the hard bits of food rattling around inside the box like stones on a tin sheet always summoned the cat, brought it running, hungry and purring about her ankles.

Except this time there was no response.

Mrs. Caputo moved cautiously toward the doorway. She stopped several steps from the open hole and tried to peer inside. The basement looked black, empty, evil.

She took a few more steps. When she was standing directly in front of the doorway a sudden calmness overcame her, as if there had been nothing to fear in the basement all along, as if there was joy and happiness to be found in its depths.

She stuck her head through the doorway, steadying herself with an arm on each side of the doorframe. The steps seemed different than she remembered; they were made of stone like the steps which led down the hill from the road at her father's home in Montecastello. And the basement appeared different as well.

There was dirt where there used to be concrete. To the right of the steps, a wagon full of hay rested with its wheels chocked. Further in the distance was the mountain she used to see every morning through her bedroom window as a child. Its sides were vibrant green in the morning sun. Straight ahead was the road that led to Cesena, a road she used to walk barefoot throughout the summer. On that road as a teenager she had sneaked cigarettes during the war. On that road she had met Mario.

"Yolanda!"

For a moment Mrs. Caputo wondered who would be calling her, for she hadn't heard her own name more than five times since Mario had died.

"Yolanda!" She heard it again and suddenly recognized the voice as Mario's. It was young and alive, the way it had sounded when they'd just married.

"Mario? Mario is that you?" She called down into the basement.

"Yes, yes, it is," came the sweet soft sound of the reply. Mario was there, standing at the bottom of the steps, dressed in the only suit he had ever owned before coming to Canada. It had been the first suit his brother Enrico made after becoming a tailor's apprentice and it fit perfectly. It was the suit he had been married in, the suit that had made Yolanda fall in love with him the first time she had seen him. "I've been waiting for you *Cara Mia*, so many years now. Why haven't you joined me?"

"Mario," she said softly as the memories of their youth came rushing back to her. "But you're . . ."

She pulled herself away from the doorway and slammed the door shut behind her. She made the sign of the cross, fell awkwardly to her knees and began to pray. She prayed to God to take the devil from her basement, to keep her free from his power, and to let Mario's soul rest in peace.

As Mrs. Caputo prayed, the cat came in from the kitchen and brushed past her. She picked it up and cradled it in her arms as if it were a child. The cat meowed once and licked a salty tear from her cheek.

#

Mrs. Caputo stayed upstairs in her bedroom most of the evening to keep some distance between herself and the basement. She had nothing to do there in her room. She didn't read; she couldn't knit anymore, and the television was downstairs in the living room. Even if she had wanted to do any of those things her mind wouldn't have allowed it. Her thoughts were drawn too strongly to what she had seen, or thought she had seen, in the basement.

But still it called to her. She tried to cover her ears, first with her hands and then with a pillow, but nothing could drown out the beckoning from the basement.

"Yolanda, Yolanda." The voice whispered up to her bedroom through the cracks in the walls and floor.

She tried praying but that only seemed to give the voice added strength, increasing its volume until her name swirled about her, filling the room like music.

"Yolanda, Yolanda . . ."

Finally Mrs. Caputo could take no more. The endless calling of her name and the curiosity about what she had seen earlier in the day had become too much. She gathered herself off the bed, put on her house coat and slippers and made her way downstairs. A rosary dangled loosely from her right hand as she mumbled prayers under her breath.

She stood in front of the basement doorway for several minutes, praying. She placed her left hand on the doorknob and made the sign of the cross with her right, the crucifix of the rosary swinging wildly from side to side.

She opened the door. The basement was gone.

Instead was the backyard of her parent's home, the mountains of her youth, the smell of grapes ripening on the vine, the light of a thousand happy days.

And coming up the road was Mario.

"Yolanda," he called. "Yolanda, there you are. I've been waiting for you. Why didn't you come when I called you?"

"Mario? Is that really you?" she said her eyes blinking and blurry with tears.

"Of course it is *cara*, how silly you are. Who else would wait for you so long, who else would call you night after night, who else loves you as much as I do?"

Yolanda's head was spinning the same way it had fifty years earlier. Mario, in love with me. Of all the girls, he chose to make me the luckiest in the village, in the province, no . . . in all of Italy.

She felt herself young again, as if the sight, sounds and smell of younger days had filled her up and rejuvenated her. Mario was as handsome as she could remember, the land was just as beautiful; everything was precisely the way she remembered it.

Mario was only a few steps in front of her now, his young blue eyes alive with the promise of a great future, his thick shock of coal black hair promising his good looks would last forever, his muscular arms and back promising there would be nights of passion once more.

"Come! Now, before it's too late and I have to wait even longer. Come now and be with me." Mario had his arms outstretched toward her.

"I can't, what will papa say?"

"Your father's here. I've already talked to him. He gives his blessing." Mario's face had such a look of love that she knew she would be safe in his arms.

She went to him.

He gathered her up and they kissed for what seemed like forever. At last they turned and, arm in arm, began walking down the road into town.

#

"Hello? Mrs. Caputo? Anybody home?"

The young man had found the front door open and was anxious to get the furnace fixed so he could get on with the day's regularly scheduled calls.

"I'm back to fix the furnace!" he called out boldly, stepping through the doorway and into the house. "La furnacia." He tried to make the word sound more Italian for Mrs. Caputo's benefit but decided he just sounded stupid.

He stepped back outside, keeping the front door open, and rang the doorbell several times. No answer. He decided to go ahead with the repair in the hopes that Mrs. Caputo would arrive before he was done.

He walked over to the basement doorway, reached for the doorknob and was startled by something brushing past his right leg. He looked down and saw the cat, sucking up to him for something to eat.

"Are you hungry fella . . . girl . . . whatever you are?"

The cat purred in anticipation of food. "Come on," the young man said picking the cat up and walking into the kitchen. "I'll fix you up. Keep you away from that door anyway. The lady would be pretty upset with me if you ended up in the basement now, wouldn't she?"

The cat was too busy lapping up the saucer of milk to answer.

Satisfied that the cat would be occupied for several moments the young man quickly walked back to the basement and opened the door.

"Holy shit!"

Mrs. Caputo's body lay bent and broken at the bottom of the stairs, a curious smile on her lips.

He ran down the steps and crouched over the body. He placed an ear to its chest and listened for a heartbeat. He placed his fingers on its neck in search of a pulse but quickly pulled his hand away. The body was cold.

"No," he said softly, his own breath and heartbeat racing.

From somewhere in the basement shadows he thought he heard a sound. It was a quick tick kind of sound, a hard soled shoe on concrete.

"Who's there?" he shouted as his mind answered the question with a hundred different possibilities.

The young man turned to face the sound, or at least where he thought the sound was coming from. "Who's there?" he called again.

There was nobody there, only a voice. It was a young man's voice with a strange accent.

"Please clo-sed door when you go." The words seem to float upon the musty, damp air of the basement.

And from somewhere in the shadows he heard a giggle. It was a young girl's giggle, and it was beautiful.

On Spec was and still is, the premiere magazine of science fiction and fantasy in Canada. I first learned of the magazine at the Context 89 convention in Edmonton and I was desperate to sell them a story. A very early story, "The Basement" is my attempt to remind people that the elderly have lived full lives, and when they were younger they were quite possibly tougher, cooler, stronger or smarter than their aged appearance might suggest. Finally, I chose Italian as the ethnicity of the central character because my mother was Italian and the neighborhood in Toronto I grew up in was all Italian, so it seemed an easy way to get the speech and mannerisms right. Write what you know, right?

Mother and Child

He looked over at her sitting in the passenger seat and, without a word being exchanged, knew what she was thinking.

"It's still not too late, you know," he said quietly. "You don't have to do this to yourself. We don't have to go back there."

She kept her eyes on the highway and didn't answer. The inside of the car was silent except for the *Shhh!* of the tires on the wet asphalt.

"All I have to do is turn the car around and we can spend the week at home. You don't have to go through with this."

Beth adjusted herself on the seat and leaned over until her head rested against the rain-spotted window. The dark green of the roadside trees passed by in a blur.

"I know I don't have to," she said finally, more like a sigh than actual speech. "But I want to, I need to be . . . reminded." She paused a beat. "I miss him so much."

Her body shook as she cried.

Barry wanted to reach over with his right hand and comfort her but stopped himself midway, his hand finally settling on the shifter between them. She wants to be alone in this, he thought. She needs to feel the pain one more time. Maybe then she'll finally be able to let go.

He kept his eyes on the road and eventually brought his right hand back to the two o'clock position on the steering wheel.

They drove on in silence.

It had been almost a year since it happened, but it seemed more like yesterday.

The three of them—Beth, Tommy and "Uncle" Barry— had rented a small two bedroom log cabin on Lake Kashagawigamog for a week last July. Beth and Tommy slept in one bedroom while Uncle Barry slept in the other. It had been a postcard perfect week of fishing trips, campfires, walks down country roads and barefoot runs through cool morning dew.

Perfect really, until the second-last day.

It was a hot and sunny Saturday afternoon. Tommy went down to the lake for a swim and Beth went out onto the porch where she could keep an eye on her son.

Realizing that Tommy would be out of the cabin for a little while, Barry put on a robe and joined Beth on the porch for a rare private moment. He stood before Beth and opened his robe. "It's been like this all week," he said.

Beth grabbed Barry's hand and led him back inside.

They made love quickly.

Even though it had only lasted a few minutes, the passion that had built up over the course of the week had made it special, one of the best times ever. And, the risk of being caught by Tommy had made it just a little bit dangerous.

But Tommy didn't walk in on them.

When Beth returned to the porch, her hair tussled and falling strangely to the left, Tommy was nowhere to be seen. She thought nothing of it at first. Probably off somewhere chasing a frog, that's all. But as the day's shadows lengthened, she began to sense something had gone wrong. Terribly wrong.

Police divers searched the weed beds for weeks but they never found a body.

The oldtimers on the lake said they'd seen it happen before. The boy had probably gotten tangled up in the weeds and drowned. After that, the body likely sank to the bottom and was sucked into the sawdust turned muck that was the only legacy of the sawmill that had operated on the lake's north shore at the turn-of-the-century.

Maybe the body would turn up in a year.

Maybe in ten.

Maybe never.

#

Something not eyes looked out and saw. Something not lungs inhaled water and breathed. Something not arms swayed in the current. Something not flesh, not blood, stirred in the depths. Something dead was alive.

Mommy? I knew you'd come back.

#

The sky brightened and the sun shone down on the damp grass, filling the air with a moist fresh scent. The flowers that trimmed the cabin opened up to face the sun with splashes of color.

Beth took the cooler out of the trunk of the car and carried it slowly into the cabin.

Barry took their luggage out of the car's back seat and followed Beth inside. He put the suitcase on the bed in the first bedroom and came out into the kitchen to look around. The walls of the cabin were the same pale knotty pine and the ceiling rafters looked like they might give way at any moment. The old vinyl floor was stained and worn and the furniture was purely functional. The windows were spotted and dirty, but the view was . . . magnificent.

Barry smiled. He turned to share the moment with Beth and saw it.

The door to the second bedroom was open. The room was dark and utterly empty; the doorway gaped before him like the yawning jaw of some great beast.

"I'm not so sure this is a good idea," he said.

Beth stopped emptying the cooler into the refrigerator, pausing in silence. "Everything is fine," she said, and then continued stocking the fridge.

Beth was a strong woman. The death of her son had been a shock to her system but she'd handled it in her own way. She was back at work a week after the funeral and never mentioned Tommy's name again. When the receipt for the down payment on a week's rental of the cottage had come in the mail, Barry wanted to send it back with a letter asking if it were some kind of sick joke, but Beth stopped him. She acted as if the receipt were a sign from God ordering her to stick her hand in the fire and proclaim her faith.

"I have to go back," she'd said. "I have to make my peace with Tommy."

Although Barry considered the trip to be a senseless masochistic exercise, he went along with Beth's wishes and said nothing more on the matter. She'd been so strong through it all, how could he deny her anything she thought might help her cope?

They finished unloading the car in silence.

#

The sun pierced the lake's surface and bands of light cut deeply into the dark murky waters, the sunbeams turning cold water into warm, turning death into life.

Mommy! I knew you wouldn't leave me here alone.

#

Beth began preparing dinner when Barry went to the camp office to pay off the week's rental fee. With the food simmering on the kitchen's two-burner hotplate, Beth poured herself a glass of wine and stepped out onto the porch.

The lake was a sheet of blue tinted glass, the sun reflecting off its surface in a bright squiggly line. The air was warm and dry; everything seemed right.

For a moment Beth thought that all she had to do was turn around and go back into the cabin and the past year would be wiped out, or perhaps transformed into nothing more than a bad dream. Tommy would be there in the bedroom, drying himself off with a towel and asking for a peanut butter sandwich.

A fish jumped at an insect on the surface of the lake. The splash broke the stillness of the water and sent rippling rings out toward shore.

Beth looked down into her wineglass and fingered the rim. She drank the rest of the wine down in a gulp and went back into the empty cabin.

#

White light shone brightly on blue and green and gray and black as leafy tendrils waved in the current.

Calling . . .

Mommy! Don't leave me.

#

"All paid up," Barry said.

Beth heard him come in and turned to greet him. There were flowers in his hand, red and pink and blue and yellow.

"I came back through the field," Barry said, holding up the flowers like a trophy. "I thought they might brighten the cabin a bit."

"They're nice," Beth said, turning back around.

Barry walked across the cabin and put the flowers in an empty jar. He came up behind Beth, put his hands on her shoulders and began to massage.

His hands felt good on her neck. Beth had thought she'd be unable to be close to Barry during the week because of what happened to Tommy, but there was something hot and warm rising up within her that told her that she was still a woman, and she was still alive.

"After," she said under her breath. "Dinner's ready."

Barry immediately slowed his massage down to a gentle caress. "I'll get the table ready."

Dinner was fine, especially the wine.

After dinner, Barry took Beth by the hand and led her to the bedroom.

Beth had feared this moment, but she was surprised to find that she was eager and responsive. She opened herself up to Barry as if sex was something new. She felt him inside her and lifted herself up to him.

They came together, life flowing warm and fluid between them.

The cool night air suddenly chilled their sweat-dampened skin and they cuddled under the covers for warmth.

Minutes later, Barry was asleep. The day's long drive had used up most of his energy, their few moments of passion had taken the rest.

Beth kissed Barry lightly on the cheek and got up from the bed. She wrapped herself in her robe and went out onto the porch. The outside air was cool and mist rose up off the still water of the lake like fog. The full moon hung over the horizon like a naked bulb, and moonbeams shone down through the mist like daggers. The shrill cry of a loon sliced through the silent night air like a scream.

#

Light and darkness came together in the depths. A limp and withered form turned toward the light. A time lost voice silently cried out.

I'm here, mommy!

Come to me.

#

Beth stepped off the porch. The grass felt cold and wet on the soles of her feet and between her toes as she walked down toward the lake.

Something . . .

After the chill of the damp night grass, the lake lapped warmly over her feet and ankles. She kicked her foot and sent water droplets shimmering through the air.

. . . called out.

Quite slowly, Beth removed her robe and dropped it behind her on the shore. The water felt warm on her legs, her knees, her thighs.

Mommy!

The water continued to rise up over her body. It felt cold on her vagina and belly. It felt cold against her breasts.

We can be together now . . .

Beth kept walking further out into the lake, the water rising above over her shoulders and encircling her neck. When it was up to her chin she began moving her arms over the surface of the water to keep afloat.

. . . forever and . . .

Something not a hand grabbed hold of her foot and pulled her . . . down.

For a moment she thought of crying out, but something told her not to. A voice somewhere in the back of her mind spoke to her and told her . . .

It will be good.

She opened her mouth in a gasp. At first the water entered her slowly, but as she went deeper the water forced its way into her mouth, purging her in a huge monstrous gush.

Something twisted around a thigh and pulled.

As the water rushed up around her, she looked up and saw the wavy disk of the moon shrinking in the distant night sky.

Something dark crawled into her arms and nestled in her bosom.

Forever and ever, Mommy.

She put her arms around it and pulled it tight against her cold, cold heart.

Yes, Tommy. Forever and ever.

The inspiration for this one comes directly from the Ray Bradbury tale, "The Lake," which I read in the collection *The October Country* -- my favorite book of all time and the reason I began writing fantasy stories in the first place. The similarities to "The Lake" are obvious but slight changes were made to make it a different story and one that is my own. Instead of a dead child calling out to a childhood friend, it now calls out for its mother, ultimately drawing her into the water and her death. A cynic might call it derivative, but I prefer to call it an *homage.*

Mark of the Beast

The cabin's silence was broken only by the sound of the rocking chair's runners as they cut into the cold hardwood floor.

Nadia Varga sat in the rocker, a knitted shawl covering her shoulders, a flannel blanket over her legs and a double-barreled shotgun sitting across her lap.

She was waiting for the beast.

And when it came she was going to kill it.

She'd been waiting for the beast ever since it took her husband last October. It had been a lonely vigil, but she'd never once broken her routine of loading her shotgun, pulling her rocker up to the front door, covering herself against the night's chill and waiting for it to come.

While she sat rocking, her mind invariably slipped backward in time to the first time the beast had come.

It had been a night just like this one . . .

#

Nadia dug her arm into the pumpkin up to the elbow and scooped out a handful of stringy pulp and seeds. She disliked the feel of the slimy mess on her hands but Thomas liked her pies so much the discomfort was little more than a minor inconvenience.

Outside, with the short October sun rapidly falling below mountains of the western horizon, Thomas was busy stacking firewood against the side of the cabin. The winter's chill had come early, and they'd had to start keeping the pot-bellied stove fired around the clock two weeks earlier than usual. Even though they had enough firewood to last for two winters, Thomas had been splitting and piling logs the past four days, just to be sure.

The day had been almost perfect, full of chores that were more like relaxation than work for the elderly couple. Their retirement had been full of many such days, the kind they'd looked forward to all their lives. Later that night, they might play cards at the kitchen table, watch a movie off the dish, or read the latest two-year-old copy of *Reader's Digest*. Or they might just go to bed early.

After a world war, four children and decades of work in the sawmills of British Columbia, the quiet uneventful hours were easy to take. They filled up their days and stretched them out until they overlapped each other like fallen autumn leaves.

That's why, when Nadia heard the first scream, she thought it was nothing more than Thomas having some fun with her. But the second scream told her that something was wrong, unnaturally wrong.

Quickly shaking the pulpy pumpkin innards from her hands, she ran outside and around the cabin to the woodpile, arriving just in time to see Thomas's mauled body being dragged by its feet out towards the forest.

His neck and chest had been ripped open and dark red blood bubbled up from the open wound like oil from the ground.

Nadia's mouth fell open in a silent scream.

"Get back," Thomas said in a thin and ragged voice, the words already sounding as if spoken by a dead man. "Get away."

"Thomas!" Nadia screamed in a shrill voice that sliced through the chill night air like a knife blade.

The beast stopped in its tracks and turned. It hesitated a moment, staring at her with wide, dark eyes and growling softly under its breath as if deciding whether or not to take her as well.

As it stood there in the twilight, Nadia clearly saw the mark of the beast cut into the thick tangle of blood matted fur on its chest—and suddenly wished her husband dead.

The beast turned back around and took two steps towards the woods before it and Thomas were swallowed up by the night-black shadows of the forest.

Nadia's eyes rolled over in their sockets. She felt her world darken around the edges and fell to the ground in a heap.

#

A couple of hikers found Thomas's remains two weeks later, fifteen miles from their cabin on the eastern shore of Pitt Lake. What they found was little more than body parts scattered across a small clearing some ten meters across. The right half of his jawbone—found underneath a foot—was enough for a positive ID.

The RCMP told Nadia her husband had been taken by a grizzly bear that had come down from the mountains looking for food. At first she couldn't be sure if the two officers believed what they were telling her or not, but once they said a police sharpshooter had shot the bear near the shores of Harrison Lake she knew they were knowingly lying to her.

But what else could they say? The police hadn't seen what she had seen. The police hadn't seen the seven-foot tall man-like beast dragging her husband away like a rag doll. They hadn't seen the huge hairy arms and legs, or the talonlike claws that tore his body apart like paper. They hadn't seen its large vulpine face, the big dark eyes or the long sharp teeth. Most of all, they hadn't seen the pentagram that was carved into its chest as if by a jagged knife.

The mark of the beast had been unmistakable.

Nadia tried to tell her story to the local newspapers but all they wanted to talk about were rabid bears, sasquatches and bigfoots.

No one wanted to know the truth.

No one wanted to hear about ravenous creatures that had once been men.

But when a 500-pound bear had been found mauled to death on the side of a nearby logging road two weeks ago, tourists and townsfolk suddenly became conspicuous by their absence.

When Nadia heard about the bear on the radio, she didn't run. She knew what was coming and she was ready for it. The two-shot gun on her lap was loaded with two shells she'd had specially made by a gunsmith in Port Moody. She'd brought the man six silver spoons and asked him to replace the lead buckshot of two shells with bits of silver.

Nadia was surprised that the gunsmith didn't laugh at her request. He simply told her he'd made silver bullets twice before and went into the back of his shop to do the work. When he'd finished the job later in the day, he gave the shells to her in an old pine box and refused to accept payment for his work. He simply gave her a look of understanding, placed a comforting hand in hers and said, "Good Luck."

#

A hard snapping of a branch outside the cabin brought Nadia back to the present.

She stopped rocking and listened.

The night had been silent save for the whispering rush of wind through the pines, but now even the wind had hushed, silenced by the same short sharp sound that Nadia had heard.

The hairs on the back of Nadia's wrist stood up on end, feeling as if they'd been charged with electricity. And she knew.

The beast had come, at last.

Although she'd had a year to prepare herself, Nadia found her body shaking at the thought of confronting the beast. Doubt slowly crept into the thinking part of her mind.

What if I miss? What if the silver isn't enough to kill it? Will I be able to kill it, or will I just die trying? What if it scratches me before it dies, and I live?

Her heart began to pound like a fist inside her chest and blood began to roar through her ears. Her hands trembled in mortal fear. The urge to flee, to find a corner and cower there hidden was strong within her, but mixed somewhere in the torrent of fear swirling through her was the single sweet thought of revenge. It wasn't enough to calm her fears, but it was more than enough to keep her seated in her rocker.

A scratching sound came from the living room window. Nadia turned in her chair in time to see the large hairy hand creeping through the small space beneath the open window. Her breath became short and choppy and her entire body began to tremble as she watched the claw-like hand crawl over the window sill, as if reaching for her.

She turned the gun around on her lap, pointing it at the window. She was about to pull the trigger, but stopped. Her whole body froze, so paralyzed by what she saw that her even her eyes refused to blink.

The beast was looking in through the open window, its angry red eyes glaring at her, boring into her as if they alone were enough to tear her body to pieces.

Then, just as quickly as they appeared, the eyes were gone, replaced by a second hand that clawed its way in, tearing at the window frame. The beast was trying to rip open a hole in the wall big enough to crawl through.

The sound of splintering wood brought Nadia out of her daze. Her heart pounded painfully, her body trembled and her hands shook violently as she reached for the shotgun. Her fingers wrapped around the stock and barrel of the gun so tightly that her knuckles turned a ghostly shade of white.

Keeping the gun close to her body to try and steady it, she picked it up off her lap, took aim . . .

. . . and fired.

The shotgun's kick nearly sent Nadia toppling over backward but she managed to keep herself upright. When the smoke cleared she saw that the window's glass was unbroken. About four feet to the right of the window was a huge hole in the wall.

Her shot hadn't even been close.

The beast had been scared off, but it would be back.

#

One more chance.

There was one shell left in the gun, one chance left to shoot the creature full of silver.

She'd only had two special shells made because she'd figured there wouldn't be time to reload the gun once the beast was upon her. There was no more room for error, she had to be sure her last shot was on target.

Her body began to shake now for a different reason. She was crying.

"Why have I been so foolish?" she said aloud, only to be answered by the sudden howl of the wind through the gaping mouth of the open window. "Stupid old woman. What makes you think you can kill it?"

The wind died down, replaced by the empty rustling of the pines.

"Why didn't I leave like the rest of them?"

Silence.

"Why did I have to stay behind?"

For Thomas.

The voice in the back of her mind spoke clearly to her, reminding her and wiping away all her fear and trembling.

"Yes," she said. "For Thomas."

She was suddenly embarrassed. *How could I have forgotten for even a moment?*

She straightened herself in her chair, adjusted the shawl over her shoulders and placed the gun comfortably in her lap. She still had one shot. It should be enough.

But even if she steeled herself against the approach of the beast, she couldn't be sure she'd aim well enough to hit it.

She'd have to shoot it at point-blank range. She would have to wait until it was nearly on top of her before pulling the trigger.

Or did she?

There was another possibility.

She'd once read that a silver bullet entering a werecreature's body at any point would bring instant death. That did not mean the bullet had to be fired from a gun.

What if . . .

She paused a moment, preparing herself for the horror of her own thought.

What if I turned the gun on myself. My flesh would be tainted with silver fragments—a deadly feast for the beast.

It could be done. She'd turned the gun on herself once before in the dark time of her life immediately following Thomas's death. She'd almost pulled the trigger, too, before the thought of revenge welled up inside her and forced her to carry on.

An icy chill ran the length of her spine as the stillness of the night slowly diminished until its silence was absolute.

Taking her own life in order to take that of the beast seemed so blackly macabre that she wasn't sure she could go through with it.

She considered her options.

If she tried to shoot the beast, she risked missing it. If that happened she'd surely end up dead. She also risked a scratch or wound before she was able to kill it. If that happened, if she became infected by the beast, she would become one herself, consigned to a lifetime of hell.

She shook her head. It was hard for her to think that by taking her own life she would have the best chance of achieving the one thing she'd lived for this past year.

She laughed. The idea seemed so . . .

The door opened, hinges creaking out a shrill cry of terror before diminishing into silence.

Claw-fingers curled around the edge of the door, pushing it open and allowing the light of the full October moon to shine into the cabin. Moonbeams streaked across the hardwood floor toward the far wall and the long, grotesque shadow there.

Nadia's heart leapt up into her throat, pounding like a thunderclap. Her breath became rapid and ragged. The gun trembled in her hands as she slowly picked it up off her lap.

The beast was upon her, so close she could smell the stench of carrion on its breath. She looked deep into its two dark eyes . . . and smiled.

Then, with a sense of pure and complete calm washing over her, she took careful aim . . .

. . . and fired.

This is the story Rob Sawyer references in his introduction, the one which *Northern Frights* editor Don Hutchinson asked me to write a story based on the cover art he'd already picked out for the anthology. I had only published a dozen or so stories by this time, so it was both an honor and a challenge for me to take on this request. The central idea is right out of werewolf lore -- that silver entering a werewolf's body by any means would cause death. The story offers two possible means of entry, both equally as lethal. Don was pleased with the end result and it was the first notch on the pulp-writer belt that Rob alludes to and I would eventually wear as a badge of honor.

Scream String

The mute twang of an unamplified electric guitar string echoed softly off the brick walls of the empty stairwell. The sound was followed by two out of tune strums, then silence.

World famous guitarist John Verrill, a.k.a. Johnny V, a.k.a. Johnny Violent, sat on the edge of a step stringing his burgundy 1969 Stratocaster. The concrete stairwell was cold and barren, the perfect place to spend a few solitary moments before the biggest gig of his life. Sure, plenty of bands had played the L.A. Coliseum before, but this concert was being televised worldwide. If things went according to plan, this one gig would make Johnny Violent and the Throbbing Purploids as popular as U2, The Rolling Stones, maybe even The Beatles.

He'd strung three new strings and was about to set the fourth when he heard the hard scrape of footsteps behind him. His eyes narrowed angrily as he turned around to see who the hell had the balls to bother him before a gig.

It was his wife, Jill.

"There you are," she said flatly as she pulled her skirt tight to her knees and eased herself down onto the landing above him. "I've been looking for you for over an hour."

Jill was a slim woman, but not especially attractive. She was in her late thirties and had been with Johnny from the very beginning. The years had not been kind to her. In the dim light of the stairwell, her eyes looked tired, cupped by large puffy bags and accentuated by crow's feet that had been scored by time's sharpest knife.

"Well, you found me," John muttered as he stretched the fourth string over the nut and set it into the machine head.

Of course Jill would have to be the one to bother him, she was the only one who could get away with it. Besides being one of the best rock guitarists in the world, Johnny Violent was also renowned for having a short fuse and an explosive temper. If it had been anyone other than Jill, they'd have been booking a flight home by now. Still, even though she could, Jill was the last person he'd expect to have bother him before a gig. She knew better than anyone that he needed his time alone.

He'd been sneaking off before gigs since the early years when he played downtown dives like the *El Mocambo* and the *Nag'sHead North* for beer and pocket change. He'd find some secluded spot and claim it as his temporary inner sanctum. Once there, he'd tune or restring his guitar, write a song, smoke a joint or just be alone with his thoughts. Now that the band had recorded six double platinum CDs, it was more important than ever that he have time alone to prepare himself before a concert.

John looked up at Jill but avoided making eye contact. "What do you want?" he asked, his voice edged with anger.

"I m sorry to bother you . . ." She made a half-hearted attempt at a smile. "But I need to talk."

"Can't it wait?"

"No, Johnny. It can t."

"All right," he said, doing his best to keep himself from telling her to *fuck off*. He pulled the fifth string from the packet on the step by his knee and let the thin steel wire coil snakelike around his fisted hand. "What's on your mind?"

"Tomorrow night's show in Seattle."

They were flying up the coast after tonight's show to play a cruddy little concert hall just outside of Seattle. The band often did things like that, not only to take a break from the tour but for the publicity it generated as well.

"What about it?" asked John.

"You said it was supposed to be just for the band and a few of the best roadies?"

"It is," John said sharply. "A one night stand in a five-hundred seat concert hall. Just like old times, and just for the boys."

Jill closed her eyes and let out a deep, long sigh. "Well, when I called the hotel to see if the case of Heineken had arrived, the concierge told me that *Mrs. Violent* had signed for it late this afternoon."

There was a long, tense silence between them. John was suddenly aware of the warm draft twisting its way up through the stairwell.

"Obviously, there's been a mistake," he said, masking the tremor in his voice by increasing its volume.

"I don't think so, Johnny. You re swinging up to Seattle for a night so you can be with *her*." The last word echoed once, then died. "Aren't you?"

"Take it easy, babe," John said in a strained voice. "It's not like that at all."

"Don't 'take it easy, babe,' me," said Jill through clenched teeth. "I'm your wife, not one of your gum-chewing, bubble-popping bimbos."

"What?"

"God, how much of a fool do you take me for, Johnny? I've been watching you closely on this tour. I know you've been cheating on me."

"No I—"

"Shut up, Johnny! Just shut up and let me finish."

John was speechless. Nobody told Johnny Violent to shut up. Nobody. Not even Jill.

"There's no use denying it. I hired a detective to follow you last month in Toronto. I've got pictures."

The short fuse leading to John's violent temper began to sizzle.

"That's why I'm filing for divorce," Jill said, rising to her feet. "I kept putting it off thinking you'd get it out of your system, but I can't wait any more. I've got to do it now, while I'm still young enough to start my life over again, on my own."

John set his guitar aside and stood up, the fifth string still in his hand. He was pissed—well past apeshit and halfway to ballistic.

Jill's eyes closed into slits and her lips cracked a blatantly malicious smile. "Don't worry about me, Johnny," she said, her voice wet with contempt. "California divorce laws entitle me to half of everything. I'm pretty sure I ll be able to make do with fifteen-million."

Outwardly, John was the picture of calm. Inside, however, was another story. The thought of losing half his wealth to Jill in one fell swoop was too much for him to handle. His mind exploded in a white-hot burst of rage; anger flared outward to every part of his body.

He bound up the steps and stood face to face with her. A vein throbbed in the middle of his forehead as he slowly pulled back his lips and bared his teeth in something that wasn't a smile.

Jill shook her head and let out a condescending little laugh. "You never grew up, did you Johnny?"

John's open hand arced out at her, his fingers and palm slapping her right cheek with a loud, fleshy *smack*.

Jill looked surprised, but remained defiant. "Do you know what the roadies call you? Little Johnny Tantrum."

John's hands shot up from his sides in a blur of motion. A moment later his strong fingers closed around her throat like a giant steel vice, squeezing off her windpipe and making it hard for her to breathe.

Within seconds he had the guitar string coiled around her neck. As he pulled on the string, it pressed sharply against her flesh, turning the skin a ghostly shade of white.

"What . . . are you—" Jill sputtered, her eyes bulging out of their sockets in a look of sheer terror.

"You're not getting a fucking thing," John said in a low, guttural voice he'd never heard himself use before. "It's mine! All of it!"

"Please don't—"

He pulled the string tightly around her neck until the thin steel wire cut into the flesh and a line of blood bubbled up from the skin.

"—kill me, Johnny."

Jill's words were little more than wet gurgles as she thrashed about, her hands desperately trying to push John's hands together and relieve the tension on the string.

It was no use. John was too strong . . . too wild . . . too freaked out to be stopped.

The string jerked in his hands as the fine steel strand snapped through the tendons in the meaty part of her neck.

Jill screamed, a keening wail that sliced through the air for a moment before dying out in the depths of her throat. The scream lived another second as an echo in the stairwell, then died there as well.

John continued to pull on the string—feeling it grate and scrape against the vertebrae in the middle of her neck—until he was almost holding the string in a straight line in his hands.

Jill's head fell limply to one side. Blood gushed freely from the open rent in her neck and splattered onto the steps like rain. Then her bowels emptied.

John released the tension on the string, his body drenched in sweat and his breath coming in hard labored gasps. Suddenly, the stink of blood and excrement brought him out of his maniacal haze. He looked at the prone body of Jill on the landing, saw the blood pooling out from her ruined neck and felt his bloody fingers beginning to stick together.

He stopped breathing and for a moment his entire body was racked by raw fear. "What have I done? What have I done?" he moaned softly, twisting and turning against the cold, hard bricks as if trying to hide in the tiny cracks between them.

Just then he heard someone shouting off in the distance. "Johnny . . . Five minutes, Johnny . . ."

For the moment, all his guilt and remorse would have to be pushed aside. He would deal with his emotions later, probably in the hotel room in Seattle. Right now, he had a show to do.

He used Jill's skirt to wipe the blood off the guitar string and his hands. Satisfied they were both clean, he jumped down a few steps for his guitar. With the quick and sure movements of an expert hand, he set the fifth string, pulled it tight and wound it into the machine head. A minute later the sixth string was set and he hurriedly began tuning the guitar.

When he was done, he started up the stairs playing a riff from *Flesh Wound*, the band's latest hit single. Although he nearly pounded on the Strat, he couldn't drown out the sound of Jill's blood dripping down the steps behind him like water from a leaky faucet.

When he got to the green room backstage, the rest of the band was waiting for him with impatient looks on their faces.

"You cut it a little too close this time, man," said Stuart Green, the band's lanky blond bass player. "This is one show we can't be late for."

"Sorry guys," said John. "I got carried away and lost track of time."

"Are you all right?" asked Bill "Burnout" Burns, the Purploids' drummer.

From the way they were looking at him, John thought his clothes were stained with blood. He gave himself a quick once-over. If there was any blood on him, it was lost in the deep purple swirls of his outfit. He was about to look up when he realized his right hand was shaking.

"I guess I'm a little nervous," John said, doing his best to crack a smile.

"We all are, man," said Green.

Burnout upended his Heineken, emptied it into his throat and belched. "I'm not," he said.

#

Rick Dees stepped onto the stage, walked up to the microphone and coughed. The crowd impatiently began cheering. Without further hesitation, the D.J. said, "Ladies and gentlemen, Johnny Violent and The Throbbing Purploids!"

The entire Coliseum broke into a roar that sounded like surf breaking over a pier. The Purploids took to the stage and immediately started into *Brain Damaged*, the band's six-year-old first hit single and signature song.

John stood backstage, feeling the pounding intro to the song beat into his head, chest and gut like a jackhammer. After just a few bars the throbbing, pulsing music overtook him, masking the deep pangs of remorse, guilt and fear that were still coursing through his body.

All he could think of now was getting on stage, drinking in the energy emanating from the hundred thousand plus crowd and letting the music envelop him like a protective shroud.

Six bars from his solo, John jumped on stage and was immediately captured in the tight, white beam of the spotlight that would be trained on him throughout the show. The crowd roared. Johnny Violent was the one they'd all been waiting for.

John strutted around the stage for a few beats to show off his long mane of obsidian black hair, and then it was solo time.

He started with a sharp A and ran a quick scale up to a high E. Even though he'd rushed the tuning of the guitar, it sounded good, real good. After a few runs down the neck, John climaxed the solo by scaling up to an A on the fifth string and holding it there. After a few beats he bent it. As the note curled over the packed Coliseum, it changed . . . slowly turning into a mind numbing, blood curdling scream.

Under the lights, John could see people in the first few rows cupping their hands over their ears to try and block out the horrifying cry. For a moment he wondered if the same thing was happening all around the world.

John spun away from the crowd and began twisting the volume and tone controls on his guitar, but they had no effect on the awful sound. He tried the toggle switch. Nothing. In fact, the scream seemed to be getting louder, like some wild pulse of feedback that had to be allowed to run its course.

John looked up. The other members of the band were still playing, but they were continually looking left and right for someone who knew what the fuck was going on.

Nobody knew a thing.

Except for John.

The scream had a familiar sound to it. It was the same sound Jill had made when he'd killed her. Her death scream had been captured on the thin steel guitar string as clearly as if it had been recorded on tape.

He ran downstage to his wah wah pedal and pushed back on it. Nothing happened. He kicked it, but the terrible scream would not die.

One by one, the band stopped playing until all that could be heard was the scream.

Then that died as well.

And the Coliseum was silent, as if it were empty.

Johnny killed me!

The words cut through the air like a knife. John stood erect in the center of the stage as if the knife had been buried deeply into the small of his back.

Johnny did it!

The voice was that of a woman, but sounded only vaguely like Jill's. It was if the words had been stretched and compressed a dozen times before being sent through the amps.

Johnny killer!

John pulled the guitar from his shoulder and held it at arm's length as if it were diseased. As he watched in horror, the fifth string—the scream string—vibrated like a displaced vocal chord.

Johnny—

Before the voice could say another word, John grabbed the Strat's neck firmly in his hands and swung the guitar over his head like an axe . . .

And in one swift motion brought it crashing down onto the stage.

Seeing Johnny Violent smash his priceless 1969 Burgundy Stratocaster in the opening minutes of the concert left the crowd dumbfounded.

Again John brought the Strat down onto the stage. Pieces of wood and metal broke away from the guitar sending a terrible black noise through the wall of speakers at each end of the stage.

When the cops stepped onto the stage, the crowd must have thought it was all part of the show because the Coliseum suddenly erupted into a standing ovation.

John kept swinging the guitar, pounding it into the stage until it was little more than junk in his hands. Then he got down on all fours and searched the debris for the fifth string.

When he picked it up, he could feel it trembling in his hand. He held it close to his ear, and felt his heart fall deep into the pit of his stomach.

Why, Johnny? Why? Jill's voice cried faintly through the string. It asked the question once more, then faded into silence.

Rough hands took hold of John and lifted him up off the stage. He looked around. There were cops everywhere.

One of them pried open his fisted right hand and slid the guitar string into a small plastic bag. Then they pulled his arms behind his back and clamped cold steel rings to his wrists.

"Mr. Violent, you have the right to remain silent . . ." The words were picked up by a nearby microphone.

And the crowd went wild.

A big part of my job in my early days of being a freelance writer was finding places to sell stories. That's what led me to get in touch with editor Jeff Gelb, sending him a letter and asking if I could contribute to any of his upcoming anthologies. Turned out he had three going on at the time and I managed to hit on all three, *Hot Blood 4*, *Shock Rock 2*, and *Fear Itself*. While I did goof around writing rock songs with a group of guys (we called ourselves The Attitude, we wrote terrible songs that used the word "Baby!" way too much) I had no real experience with rock music. And so, with the help of David Nickle, I was put in touch with another newspaper reporter named Stuart Green who also happened to play in a grunge band called, Crawl. Stuart and I talked about guitars and what type of strings were the best for killing people and the result was "Scream String." Such were the sorts of discussions I had with people back in the day.

S.P.S.

My husband died during childbirth.

Now I know that sounds incredible, but if you know anything about S.P.S. you wouldn't think so.

In fact, if you knew anything at all about Sensory Perception Simulators you'd probably have nothing but sympathy for me.

Well, save it. I don't need it.

I've learned to get along quite nicely in a world without Marty—that was my husband—and with S.P.S. Perhaps I should explain.

It's been six years since we went to Sim Shack to buy our S.P.S., but I can still remember the salesman's knuckle ball as if it were yesterday.

"The Phillips S.P.S. XR 2000 is the ultimate in sensory perception simulation on the home entertainment market today," came the windup.

My husband Marty paid close attention. He was the one who wanted an S.P.S., after all. I tried hard not to listen; the salesman's voice was too automatic and precise for my liking. It sounded as if he could make the same pitch in his sleep.

". . . say you're watching the World Cup downhill on television and you suddenly wonder what it feels like to ski down the side of a mountain at a hundred kilometers-per-hour. Well, with the S.P.S. you don't have to wonder anymore. With a World Cup cassette and the seven electrodes connected to the right spots on the head and back of the neck—there," he connected Marty up as he spoke, "you can feel all the terror and excitement of the real thing in the safety of your own home."

The salesman touched a pressure sensitive pad on the S.P.S. and Marty's body snapped stiff, his eyes clamped down tight. He began to sway and then bent his knees and went into a tuck, just like a skier. He leaned first to one side and then another. Inside his head was Kitzbuehl, San Moritz, Whistler and Vail all rolled into one two minute ski ride through hell.

"You see," the salesman continued, now finding me his only audience, "the S.P.S. can duplicate any experience you might want to try. The XR 2000 model comes ready-to-use with twenty cassettes programmed with over one-hundred basic life experiences. And, you can buy additional cassettes if you feel those are, uh . . . too tame."

"How does it work?" I asked, not really interested but afraid of having to wait in silence while Marty finished his run.

"That's a good question, not too many people want to know. What S.P.S. does is stimulate the precise nerve endings and constrict the right muscles to create, within your body, an experience which is almost indistinguishable from the original. To enhance the effect, it can increase your heart rate, cause adrenalin to flood your system . . . it can even crack the right bones with some of the more exotic programs. Basically, it's all just clean fun, helps you to feel more alive."

I nodded numbly, dreading the possibility of having one of these tiny technological monstrosities in our home.

Marty's body suddenly went limp. He opened his eyes; they looked dopey. "I'll take it," he said.

"Marty, I don't want that thing . . ." I began, but he refused to hear me out. He dismissed me with a wave of his hand and one of his usual, "not-to-worry-dear" looks. He'd made up his mind that he was going to buy himself an S.P.S. — period, end of discussion.

Marty's face brightened as he turned away from me and looked back at the salesman. It was a little boy's look, the one I'd fallen in love with for some reason or another. "It's the greatest thing I've ever . . ." He stopped, searching for the right word. ". . . felt!"

#

At first it wasn't so bad having an S.P.S. of our own. Marty kept his use recreational, nothing more than a cassette or two a night.

I even used it from time to time.

I'd float on the Dead Sea, listen to the rain fall in the Amazon and cruise the coast of Alaska following the migration of the whales.

But no matter how much pleasure I got from these experiences, Marty was always waiting impatiently for me to finish so he could go flying with the Thunderbirds or hunt Bengal tigers with a slingshot.

Over time, he slowly became obsessed with S.P.S. and wound up practically living for it. He'd trudge off to work in the morning like an automaton and come home each night with all kinds of enthusiasm because he knew he'd soon be simulating through the night.

Even so, it didn't bother me all that much that he spent more time with S.P.S. than he did with me. What did concern me was the kinds of things he was simulating. If there was some cassette that taunted death, that called up the devil and challenged him to take a soul, Marty had to have it.

We spent some evenings together in the living room. I'd be watching some romantic police drama on television when over on the couch Marty would suddenly gasp in wonder or let out a terrifying scream because he had just made the jump to light speed or been buried under an avalanche in the Swiss Alps.

Once I asked him why he put himself through such horrible experiences and he told me it helped him feel more alive.

The irony of it kept me awake nights crying.

#

General Electric developed the first S.P.S. models for use in hospitals. They were designed to stimulate nerve endings and muscles in quadriplegics. Later they were used as a recreational tool for the blind, allowing them to see and feel a world around them they had never known. But as S.P.S. technology progressed and every hospital in the world had several S.P.S. machines, companies began developing home versions.

The prototype and first-generation machines were as big as Japanese cars, but they shrank in size over time until they became both portable and affordable to the general public.

They were as popular as Compact Disc players had been when they'd first hit the market fifty years earlier. But while listening to better quality music reproduction can stimulate your mind and body beneficially, unlimited access to S.P.S. proved to be addictive, and in some cases destructive.

#

Marty started looking sick, older, withered.

"Look at you," I said to him one night. "Thirty-years-old going on sixty-five. Are you trying to keep pace with that machine of yours? Are you trying to beat it? You might think you ve got a life with that thing, but it's killing you!"

His face was gaunt, his hair had whitened around the edges and his eyes seemed to be slightly recessed in their sockets. S.P.S. was sucking the life out of him, killing him with a thousand tiny deaths.

I had to act before it was too late.

I told Marty I wanted a child. In fact, I demanded that he give me a child. S.P.S. could take his life, but I needed a little of it within me before what little he had left was gone. If he didn't want to share his life with me, he could at least provide me with someone with whom I could share mine.

He wasn't very receptive to the idea until I threatened to separate him from his technological marvel.

"Either you give me a child or I'll destroy it," I said, fully intending to carry out the threat.

Marty either feared for his machine or for what his life might become without it. Whatever the reason, he gave in to my demand.

#

So we did it.

We didn't make love or fuck or anything like that, we just performed the act of sexual intercourse. I wasn't surprised, it was what I expected, really. Real sex bored Marty. After all, he had five-hundred-and-sixty-seven female sex cassettes in his collection and had probably made love to a thousand exotic women through S.P.S. I wasn't jealous; how could I be? How could flesh and blood compete with direct and acute nerve and muscle stimulation?

I didn't do it for the sex anyway. I wanted a child and if you had to have sex to have one, so be it.

#

Nine months later I was ready to bring my child into the world.

Marty took me to the hospital. I was happy that he came along, not because *he* was with me but because *someone* was with me and I wouldn't have to go through childbirth alone. Little did I know.

I was in labor for close to six hours. Marty was there, too, but he wasn't really there. He was present in the room hooked up to S.P.S. and off in his own little world having a baby of his own.

He'd wanted to experience childbirth with me, so he bought a childbirth cassette and took it with him to the hospital. He wanted to know what giving birth felt like. I could have told him if he had only asked.

It felt like white hot knitting needles were stuck through my abdomen, pinning me down onto the delivery room table. It felt like my belly was on fire, like my back muscles were locked tight with a staple gun, like my throat was dusted with Sahara sand, like my head might explode any second.

It felt as if I was creating life where there had been none before.

I lived through it.

Marty didn't.

I don't remember much of the birth, it's all one huge blur in my mind　　—all except the final few moments. Those last few seconds were the most painful of my life and I can remember quite vividly screaming in agony, seemingly walking a line of pain with consciousness on one side and unconsciousness on the other.

It was that moment that Marty wanted to experience most—the ultimate human experience.

The S.P.S. had been keeping him in an extended labor that mirrored my own. He had set up the machine so that when I finally gave birth he would be able to simulate the experience at the push of a button.

The doctors told me later that he'd suffered a massive coronary.

The autopsy concluded that the S.P.S. program had simulated the pain of childbirth by giving Marty a lethal jolt of electricity. His heart just stopped beating.

Marty had experienced death through life.

This time I couldn't help but laugh at the irony.

#

I know it sounds terrible, but I can't say I miss Marty much.

What's to miss?

Anyway, S.P.S. has taken his place quite admirably.

Sometimes I sit in the baby's room gently rocking my daughter's cradle with the S.P.S. in my lap.

I've often wondered what it felt like to have your husband come home from work to find supper ready and the dinner table set with candlelight and wine.

It's nice.

I'd sometimes wondered what it felt like to be a family on Christmas morning, with dozens of presents under the tree crying out to be opened.

It's wonderful.

I could never imagine what it might feel like to make love on an isolated beach, on a warm summer night full of stars.

Now I know.

It's heaven.

In 1993, what we now know as Virtual Reality was just getting its start and the subject matter seemed ripe for a story. Like all science fiction and fantasy, this story works on a "What if?" scenario, that being, "What if someone became addicted to virtual reality and substituted that virtual world for their own reality?" That's an ambitious story to tell, and one I was never really sure I was a good enough writer to pull off, especially in those early days of my writing career. However, I recently stumbled upon a review of the story by 18-time Hugo award nominee Stephen H. Silver (he's never won one, crazy I know, but I had to check) who read the tale in it's original publication, *Tails of Wonder*, and says that the story mostly succeeds and he's glad that it was rescued from a one-and-done magazine and published in this collection.

The Cold

Artie Mann rolled to the edge of the bed and placed a foot on the bare hardwood floor. An unbelievable feeling of cold shot up his leg and spread through his body like a hyperactive arctic cancer ravenously consuming his body's warmth.

There are two kinds of cold. One is the bitter cold that nips at noses on midwinter walks. The other is the angry cold that pierces the skin like a silver-steel blade wielded by a sinister Jack Frost; it chills to the bone with a single touch.

It was this second kind of cold, the angry cold, that Artie felt as he rolled out from the warmth of his bed on this first day of winter. His body ached as if his skeletal system had been replaced by an intricate network of icicles. Whatever the reason for the cold, he was consumed by it totally.

Artie left the bedroom and went into the hall.

The thermostat insistently pointed to a comfortable twenty-degrees Celsius, but Artie's teeth chattered and his body quaked with uncontrollable shivers. And no matter how many blankets he wrapped about himself as he moved through his well-appointed surroundings, he felt the cold within him.

Seeking warmth, Artie took a long, steamy shower. The pounding of hot water against his body helped Artie little, about as much as a warm day in February helps thaw a winter's worth of ice and snow. After he got out of the shower, he dressed quickly in heavy corduroy pants and a thick wool sweater to put a barrier between himself and the relentless cold.

As he sat at the kitchen table drinking his second cup of deliciously hot coffee, the cold within him finally began to dissipate.

From down the hall Artie could hear his wife Jennifer approaching. When she entered the kitchen Artie was surprised to see her dressed in a skimpy black silk teddy.

"Aren't you cold in that thing?" he said.

"And a good morning to you, too."

"I'm sorry, good morning. It's just that when I woke up I felt like I'd slept the night outside on the porch. Were you cold this morning?"

"Not at all. Actually, I find it quite warm in here. Did you know the thermostat is set at twenty-degrees?"

"Yeah, I know," Artie said.

"You must be coming down with something. Maybe you could do with some time off. How's a week in Mexico sound?"

"What are you, nuts? It's the first day of winter." He walked over to the sink and looked out the window. The backyard trees were topped with a healthy frosting of snow. "You know it's the best time of the year for business. I can't take off now—maybe in a couple of months, in the spring."

"Artie, if you haven't got your health, you haven't got anything."

"And if you haven't got money, you ain't got nothing," Artie said.

"The are other things in life besides money, you know."

"Maybe, but none more worth having."

#

Artie owned *Artistic Furs,* a trendy store on Toronto's Spadina Avenue. He arrived at the store early that morning and did some tidying up in preparation for what he knew would be the first big day of the season. He spent time polishing the seemingly endless lengths of brass rails, vacuuming the thick gray pile carpet and cleaning the wall-length mirrors placed at strategic points throughout the store. Expensive items like furs needed to be complimented by proper surroundings, and Artie was never one to spare an expense if it could help generate sales.

With the store clean, Artie shuffled his inventory slightly, hanging some of his most expensive coats in the store's front window. He dusted each coat lightly with Styrofoam chips that looked a little like snow, then clipped the price tags from each. Presentation was an important aspect of his business; customers only need to know the price of a coat *after* they've decided they want it.

Customers began arriving around ten-thirty—the coffee break crowd. They were a cross-section of the downtown Toronto workday community. Secretaries browsed, dreaming of luxury they couldn't afford, and executive types scanned the store quickly, looking for a special little something that would make up for last month's forgotten anniversary. The rest, mostly wives out shopping for the day, were looking for a coat that would keep them warm while showing the world they had money to burn.

Sales were good through the first part of the day, and Artie did nothing but smile as he treated each potential customer like a longtime friend.

"That coat makes you look like a million," he would say to some seventy-year-old woman who might look like a couple thousand if she had her cheeks pinned back behind her ears.

"No, no, that coat doesn't suit you at all," he would say to some middle-aged housewife who looked to be buying the first and perhaps only fur of her life. "With all due respect madam, it makes you look like an alley cat in heat. If you're going to buy a coat, I suggest you pamper yourself with the best."

Artie even treated some customers like longtime enemies.

A woman, dressed in an old cloth coat strolled nervously through the aisles. She carried a plastic mesh shopping bag in one hand, and led her four-year-old son along with the other.

"May I help you with something, ma'am?" Artie asked, sizing the woman up.

"Oh no," the woman answered shyly. "I could never afford a fur coat." She sighed. "My husband would kill me if he knew I was even in here." She motioned her child toward the door. "Nonsense," Artie said. "We have several payment plans. I'm sure we could work out something that you would find easily affordable."

The woman stopped, hesitated, then walked back in Artie's direction.

I've got her now, thought Artie. *Just get the coat on her back, just get her to try it on.*

He was interrupted by a growing noise coming from the sidewalk in front of the store where a sizable crowd was gathering.

Inside, customers and staff moved to the store's front window to see what was going on.

"Try it on," Artie anxiously told the woman. "I'll be right back." He went to the front of the store to look out the window.

On the sidewalk out front, the International Friends of Animals (IFA) were staging one of their infamous protest demonstrations. The IFA was a strong lobby group run by people who knew how to get their message across. They took action on behalf of the world's wildlife in the courts and especially in the streets where they were most effective.

Artie had heard from others in the business that the IFA would be coming through Toronto, but their appearance in front of his store still came as a surprise, as well as a bit of a shock.

As Artie watched and listened, the leader of the group stood on the sidewalk using a bullhorn to tell passersby about what the IFA believed was an injustice being done to the world's wildlife.

"You sir!" the man said through the bullhorn, his voice carrying on down the sidewalk and across the street. "Do you know what this is? This . . . is a leg hold trap. It snaps around the leg of an animal, usually causing it to bleed to death." He placed the trap down on the sidewalk, set it and sprung it with a wooden stick. The trap's claws ripped through the wood, snapping it in two and sending splinters flying in every direction.

"Can you believe that some animals chew through their own flesh and bone to escape this cruel, cruel trap—only to bleed to death hours later. Although illegal in many countries, these horrific devices are still being used around the world, even in so called civilized countries like our own."

He then held up huge, full color laminated blow ups to illustrate his point. The crowd let out a long collective moan.

The demonstration continued for several minutes before climaxing with two "friends" acting out the trapping and skinning of a rabbit. The friend playing the rabbit stepped out from a parked car wearing a pair of floppy ears on his head and a big ball of cotton pinned to his behind. He wore a coat made of synthetic material that had the look of real fur. He hopped about on the sidewalk and tried to twitch his nose, much to the delight of the crowd.

Then the rabbit suddenly writhed and twisted in mock pain as its leg was snapped into a leg hold trap made of cardboard and aluminum foil. As the rabbit tried desperately to pull his leg free, a second friend jumped out of the car and pushed his way through the crowd. Brandishing an oversized ceremonial dagger, he pretended to skin the rabbit alive, unbuttoning the rabbit's coat along a line traced by the dagger.

The crowd in front of the store grew larger. Television cameras began to appear around the periphery.

The rabbit's body twitched and heaved on the sidewalk. It screamed horribly as the coat was ripped from its body in a series of violent jerks.

The stunt was dramatic, though not an accurate portrayal of what goes on in the wild; but it was the type of thing the media zealously gobbled up and spit out over the airwaves. At one point or another, the IFA had been on the cover of every major magazine and newspaper in the world. Their efforts appealed to people's consciences, and people usually eased their consciences by making donations to their cause—often large ones. As a result the IFA had become both financially and politically powerful over the years.

And with financial power, some of their tactics had become more and more extreme—even for some of the more fanatical among them. Last year the captain of a Japanese whaling ship was found pinned to his bridge by several harpoons. In Africa a group of ivory poachers were found lying in a circle, a hole through their foreheads and all of their teeth missing. In both cases the murderers were never found, but many speculated that it had been the work of IFA zealots.

On a smaller scale, the demonstration in front of Artie's store had had its desired effect and customers began to leave.

Artie was incensed by the demonstration and was about to run out onto the sidewalk and chase everyone away when he noticed the television crews skirting the crowd. Wisely, he decided to remain inside until he calmed down.

When the demonstration ended and the crowd had dispersed, a reporter from a local station asked Artie if he would agree to be interviewed on camera. He agreed.

"What do you think of this kind of grandstanding?" the cute Asian reporter asked him as they taped the interview on the front steps of his store.

Artie thought about the question for a few moments before answering. "Well, what can I say?" he began. "This is a free country and they have the right to express their opinion. But at the same time, I have the right to express *my* opinion and I think they're idiotic for demonstrating on city streets when they'd be better off lobbying the government in Ottawa. As long as it's not illegal to sell furs and there's people willing to buy them, there will always be merchants like me to sell furs."

"Does this kind of stunt make you think differently about the furs you sell?"

"What do you mean?"

"Well," the reporter paused a moment, as if surprised she had to explain herself. "Does it make you think about the furs once being part of a living thing?"

"Why should it? I'm just a businessman and this is my business."

It was true. Artie had never really given much thought to the idea that furs came from living things. His furs came out of the back of a truck every other Monday.

The reporter paused again, then said, "Thank you very much, Mr. Mann."

"Hey, when will this be on?"

The woman looked at her watch. "We're too late for six. Probably the eleven o'clock news."

As he drove home that night Artie thought about his interview, specifically about the question, "Does it make you think about furs once being part of a living thing?"

The answer was no.

Artie didn't think in terms of living things and he knew absolutely nothing about animals. What he knew about was coats.

He knew that his top-of-the-line coats had a three-to-four-hundred percent mark-up and that when one of them walked out of the store Artie Mann was that much closer to his second Mercedes-Benz. He also knew that he sold twenty-five seal skin coats last year and that pushed his gross sales over two-million dollars for the fourth year in a row.

No, Artie didn't think about living things and he didn't want to think about them either. What he knew about the fur business had kept him in business for twelve years, through two of the toughest recessions in the country's history.

What else was there to know about?

#

By the time Artie got home, exhaustion had caught up with him. The day had taken such wild turns that all he wanted was to see it come to an end.

Jennifer made him a stiff drink of Vodka on the rocks, and together, they sat down in front of the television and waited for the eleven o'clock news.

The IFA demonstration turned up as the fourth item of the newscast and was teased before the commercial break.

"When we come back," said the news anchor. "Furor over furs."

Artie could just pick himself out, watching the demonstration from inside the store, before the commercial kicked in. "Did you see me?" he said, pointing to the screen which now showed a man on the verge of nervous breakdown because of ring around the collar.

"Yes, I saw you," Jennifer said flatly.

When the news came back on, the report opened with the demonstration and the reporter giving some background on the IFA. A "friend" was interviewed on camera next, basically repeating the speech he'd given to the crowd through his bullhorn. A brief shot of the exterior of the store was followed by Artie's interview.

But the reporter was still doing her voice over while Artie was on camera.

"Many fur sellers turn a blind eye to the slaughter of animals that goes on around the world year after year. Artistic Furs owner Artie Mann is aware of the brutality, but says it doesn't bother him."

At last Artie's voice was allowed to be heard.

"Why should it? I'm just a businessman and this is my business."

The reporter came back, on camera this time, and made her closing commentary. "Besides organizing demonstrations in cities like Toronto, the IFA also works in the wild to try and prevent the carnage of the world's wildlife. Their efforts are often heroic, but the battle is a long one and converts come slowly. For some fur advocates, like Artie Mann, members of the IFA are, quote: *idiotic*.

"In front of Artistic Furs on Spadina Avenue, this is Victoria Sung reporting."

And with that, the report ended.

Artie sat back in his chair in numb silence.

Jennifer looked at him, but said nothing.

Finally Artie spoke, his voice little more than a whisper. "That's not what she said before she asked me the question. She asked me if the demonstration bothered me, the demonstration, not the animals." He fell silent again as if gathering strength. "And that *idiotic* thing . . . Do you like how she used that? It was one word. I talked for over a minute and she pulls out one damn word." He was silent once more, overcome by shock.

"I'll sue her . . . and the station she works for. I swear to God, I'll sue." He slumped back in his chair, unable to continue.

The newscast continued with a special feature on the fur trade. On the screen furs were being modeled at some big European fashion show. Spindly-legged models paraded up and down the runway with mink, muskrat and seal skin coats draped over their shoulders.

But something went wrong. The furs dragged across the runway began to trail wide swaths of crimson behind them. Then, as the models whirled in circles, blood flew and splattered across the faces of the beautiful people gathered to celebrate the new collection.

Artie wanted to switch channels, but he couldn't. His flare of anger had left him drained and all he could do was sit wide-eyed in front of the television and take in everything as it was broadcast to him.

The fashion show sequence dissolved into images of frozen ice-drifts and the annual seal hunt of Canada's north.

On the screen an IFA volunteer was chasing a seal pup across the floe until it dove under the ice to safety. "Some of the seals aren't as lucky," the narrator said as the image on the screen turned violent.

"Bullshit scare tactics!" Artie said in disgust when it was over. He believed showing an episode like that on television was like showing a full-color photo of a cancerous lung to a smoker. Great immediate effect, but once the photo is gone so is its effect.

He decided he'd call his lawyer in the morning to see what could be done about his on-camera interview. He also vowed to try to not let things bother him. Still, whatever good intentions Artie had, the day's events—the cold, the demonstration, the interview, the newscast—were with him like a cancerous lung.

And cancer, like rust, never sleeps.

As they prepared for bed, Jennifer did her best to comfort Artie, but what could be said to a man who had just been made out to look like a Shylock in front of an entire city.

"Nobody was watching the news tonight anyway, hon. There were two west coast hockey games on and . . ."

"Everybody was watching," Artie said, turning on the water faucet in the bathroom with a hard, quick turn. "Everybody was watching. I'll be lucky if I just break even this year. That's just what those guys want, you know. The IFA wants everybody in the industry to look like saliva-drooling, bloodthirsty monsters when it's probably more true the other way around. I wouldn't be surprised if that reporter was a fucking *friend* herself."

Jennifer had left the bathroom while Artie ranted. She returned just as he finished.

"Here, take this," she said, holding out a tiny white pill. "A Valium? I don't need . . ."

"Just take it. It'll help you sleep better, and God knows you're going to need your sleep tonight."

Artie said nothing for a few moments. Finally, he took the pill and popped it into his mouth. "Thanks," he said.

#

Even with the help of the tranquilizer, Artie's mind was reeling through the day's events as if they were part of some all-night movie. He tossed in his sleep, the sheets twisting around his body until they restricted his movements and he was trapped within them.

The image of the seal hunt replayed in his mind a hundred times over. The spike-end club crashing down, piercing the skull with the first blow and then bashing the head to a bloody pulp again and again and again . . . Finally, the seal lay dead, blood-red oozing from its ruined head, discoloring all the surrounding white. Then Vicki Sung rose up from a hole in the ice by the seal, her hair wet from a mix of water and seal's blood.

With one hand she petted the dead seal as if it were a sleeping dog. In her other hand she held a microphone and repeated over and over, *Does it make you think about the furs once being part of a living thing?*

She continued speaking, stroking the seal all the while. With every stroke of her hand something about the seal's head became more familiar to Artie. Every pass of her hand wiped away a little more blood until an image became recognizable. Artie's mind brought the seal's head in for a close up and that's when he saw it: his own head split open on the ice, bloody brains clearly visible through the rent in his skull.

It's just a business after all. Just a business. This is Vicky Sung reporting, she said before slipping back into the water and disappearing beneath the ice.

At last it was over. Artie sat up, his hair wet and pasted down onto his head, his body cold and damp with sweat.

The angry cold had returned.

He looked over at Jennifer sleeping peacefully by his side. Only half of her body was covered by the bed sheets while the other half was exposed to the air. Still, she looked warm and comfortable.

Artie shivered.

It was five in the morning, hardly enough time to fall back to sleep, even if he wanted to. He decided to get an early start on the day.

He moved slowly through the house, still feeling the effects of his nightmare and the cold.

He went through his morning ritual of a shower and a hot cup of coffee, but nothing could wash away the images of the night or the cold within his body. He could see the dead seal as clearly as if he were still watching it on television, and the reporter's words echoed through his head as if he were wearing a set of headphones that could never come off.

For the first time in his life, Artie began to think differently about furs, began to think of them as being part of a living thing rather than just an item of merchandise. It was an uncomfortable feeling. Still, as he left for the store, he felt confident he would regain his usual profit-driven perspective well before it came time to open for business.

By seven Artie was standing at the front steps of his store. The morning sun, just beginning to snake its beams through the maze of downtown buildings, felt refreshingly warm on the back of his black leather jacket. Artie stood still a moment to collect some of that warmth, then slid the key into the door and unlocked the deadbolt.

Though the morning sun shone brightly—and usually illuminated the store well through its windows and door— the inside of the store on this morning was completely black. Artie couldn't see two feet in front of himself, but instinctively knew the way to the light switch on the far wall. He suddenly felt uneasy as his foot brushed something on the floor. It moved abruptly in the darkness as he touched it, like a cat rudely awakened from sleep.

He reached the light switch and placed his back to the wall. He lifted the switch and the lights shone five times brighter than Artie could ever remember. At the same moment, the morning sun blazed through the windows, bathing the inside of the store in a blindingly bright white light.

Artie shielded his eyes with his hands as best he could, his eyes squinted shut; but through the slits he could just make out the horror that undulated beneath his feet: The floor was covered in a writhing mass of bleeding flesh.

They appeared to be animals . . . naked and bleeding animals. Artie hadn't recognized them at first because they looked like human fetuses with all their muscles, tendons and ligaments clearly visible without the protective covering of skin and fur. But as Artie's eyes adjusted to the light, he saw that the entire store was covered in a sea of twitching pink and red. Muskrats, minks, foxes, beavers, and God knows what else crawled across the floor toward him. They were on top of the cash and clung to the racks on which, row upon row, their furs were hung.

They moved in an awkward kind of unison, as if in constant pain, until they surrounded Artie, not allowing him to move a muscle.

Artie took a deep breath and closed his eyes, hoping the horror would be gone when he reopened them.

It was then that he felt the first animal clutching at the material of his pants. A moment later a more forceful claw grabbed his leg. In seconds his legs were covered with animals, claws and teeth grabbing, ripping and tearing at his skin.

Just before he fell unconscious, Artie heard what sounded like a tiny voice in his head crying out in a whisper.

It's cold. It's so cold.

As his body hit the floor, the lights went out and the store returned to utter darkness.

#

It was nine thirty before the detective flashed his badge and stepped under the line of yellow tape surrounding Artie's store.

"What can you tell me so far?" he asked a young uniform who had been on the scene for half-an-hour.

"As far as we can tell, it happened early this morning. Probably some nut high on something, getting his kicks . . . Nothing was taken from the store."

"All right. Let me know if anything turns up out here," the detective said, making his way into the store.

Inside, Artie Mann lay face down in the middle of his showroom, the tips of his fingers submerged in a pool of blood. His skin had been ripped from his body, exposing all that was underneath to the light.

There was an angry cold in the air on this winter morning, but the inside of the store was warm.

All except for Artie.

Artie was motionless . . . and cold.

This was my first-ever short story. I think the genesis for it came from when I was a teenager and spent a few days helping my father do some exterior sheet metal work (the job he did as a tradesman all his life) on the building that housed the Paul Magder Furs shop in downtown Toronto. After peeking in the store's windows and seeing all those fur coats on the racks, I'm sure my teenage mind thought, "What if all those animals came back for their fur?" And so, many years later, a horror tale was born.

Blood Count

The dressing room door opened slowly. "Five minutes, Vlad."

Boris Bronsky, a professional wrestler known to millions of wrestling fans the world over as Vlad, The Impaler, pulled hard on the laces of his big black boots. "Right."

Dean Kiniski, the hunched-over old man who'd worked in the Garden for what seemed like forever lingered in the doorway, looking at the wrestler with a mixture of admiration and sorrow. "I'm gonna miss you, Vlad."

Vlad pulled the black singlets over his broad shoulders, the dark straps standing out in high relief against his pale white of his skin, then looked over at Kiniski. When he saw the expression on the old man's face, he smiled, exposing the two long fangs that had been his trademark since his days wrestling in carnivals and county fairs. "Yeah, well I'm going to miss some of it, too."

The old man swung the dirty white towel he'd been carrying over his shoulder and stepped into the dressing room, closing the door behind him as if he'd just entered the wrestler's inner sanctum. "Really? Which part you gonna miss most?"

He'd been asked this question dozens of times by garrulous ring announcers and television pitchmen during his six-month farewell tour through the southern states, but he'd never answered it honestly. Since he was finishing his career as a heel, his one pat answer had been, "Inflicting *pain* on mine opponents," followed by an insane, wide-eyed stare into the camera and a final menacing sneer that showed off his deadly white fangs.

But that wasn't the part he was going to miss at all. "What I'm going to miss most," he said, "is the way it was in the old days. You know what I mean?"

Kiniski showed him a dirty, gap-toothed smile. "Yeah, you were something to see back then, Vlad. Nobody could touch you. I remember when you fought Gorilla Kilpatrick here in '82 . . ."

As Kiniski's voice droned on, Vlad pressed the back of his head against the concrete wall behind him and stared blankly across the room as if he were looking back across the years.

The good old days . . . When wrestlers fought in smelly, run-down arenas just to make the rent and baseball players were the athletes people looked up to. *The good old days* . . . When steroids were something only veterinarians knew about and muscles were something you made by lifting weights and eating steak. The *good old days* . . . When wrestlers didn't wear make-up and the blood that flowed from foreheads night after night was real . . . and pure.

He closed his eyes and the memories faded.

Today's fans didn't want blood as much as they wanted an act, a show. Wrestlers with flair and charisma. Drug-pumped pretty boys with a costume and a gimmick, putting on a play, following a script.

Entertainment.

Vaudeville.

Vlad, The Impaler was a throwback to the days when professional wrestling had been more like the Grand Guignol.

He was a brawler who hit with a closed fist and tore flesh when he bit. He had size, strength, an eerie physical presence and a proclivity toward blood and violence unrivaled by any of his opponents. It had all come to him so naturally. All he'd had to do was deny his bloodlust and he was transformed into an inhuman wildman in the ring—the perfect heel without even trying.

And even on those rare occasions when he was overcome by his thirst for blood, the crowds were such that they cheered him on as he lapped at the ruined heads and faces of his opponents. In fact he'd never been more popular than in the late '80s after he'd bitten off the tip of Dutch Holland's nose in a Texas cage match.

These days, not only wasn't bloodletting allowed by the wrestling associations, but with the way needles were being passed around the dressing rooms, it was also downright dangerous.

Now, without the periodic taste of blood inside the ring, it had become more and more difficult for Vlad to keep himself in check. If he was to give into his bloodlust now, he'd likely kill his opponent. Best to get out now, before he was forced out, or put in jail, or lynched by an angry mob.

Besides, there were easier ways of procuring blood. Sure, it would take time to adjust, but he'd survive. His kind always did.

He opened his eyes and looked over at Kiniski, still yapping away.

". . . and Kilpatrick waving at the referee, begging him to stop the fight." Kiniski shook his head. "Who'd ever have thought that biting a man's leg could be used as a submission hold?"

The door popped open then and one of the network producers stuck his head into the room. "Come on Vladdie," he said, like he was talking to a kid. "They're waiting for you."

Years ago Vlad would have smacked the guy on the side of the head for daring to address him like that. But, these were the nineties and television producers wielded power, real power. Even though this was his final fight, broadcast live on *Saturday Night's Big Ticket*, who could tell? Maybe he'd want back into the ring in a few months. Maybe bloodbaths would come back into style one day. Either way, it was best not to burn any bridges.

"I'm ready," he said.

The producer spun on his heels and hurried off.

Vlad draped his black silk cape over his shoulders and slowly got to his feet, his six-foot-six frame towering over Kiniski as if he were a child.

The old man stood and looked up.

"Give 'em hell, Vlad."

Vlad smiled, sliding into character. "Maybe I vill."

#

"Ladies and Gentleman!" boomed the amplified voice of the ring announcer. "Making his final appearance in the squared circle, ending a distinguished twenty-year career as a professional wrestler, the two-time former world heavyweight champion, the three-time former intercontinental champion, the two-time former television champion, and a future member of the Professional Wrestling Hall of Fame . . ." A pause. "Weighing in at two hundred and seventy five pounds . . ." A longer pause. "From somewhere deep within the Carpathian Mountains, Vlad, The Impaler."

Vlad stretched out his arms, holding the ends of the cape out like a pair of bat wings. The capacity crowd erupted in a standing ovation and for a moment he imagined people all over the world—tens of millions of them—were cheering him as well.

It gave him a thrill he hadn't felt in years.

And his bloodlust stirred, gathered strength.

Vlad was made to wait as the current champ, Colt 45, was introduced to the crowd. Colt 45 was a blonde-haired, bronze-skinned Californian who wore silver boots and bullet shaped patches on the butt of his trunks.

As the crowd cheered the champ, Vlad circled the ring, pacing like a caged animal ready to escape the moment the door is left unattended. Some fans up front began taunting him, calling him a bum, but he played up to them by climbing onto the ropes and inviting them up into the ring.

After Colt 45 had been introduced, the referee had a few words to say to the combatants about fighting clean and putting on a good show.

When the referee was done, Colt 45 extended his hand. "I watched you wrestle when I was a kid, man. I'm honored to be your last opponent."

Vlad's cold stare remained unchanged. The tribute from the champ had been caught by the ring mike. Vlad couldn't let an opportunity to play the heel go to waste. "Tank you," he said. "And I honored to be *your* last opponent, too." Vlad finished by baring his fangs in something that wasn't a smile.

The one-upmanship continued until the two men suddenly came together, pushing and shoving at each other for a few moments before the referee and others in the ring were able to pull them apart.

Once the slight skirmish had been quelled, the ring quickly cleared and it was showtime. The bell rang and the two men circled the ring, staring each other down as if searching for a weakness.

Colt 45 was a classic example of the new breed of wrestlers. Blessed with good looks, a large frame and a gift for gab, he'd been *made* into a wrestler by slick managers and promoters who'd recognized his appeal. Within a year he'd bulked up to nearly three-hundred pounds and was a champion headlining cards all over Japan and North America.

But for Vlad, Colt 45 was the worst sort of opponent to have. The man's blood pressure was abnormally high from steroid use and his veins stood out in sharp relief against his smooth, tanned, skin. To see all that glorious blood pulsing so close to the surface and not be able to tap it was enough to make his fangs ache with hunger.

At last the two wrestlers met in the middle of the ring, grappling one another and whispering instructions for the first series of moves.

Vlad broke the clutch with a head butt, sending Colt backwards into the ropes. With Colt seemingly staggered by the blow to his head, Vlad followed up with a series of roundhouse right hands to the chest.

When the flurry of punches ended, Colt fell to his knees. Vlad circled the ring again and came up behind him. After dramatically raising his claw-like fingers high in the air, Vlad clamped them onto the downed-man's shoulders. With a sinister laugh, he bared his fangs in preparation to bite.

The crowd loved it, screaming, "No, no, no."

Even Colt managed a terrified look as he glanced up at Vlad.

But just as he was about to sink his teeth into the soft flesh of Colt's shoulders, the referee intervened, reminding Vlad that biting was *not* in the rule book.

Vlad shot the referee a contemptuous look (no acting there), then showed his disgust by pushing Colt face-first into the mat. Next, he stomped after the referee, explaining with wildly exaggerated gestures that one little bite wasn't going to hurt.

But as Vlad's attention was concentrated on the referee, Colt was able to make a miraculous recovery. With surprising speed and agility he rose up from the mat and hammered Vlad from behind with a two-handed, forearm smash.

Vlad stumbled forward onto the mat, then rolled over onto his back, allowing Colt the opportunity to attempt one of his patented legdrops.

As the blond-haired Californian sailed through the air, a groggy Vlad rolled over onto his stomach, leaving Colt to land squarely on his own silver-bulleted butt.

Both wrestlers rolled around the mat in mock pain.

As Vlad looked about, he was aware of Colt's leg just inches from his mouth. He could sense the hot blood flowing through the man's thick femoral artery and had to lick his lips and roll away just to keep his instincts in check.

After a few moments, the combatants staggered to their feet and met once more in the center of the ring. Quickly, the next series of moves was decided on and Colt ended the encounter by taking Vlad's feet out from under him with a diving leg-trip.

Vlad landed heavily on the mat, surprised by the move since it hadn't been one they'd agreed upon. Vlad turned his head and saw the smile on Colt's face as the man twisted Vlad's legs into a figure-four leglock.

There was pain to be sure, but nothing Vlad couldn't handle. He slapped the mat a few times with his arms, begging for mercy, but he was really more concerned about the apparent deviation from their fight plan.

Colt continued to apply the leglock, putting more strain on Vlad's knees and ankles.

Is this a real fight? thought Vlad, or just an isolated improvisation?

Vlad rolled over, first breaking, then reversing the leglock. He was tempted to snap Colt's leg in two, but decided it was best to regroup and find out what was going on.

He let Colt break the leglock and the two soon found themselves in a clench, pressed up against a turnbuckle.

"What was that all about?" asked Vlad.

"Thought you might be up to a real fight, old man."

Vlad sneered to hide his smile. His body ached for an old-fashioned type blood-brawl, but he knew that if a single drop of blood was spilled inside the ring, it would be followed by a torrent. "Better stick to the plan, boy," said Vlad.

"Suit yourself."

The referee broke up the clutch and grab. "Come on, guys. People come to see a fight. Let's mix it up."

After an exchange of open-handed punches, Vlad sent Colt running into the ropes with a mighty push from behind, then greeted his return to the center of the ring with a powerful drop-kick to the chest. Colt backpedaled into the ropes, deciding to rest there for a moment as if the wind had just been knocked out of him.

Vlad leaped up off the mat, grabbed Colt by the arm and gave him an Irish whip that sent him hurtling toward a corner turnbuckle.

Colt took a few awkward steps, then stumbled. He reached out desperately to try and steady himself, but his flailing arms missed the ropes completely. He shot past the padded part of the turnbuckle and slammed head first into the steel post it was secured to.

People near that corner of the ring squealed in delight over how real the move had looked, but as Colt staggered out of the corner it was obvious he'd been seriously hurt.

A gash had opened up from the left side of his hairline to just over his right eye. Blood flowed freely from the wound, running into Colt's eyes and painting his entire face a rich, bright red.

Vlad stood motionless in the ring watching his opponent bleed . . .

So much blood . . .

And felt years of denied bloodlust wash over him with all the force of a tidal wave.

Colt continued to walk the ring in a daze.

Vlad followed him, closing the distance between them with each step, as if going in for the kill.

He knew this was live television, knew he wasn't supposed to win the match, knew that the man needed immediate medical attention . . . but he didn't care.

There was too much blood for him to care.

In a flash, Vlad soared through the air, hitting the champion square in the chest and knocking him to the mat. An instant later his mouth was on the wound, lapping at the blood as it pulsed up through the tear in the flesh.

The blood was of poor quality, tainted by drugs, and tasting thin and bitter. It would make Vlad sick, but he couldn't stop.

There was just so much of it.

So much blood . . .

People in the front rows screamed, fainted.

Others watched in horror.

The referee quickly began pounding out a three count in the hopes that a pinfall would end the carnage, but Vlad halted the referee after each count of two by grabbing a handful of Colt's matted hair and lifting the man's shoulders off the mat.

And then, before the count could resume, he was back sucking at the wound, sating his hunger, draining the life from the champion.

At last the referee called for the bell, disqualifying Vlad and giving the victory to the prone Colt 45.

The match was over, but Vlad didn't care.

When the wound on Colt's forehead ran dry, he sank his fangs into his neck, piercing the carotid artery and feeling the weak pulse dribble more blood into his mouth.

Suddenly hands were on him, lifting him away.

He glanced around and saw other wrestlers pouring into the ring. Each one grabbed a piece of him: a leg here, an arm there. One of them was even foolish enough to put a hand over his mouth. Instinctively he bit at the flesh, sucked at the wound . . . and then the hand was gone, the skin tearing open as it jerked away.

An inhuman strength raged through Vlad's body. He shook his arms and kicked his legs. Wrestlers fell away in different directions. He moved back in on Colt, in the hopes of one last taste of the man's bittersweet blood.

But then even more hands were upon him, pushing him down, pinning him to the mat.

The crowd was going wild.

Objects were starting to fly into the ring. Cans and bottles and chairs.

A face suddenly appeared before him. It belonged to a suit from the network. "I don't care if you're retiring or not, asshole. You're finished . . ."

The man continued on, screaming at him about lawsuits.

But Vlad just laughed at him, laughed at all of them.

Just like he had in the good old days.

I used to be a huge fan of the WWF (now the WWE) in the era of Hulk Hogan and Andre the Giant. But, my favorite wrestler of that time was the Iron Sheik, who made it his schtick to badmouth the United States, (Iran number one, USA, -- then he would spit.). I liked him because he had been a competitive wrestler in Iran -- and could suplex better than anyone -- but was also a coach for the US Olympic team in the 1970s. With all the blood that was flowing in the ring back then, I wondered what it might be like if one of the wrestlers was a vampire and "Blood Count" was the result. And, for those who didn't recognize it, Colt 45 is a very thinly veiled Hulk Hogan.

Ice Bridge

The continuous diesel-driven thrum of the loader was only occasionally drowned out by the crash of logs being dumped into place. The loud noise was followed by the faint groan of metal and the slight rumbling of frozen earth as the truck dutifully bowed to accept its load.

Rick Hartwick mixed his coffee with a plastic stir-stick and walked casually toward the far end of the office trailer. At the window, he blew across the top of his steaming cup and watched his breath freeze against the pane. Then he took a sip, wiped away the patch of ice that had formed on the glass, and watched his truck being loaded one last time.

As always, the loader, a Quebecois named Pierre Langlois, was making sure Rick's rig was piled heavy with spruce and pine logs, some of them more than three feet in diameter. Langlois liked Rick, and with good reason. Every other week throughout the season, Rick had provided Langlois with a bottle of Canadian Club. He'd been doing it for years now, ever since he'd called a loader an asshole during a card game and wound up driving trucks loaded with soft wood and air the rest of the winter.

He'd been lucky to hang on to his rig.

The next winter he began greasing Langlois' gears with the best eighty-proof he could find and since then had never had a load under thirty tons and only a handful under thirty-five.

He owned his rig now, as well as a house in Prince George. As he continued to watch the loading operation, Jerry Chetwynd, the old-timer who manned the trailer for the company came up behind Rick and looked out the window. "That's a good load you got going there."

"Not bad," said Rick, taking a sip.

"Are you gonna take it over the road, or take a chance on the bridge?"

Rick took another sip, then turned to look at the old man. They said Chetwynd had been a logger in the B.C. interior when they'd still used ripsaws and axes to clear the land. Rick believed it, although you wouldn't know it to look at Chetwynd now—all thin and bony and hunched over like he was still carrying post wood on his back. "Is the ice bridge open?"

Chetwynd smiled, showing Rick all four of the teeth he'd been able to keep from rotting out. "They cleared the road to MacKenzie last night and this morning," he said. "But the company decided to keep the bridge open one more day seeing as how cold it was overnight."

Rick nodded. Although the winter season usually ended the last two weeks of March, a cold snap late in the month had lingered long enough for them to keep the bridge operating a whole week into April. And while they'd been opening and closing the ice bridge across Williston Lake like a saloon door the past couple days, the few extra trips Rick had been able to make had made a big difference to his finances—the kind of difference that translated into a two-week stay at an all-inclusive singles resort on Maui.

"Anyone use the bridge today?"

Chetwynd scratched the side of his head with two gnarled fingers. "Not that I know of. Maybe an empty coming back from the mill. Harry Heskith left here about an hour ago . . . But he said he wasn't going to risk the ice. Said the road would get him there just the same . . ."

"Yeah, eventually," Rick muttered under his breath.

The ice bridge across Williston Lake was three kilometers long and took about four minutes to cross. If you took the road around the lake you added an extra fifty kilometers and about an hour's drive to the trip. That might have been all right for Harry Heskith with a wife, mortgage, two-point-three kids, and a dog, but Rick had a plane to catch.

Maui was waiting.

"Up to you," Chetwynd said, shrugging his shoulders as he handed Rick the yellow shipping form.

The loader's throaty roar suddenly died down and the inside of the trailer became very quiet.

Uncomfortably so.

Rick crushed his coffee cup in his hand and tossed it into the garbage. "See you 'round," he said, zipping up his parka and stepping outside.

"If you're smart you will," said Chetwynd to an empty trailer. "Smart or lucky."

#

The air outside was cold, but nothing like the minus thirty-five Celsius they got through January and February. Between minus fifteen and minus thirty-five was best for winter logging—anything colder and the machinery froze up, anything warmer and the ground started getting soft. The weather report had said minus fifteen today, but with the sun out and shining down on the back of his coat, it felt a lot warmer than that.

Rick slipped on his gloves and headed for his rig, the morning's light dusting of snow crunching noisily underfoot.

"You got her loaded pretty tight," he called out to Langlois, who had climbed up onto the trailer to secure the load.

"Filled the hempty spaces wit kindling," Langlois said with obvious pride in his voice.

"Gee, I don't know," chided Rick. "I still see some daylight in there."

"All dat fits in dare, my friend, is match sticks hand toot picks," Langlois said, his French-Canadian accent still lingering after a dozen years in the B.C. interior.

Rick laughed.

"You know, I uh, I haven't seen you in a while and I been getting a little tirsty . . . You know what I mean?"

Rick nodded. Of course he knew what Langlois meant. He was trying to scam him for an extra bottle before he went on holidays, even though he'd given the man a bottle less than a week ago.

"I'll take care of you when I get back next week," Rick said, knowing full well he wouldn't be back for another two.

Langlois smiled. "Going somewhere?"

"Maui, man," said Rick, giving Langlois the Hawaiian 'hang loose' sign with the thumb and little finger of his right hand.

"Lucky man . . . Make sure you get a lei when you land dare."

"When I land," Rick smiled. "And all week long."

The two men laughed heartily as they began walking around the truck doing a circle check on the rig and making sure the chains holding the logs in place were tight and secure.

"You load Heskith this morning?" Rick asked when they were almost done.

"Yeah."

"What do you figure you gave him?"

"Plenty of air," Langlois smiled. He had struggled to pronounce the word *air* so it didn't sound too much like *hair*.

"How much?"

"Twenty tonnes. Maybe twenty-two."

"He complain about it?"

"Not a word. In fact, he ask me to load him light. Said he was taking the road into MacKenzie."

Rick shook his head. "Dumb sonuvabitch is going to be driving a logging truck into his sixties with loads like that.

"Well, he's been doing it twenty years already."

"Yeah, and maybe he's just managed to pay off his truck by now, huh?"

"He seem to do okay," Langlois shrugged. "But it's none of my business anyway, eh?"

"Right," said Rick, shaking his head. The way he saw it, truck logging was a young man's game. Get in, make as much as you can carrying as much as you can, and get out. So he pushed it to the limit every once in a while. So what? If he worked it right he could retire early or finish out his years driving part time, picking and choosing his loads on a sort of busman's holiday.

They finished checking the rig.

Everything was secure. "How much you figure I got there?" asked Rick, knowing Langlois could usually estimate a load to within a ton.

"Tirty-six. Tirty-seven."

"You're beautiful, man."

Langlois nodded. "Just get it to the mill."

"Have I failed you yet?"

"No, but dare will always be a first time."

"Funny. Very funny."

There was a moment of silence between them. Finally Langlois said, "So, you taking it over the ice?"

"The bridge is open isn't it."

"Yeah, it's *open*."

Rick looked at him. Something about the way he'd said the word *open* didn't sit right with him. It sounded too much like *hope* for his liking. "Did Heskith say why he wasn't taking the bridge?"

"Uh huh," Langlois nodded. "He said he had no intention of floating his logs to the mill."

Rick laughed at that. "And I got no intention of missing my flight."

Langlois nodded. "Aloha."

For a moment, Rick didn't understand, then he smiled and said, "Oh, yeah right. Aloha."

#

The interior of the Peterbilt had been warmed by the sunlight beaming through the windshield. As Rick settled in he took off his hat and gloves and undid his coat, then he shifted it into neutral and started up the truck. The big engine rattled, the truck shivered, and a belch of black smoke escaped the rig's twin chrome pipes. And then the cab was filled with the strong and steady metallic rumble of 525 diesel-powered horses.

He let the engine warm up, making himself more comfortable for the long drive to the mill. He slipped in a Charlie Major tape, and waited for the opening chords of "For the Money" to begin playing. When the song started blaring, he shifted it into gear and slowly released the clutch.

His first thought was how slow the rig was to get moving as the cab rocked and the engine roared against dead weight of the heavy load. It usually didn't take so long to get underway, Rick thought. Must be a bit heavier than Langlois had figured.

Inch by inch, the truck rolled forward. At last he was out of first and into second, gaining small amounts of momentum and speed as he worked his way up through the gears.

A light amount of snow had begun to fall, but it wasn't enough to worry about, certainly nothing that would slow him down.

The logging road into MacKenzie was wide and flat, following the southern bank of the Nation River for more than a hundred kilometers before coming upon the southern tip of Williston Lake. There the road split in two, one fork continuing east over the ice bridge to MacKenzie, the other turning south and rounding the southern finger of Williston Lake before turning back north toward the mills.

Rick drove along the logging road at about sixty-kilometers-an-hour, slowing only once when he came upon an empty rig headed in the opposite direction. Out of courtesy, he gave the driver a pull on the gas horn and a friendly wave, then it was back to the unbroken white strip of road cut neatly through the trees.

The snow continued to fall.

When he turned over the Major tape for the second time he knew he was nearing the bridge. He hated to admit it, but a slight tingle coursed through his body at the thought of taking his load over the ice.

When Rick first began driving logging trucks, the idea of driving across lakes didn't sit all that well with him. To him, it was sort of like skydivers jumping out of perfectly good airplanes—it just wasn't right. Six-axle semi-trailers loaded with thirty-five tons of logs weren't meant to be driven over water—frozen or otherwise.

It was unnatural . . .

Dangerous.

But after his first few rides over the ice, he realized that it was the only way to go. Sure, sometimes you heard a crack or pop under your wheels, but that just made it all the more exciting. The only real danger about driving over the ice was losing your way. Once you were off the bridge there were no guarantees that the ice beneath your rig would be thick enough to support you. And if you did fall through, or simply got stuck, there was a good chance you'd freeze to death while searching for help.

Even so, those instances were rare, and as far as Rick knew, no one had ever fallen through the ice while driving over an open bridge.

And he sure as hell didn't intend to be the first.

Up ahead the roadway opened up slightly as the snow-trimmed trees parted to reveal the lake and the ice bridge across it. In the distance, he could see the smoke rising up from the stacks of the three saw mills and two pulp mills of MacKenzie, a town of about 5,000 hardy souls.

He turned down the music, then shut it off completely as he slowed his rig to a stop at the fork in the road.

He took a deep breath and considered his options one last time.

Across the lake at less than three kilometers away, MacKenzie seemed close enough to touch. But between here and there, there was nothing more than frozen water to hold up over thirty-five tons of wood and steel.

He turned to look down the road as it curved to the south and pictured Harry Heskith's rig turning that way about an hour before, his tracks now obscured by the continuing snowfall.

The road.

It was Heskith's route all right . . .

The long way.

The safe way.

But even if Rick decided to go that route, there were no guarantees that the drive would be easy.

First of all he was really too heavy to chance it. With its sharp inclines and steep downgrades there was a real risk of sliding off the snow-covered road while rounding a curve. Also, although it hadn't happened to him yet, he'd heard of truckers coming across tourists out for Sunday drives, rubbernecking along their merry way at ten- or fifteen-kilometers-an-hour. When that happened, you had the choice of driving over top of them, or slamming on the brakes. And on these logging roads, hard braking usually meant ending up on your side, or in the ditch, or both.

And that might mean a month's worth of profits just to get back on the road.

But even if he *wanted* to take the road, it would mean spending another hour behind the wheel and that would make him late for his flight out of Prince George. Then he'd miss his connecting flight out of Vancouver which meant . . .

No Maui.

And he wasn't about to let that happen, especially when he'd been told that the resort he'd be staying at discreetly stocked rooms with complimentary condoms.

Man, he couldn't wait to get there.

He looked out across the lake again. The snow was still falling, but a light crosswind was keeping it from building up on the ice. He could still clearly see the thick black lines painted onto the ice surface on either side of the bridge. With those lines so visible, there was really no way he could lose his way.

He took one last look down the road, thought of Heskith heading down that way an hour ago and wondered if he'd catch up with good old Harry on the other side.

If he did, maybe he could race him into Mackenzie.

The thought put a dark and devilish grin on Rick's face.

He slid the Charlie Major tape back into the deck, turned up the volume and shifted the truck into gear.

"Here goes nothing," he said. The rig inched forward.

#

It took him a while to get up to speed, but by the time he got onto the bridge he was doing fifty, more than enough to see him safely to the other side.

The trick to driving over the ice was to keep moving. There was incredible amounts of pressure under the wheels of the rig, but as long as you kept moving, that pressure was constantly being relieved. If you slowed, or heaven forbid, stalled out on the ice, then you were really shit-out-of-luck.

He shifted into sixth gear, missed the shift and had to try again. Finally, he got it into gear, but in the meantime he had slowed considerably and the engine had to struggle to recover the lost speed.

Slowly the speedometer's red needle clawed its way back up to sixty, sixty-one, sixty-two . . .

And then he heard something over the music.

It was a loud sound, like the splintering of wood or the cracking of bone. He immediately turned down the music and listened.

All he could hear was the steady thrum of his diesel engine.

For a moment he breathed easier.

But then he heard it again.

The unmistakable sound of cracking ice.

It was a difficult sound to describe. Some said it was like snow crunching underfoot, while others compared it to fresh celery stalks being snapped in two. Rick, however, had always described it as the sound of an ice cube dropped into a warm glass of Coke—only a hundred times louder.

He looked down at the bridge in front of him, realized he was straddling one of the black lines painted onto the ice and gently eased the wheel to the left, bringing him safely back between the lines.

That done, he breathed a sigh of relief and felt the sweat begin to cool on his face and down his back.

"Eyes on the road," he said aloud. "You big dummy—"

Crack!

This one was louder than the others, so loud he could feel the shock waves in his chest.

Again he looked out in front of his truck and for the first time saw the pressure cracks shooting out in front of him, matching the progress of his truck meter for meter.

Finally Rick admitted what he'd known all along.

He was way too heavy.

And the ice was far too thin.

But 20/20 hindsight was useless to him now. All he could do was keep moving, keep relieving the pressure under his wheels and hope that both he and the pressure crack reached the other side.

He stepped hard on the gas pedal and the engine responded with a louder, throatier growl. He considered shifting gears again but decided it might be better not to risk it.

He firmed up his foot on the gas pedal and stood on it with all his weight.

The engine began to strain as the speedometer inched past seventy . . . He remained on the pedal, knowing he'd be across in less than a minute.

The sound grew louder, changing from a crunching, cracking sound to something resembling a gunshot.

He looked down.

The crack in front of the truck had grown bigger, firing out in front of him in all directions like the scraggly branches of a December birch.

"C'mon, c'mon," he said pressing his foot harder on the gas even though it was a wasted effort. The pedal was already down as far as it would go.

Then suddenly the cracking sound grew faint, as if it had been dampened by a splash of water.

A moment later, crunching again. Cracking.

He looked up. The shoreline was a few hundred meters away. In a few seconds there would be solid ice under his wheels and then nothing but wonderful, glorious, hard packed frozen ground.

But then the trailer suddenly lurched to the right, pulling the left front corner of the tractor into the air.

"C'mon, c'mon," Rick screamed, jerking back and forth in his seat in a vain attempt to add some forward momentum to the rig.

Then the front end of the Peterbilt dipped as if it had come across a huge rent in the ice.

"Oh, shit!"

The tractor bounced over the rent, then the trailer followed, each axle dipping down, seemingly hesitant about coming back up the other side, and then reluctantly doing so.

And then, as if by some miracle . . .

He was through it.

Rolling smoothly over the ice. Solid ice.

And the only sound he could hear was the throaty roar of his Peterbilt as he kept his foot hard on the gas.

He raced up the incline toward the road without slowing.

When he reached the road, he got off the gas, but still had plenty of momentum, not to mention weight, behind him.

Too much of both, it seemed.

He pulled gently on the rear brake lever, but found that his tires had little grip on the snow-covered road. His rear wheels locked up and began sliding out from behind.

He turned the wheel, but it was no use.

He closed his eyes and braced himself for the rig to topple onto its side.

He waited and waited for the crash . . .

But it never came.

Suddenly all was quiet except for the calming rattle of the Peterbilt's diesel engine at idle.

Rick opened his eyes.

He breathed hard as he looked around to get his bearings.

He was horizontal across the highway, pointed in the direction he'd come.

He looked north out the passenger side window, saw the puffing smokestacks of MacKenzie and smiled.

He'd made it.

Made it across the bridge.

The moment of celebration was sweet, but short lived . . .

Cut off by the loud cry of a gas horn, splitting the air like a scream.

He turned to look south down the highway.

Harry Heskith's rig had just crested the hill and was heading straight for him.

Rick threw the Peterbilt into gear, stomped on the gas and popped the clutch.

The rig lurched forward, but he was too slow and too late.

All of Heskith's rear wheels were locked and sliding over the snow like skis. Heskith was turning his front wheels frantically left and right even though it was doing nothing to change the direction he was headed.

And then as he got closer, Rick could clearly see Heskith's face. What surprised Rick most was the realization that the old man was shaking his fist at him.

Shaking his fist, as if to say he was a crazy fool for taking the bridge.

But as the two trucks came together, all Rick could think of was how *he'd* been right all along.

The dangers of the ice bridge had been a cakewalk compared to—

When I was growing up our family had a daily subscription to *The Toronto Star* newspaper. Each night my dad was sit back in his chair and read the paper, then go over it again while he ate his breakfast the next morning. I remember a story in the Saturday edition about how logging trucks would take loads over the frozen lakes in British Columbia during the winter months and all the dangers that entailed. I remember discussing the story with my brother and father at length one night at the dinner table, and years later when looking for a subject to write about for another *Northern Frights* anthology, this seemed a natural with no small amount of suspense built right in. Then, when I knew exactly the type of story I wanted to write, I called up the *Prince George Citizen* and asked to speak to their forestry reporter. While I'm sorry to say I don't remember the man's name, I do recall speaking to him for an hour, asking questions about the industry and how the ice roads worked. He told me his wife was a big horror reader and he knew just what I was looking for. Turned out his was right. Finally, it was the trucking details in this story that prompted *Truck News* editor John G. Smith to ask me to write a serial story that was "Trucking Industry Positive" for his magazine. That resulted in me writing 55 stories for my trucker detective series *Mark Dalton: Owner/Operator*, which ran continuously in *Truck News* for 15 years. I also wrote three novels featuring the character for Natural Resources Canada, (Yes, I've had three novels published by the Canadian government) and two audiobook collections from GraphicAudio.

No Kids Allowed

The silver-haired landlord pulled the key from the lock and pushed the door open. The hinges protested by moaning a crackling, staccato rhythm.

The old man mumbled something about oil, stepped back to let the young couple pass and then followed them inside.

"It's not in too bad a shape," he said, closing the door behind him. "Not for what I'm asking, anyway."

The couple wandered through the two-bedroom apartment, peaking behind corners and looking into shadows as if they expected to find something hidden in the dark that might explain why the rent was so low.

"And the other two apartments on this floor are being used for storage so there's plenty of privacy."

The couple nodded politely, but neither said a word.

"Of course, if you do decide to take it, I'll patch up some of the holes in the walls, give the place a coat of paint. You know, fix it up a little."

They stopped in the middle of the living room. The woman, Mary Williams, was in her late twenties, a little bit heavy but neither fat nor unattractive. She stood up straight next to her husband Alex, a six-foot telephone pole of a man with a beard and short-cropped hair, and whispered something in his ear.

The landlord looked up at the ceiling, but his ears strained to hear what she was saying. She whispered too softly for him to decipher her words.

"Uh," the man said, before pausing to take a breath. "Why are you asking so little for this place? We've been looking at apartments for months and we've seen a lot worse than this for a lot more money. What's the catch?"

The old man took a roll of Certs from his pocket and popped one into his mouth. "There's no catch. I know I could get a lot more for this place than I'm asking. Don't think I don't know what this place is worth, because I do—I look through the classifieds, you know." He puckered his lips and sucked on his breathmint. "It's just that I've got one firm rule with my tenants. No kids! Period."

The husband and wife looked at each other, relieved.

"I don't care if you keep cats or dogs, sheep or donkeys. As long as your neighbors don't complain about them, I couldn't care less. But I simply will not allow children to set foot in this building. Personally, I like kids. But the snot-nosed little bastards like to write on walls, throw rocks through windows, scratch cars in the parking lot—and that's the ones that are behaved. The other ones pee in the stairwells and drop things from balconies onto people on the sidewalks." The old man looked to the floor and shook his head in disgust.

"That's terrible," the woman said.

The old man's head stopped shaking. He raised it slowly, lifting his eyes to look up at the couple. "You don't happen to have children, do you?"

"No, I'm afraid not. My husband and I are unable to have children," the woman said, putting an arm around her man and pulling him close.

"That's good," the old man said flatly. "You're a nice looking couple and I'd hate to have to throw you out on account of some pukey little kid with a diaper full of shit. Because if you did have a kid in here, I'd find out about it. I can smell 'em a mile off. It's an instinct I have, a sixth sense.

"You don't have to worry about us. We've decided to concentrate on our careers," the woman said, standing straight up and throwing her chin out a fraction of an inch. "My husband is a copy writer for an advertising company and I'm a high school teacher. Our lives are hectic enough as it is."

The old man nodded. "Then you'll take it?"

"Uh," said the husband. "We'd like to have a minute to talk it over."

"Sure. Go right ahead."

"Between ourselves . . . if you don't mind."

"All right, but make it quick. *Jeopardy* is on, and I don't like to miss it," the old man muttered, stepping into the hallway.

They'll take it all right, the old man thought as he lit up a cigarette and waited. Where else were they going to find two bedrooms for six-fifty a month? Sure, it's a little outside of the city and there's a rat or two in the basement, but it's still a lot better than the twelve-hundred-a-month broom closets downtown they try to pawn off as condominiums. This place is perfect for a couple of double-income-no-kid dinks like them. They'll live here a year or three, save their money and buy a starter home or condo in a bedroom town north of the city. Then maybe their careers won't matter so much and they'll look for a good fertility doctor who'll give them a kid.

Yes, dear God. Please let them have their children then.

The old man inhaled one last time and held his breath as he pinched the cigarette out and dumped the butt into his shirt pocket. He felt the thick smoke inside him, eating away at his lungs like termites on wood, and smiled.

He exhaled and knocked on the door. When he opened it, the man and woman were hugging.

"We'll take it," Mary said.

#

By the middle of the month Alex and Mary were comfortably settled into their new apartment.

The landlord had kept his word about patching the holes and giving the place a coat of paint before they moved in. They had steam cleaned the carpet themselves and scrubbed everything else from the bathroom walls to the inside of the kitchen cupboards. By the time they'd finished, every trace of the previous tenants had either been covered up or washed away.

It was *their* home now.

And in the comfort of their home, Alex lazed back on the couch watching a hockey game on the all-sports channel. The home team was down by four.

During pauses between the play-by-play announcer and color commentator's banter, Alex could hear the music coming from Mary's portable radio. She was at her desk in the spare bedroom marking test papers. Alex sighed. She always seemed to be marking test papers, even during the first week of school.

A third sound, that of the telephone ringing, cut through the television and radio noise and made Alex sit up on the couch. "I'll get it," he said, reaching over for the phone without taking his eyes from the screen.

"Hello?" The inflection in his voice made the word sound more like a question than a greeting.

"Alex, it's John."

"It's my brother," Alex shouted in Mary's direction. He put the receiver back to his ear. "Hey, John. How's it going?"

They made small talk for a few minutes. John was watching the hockey game, too.

"Listen, Alex." John's voice suddenly turned serious. "Now that you've got a bigger apartment and plenty of room, Cynthia and I were wondering if you could babysit the twins this weekend. We need a little time to ourselves and we thought if you could help us out, we could book a secluded cabin somewhere for a few days . . ."

"I don't know, John," Alex said, wondering if it were actually possible for him to say no to his brother. He shifted the receiver over onto his other ear. "The landlord is pretty strict about having kids in the building. He mentioned it several times the night we looked at the place."

"It'll be only be for two days, you won't even have to take them anywhere. I'll bring over a few video tapes and you can set them up in front of the television all weekend. They're good kids. They won't bother you at all."

"Uh . . . I don't—"

"C'mon, Alex. They're your nieces too, don't forget."

Alex pulled the receiver away from his ear for a moment and looked at the ceiling. "All right," he said with a sigh. "Drop them off around six-thirty, Friday."

"Thanks Alex. I knew you wouldn't let your brother down."

Alex hung up the phone and slumped back on the couch. He knew he'd taken a risk agreeing to babysit the twins, but what else could he have done. John was his brother and he couldn't refuse a favor to family. Besides, what was the landlord going to do to them, evict them for having some kids sleep over for a couple of nights? The old man couldn't just throw them out onto the street; there were laws against that sort of thing.

"What did he want?" Mary called from the spare bedroom.

"He uh . . . he asked if we wouldn't mind babysitting the twins for the weekend."

"And what did you say?" Mary asked, quickly making her way to the living room.

"I said yes."

Mary's shoulders slumped and she dropped her arms limply to her sides. "How could you? You know we can't have children in the building. You heard what the landlord said."

"I know, dear. But he's my brother. I couldn't say no to him."

"Tell that to the old fart when he asks where the kids came from," Mary said, resting her fisted hands on her hips.

"The landlord won't even know they're here." He knew he was wrong, but he struggled on as if in the right. "We'll keep them inside all weekend, they won't cause any problems. I promise."

"They're kids, Alex. They need to go out and play. They'll need fresh air and sunshine."

"It'll be all right, Mary. I promise."

"I just hope your brother doesn't refuse *us* when we show up on his doorstep Monday looking for a place to live." Mary turned around and walked back down the hall. She turned her radio up loud.

Alex went back to watching the game, clicking up the volume a few numbers before settling back on the couch for the third period.

#

John and Cynthia dropped the twins off at precisely six-thirty the next night. They were gone and headed for a cabin somewhere up north and precisely six-thirty-five.

The twins were adorable. Janice and Janet were four-and-a-half-years-old, Janice being the older sibling by six minutes. They were identical blonds, their long shimmering locks more like fleece than actual hair. Their eyes were powder-blue and their skin was pale pink and as soft as cotton balls.

Mary's anger over having to babysit went away almost immediately after the twins stepped into the apartment. Alex would never admit it, but he liked having the twins over just as much as Mary did. Just having them around seemed to put a spark back into their relationship. The whole apartment seemed to brighten in the glow of youthful innocence.

"Who wants popcorn?" Mary said as she came into the living room with two heaping bowls in her hands.

"I do," said Janice.

"I do," said Janet.

"I do," said Alex.

Mary laughed. She put the bowls down on the living room table, one in front of each of the girls, and went back to the kitchen.

Alex watched his wife closely, marveling at the color in her cheeks and the bounce in her step.

Mary came back from the kitchen with a two-liter bottle of Coke and four glasses. "Is it good?" she asked the girls as she put the pop bottle on the table.

The girls, mouths full of popcorn, nodded dramatically.

Mary sat down on the couch behind the twins. "Well, how about a movie?"

"Yeah sure," Alex said, moving over in front of the television. "What do you want to see?"

"*My Little Pony*!" the twins cried in unison. "Again?" Alex said. "We saw that one the last time we babysat you two, at our old apartment. How about something else? Something newer? How about . . . *Robocop 2*?"

"*My Little Pony*," they shouted.

Alex looked over at his wife. Mary tilted her head to one side and shrugged.

"All right," Alex said, sliding the tape into the VCR and pressing the play button. "*My Little Pony* it is."

He moved back to join the girls, grabbed a handful of popcorn and sat down next to his wife. Mary put her arms around her husband, hugged him, and kissed him on the cheek.

The movie was exactly as Alex remembered it.

#

The old man turned off the taps and shook the water from his hands. As he dried off, he rubbed the damp towel against his face, over his head.

He'd been working in the basement all day preparing the boiler for the winter and his muscles and joints ached from the strain.

He hung the towel around his neck and lifted his hands closer to his face. He blinked several times and finally moved his hands away, settling on a distance that allowed his aged eyes to make out some detail. The skin on the back of his hands was showing its age well, beautifully covered in dark brown spots and long deep wrinkles. He balled his hands into fists several times and rejoiced at the weakness of his grip, the languor of his muscles.

I'm getting old, he thought.

As he walked into the living room, his joints cracked and snapped like twigs. He felt a faint murmur in his heart and smiled. It felt good to be dying.

He sat down in his recliner and clicked on the television. He scanned the channels until he found a movie he liked and eased the chair back until he was horizontal. His eyelids immediately began to droop as sleep gladly overcame him.

Minutes later he felt something course through his body like a shiver. He opened his eyes and sniffed at the air.

He could smell it.

#

"What was that?" Alex said under his breath. He sat up in bed, ear straining to hear the sound again.

Silence.

Mary was asleep by his side, the regular rhythm of her breath suggesting that nothing out of the ordinary had happened.

But Alex was certain he'd heard something.

It took a moment for him to remember the twins, but when he did he quickly padded over to the spare bedroom and opened the door. The twins were huddled together, asleep in the middle of the fold-out bed looking like angels.

Alex took a deep breath and sighed.

He was on his way back to bed when he heard it again. It was a soft sound, the bated cry of a dog perhaps, or the far-off howl of a wolf.

Alex stopped still and listened. It sounded as if the cry were coming from the hall. He went to the door and heard it clearly: the sound of a dog whimpering on the other side of the door.

Alex flipped the locks and slid the chain free before opening the door a crack. He looked down at the floor expecting to find a dog, but there was nothing there. He opened the door wider and stuck his head out into the hall, looking down the corridor in both directions.

He looked both ways again, just to be sure, and went back inside. He closed the door and checked the locks twice before heading back to bed.

It was almost light out when he finally got back to sleep.

#

The bed shook and Alex felt something heavy crawling over his legs.

He opened his eyes and peered down the covers at his feet. A pair of pale smiling faces looked back at him. "It's almost seven-thirty, Uncle Alex. Aren't you gonna get up?" Janet asked. She had both hands on his legs and was nudging him endlessly. "Aunt Mary said you never sleep in this late on Saturdays."

"She said wha—"

"You're gonna miss half the cartoons," Janice said, joining her sister in giving her uncle a shake.

"All right, all right. I'm up already," Alex said, rolling over and covering his head with a pillow. "I'll be out in a few minutes."

The twins clambered off the bed and scooted out of the room. In the silence, Alex wondered how it was possible that little monsters could be so cute.

A few minutes later, Alex was dressed and sitting at the kitchen table. The room was full of the aroma of fresh-brewed coffee and the smell of eggs and bacon frying up on the stove. With the twins around, Alex noted, at least they paid more attention to what they ate. Normally, Saturday breakfast was nothing more than coffee and a couple of cookies.

"I thought I'd take the girls out shopping with me today," Mary said, pouring a cup of coffee for her husband. "I'm going downtown for some shoes; it might be fun for them."

Alex stirred sugar and cream into his coffee and slurped a long sip.

The twins were in the living room watching the Ninja Turtles. They kept repeating "Kowabunga Dude" over and over, echoing the phrase each time with a giggle.

Alex smiled. "I thought we agreed to keep them in the apartment?"

Mary busied herself in front of the stove. "What harm can taking them shopping do?"

Alex didn't have an answer. He sipped his coffee instead.

"Oh, this is ridiculous. We pay rent here. We have a right to have whoever we want stay over with us whenever we want. Why don't you just go up to see the landlord and tell him we have the twins over for the weekend? It's just for one more night. What is he going to do to us, throw us out onto the street?" She dropped Alex's breakfast plate on the table with a clang to emphasize her point.

Alex pictured the landlord spouting off about snot-nosed little rat-faced bastards and suddenly taking the twins out of building didn't seem like such a bad idea. "All right," he said, moving the plate in front of him with the push of an index finger. "Downtown sounds fine, just make sure the coast is clear when you get back."

Mary's face brightened. "Do you need anything?" She kissed him on the cheek on her way out of the room.

"No I'll be fine. You girls have fun," Alex said to the empty kitchen.

An hour later the apartment was silent. Alex sat on the couch across from the television and sipped his third cup of coffee. The Turtles were still on—on yet another channel—but Alex chose to watch the Three Stooges instead.

When the Stooges were over, all the television stations seemed to join in a conspiracy of woodworking, home improvement and lawn and garden shows. Alex clicked off the television and slumped back on the couch. Bored.

He would have read the paper if they got home delivery on Saturday . . . He would have washed the car if Mary hadn't taken it . . . He would have read a book if he liked to read . . . His options rapidly diminishing, Alex thought of doing the laundry.

With a full basket of whites tucked under one arm, Alex stepped onto the elevator and pressed B. The elevator was dark and smelled a little of urine, but it was a fast one and the trip to the basement didn't take long.

As he stepped out of the elevator, Alex bumped against one of the doors and knocked several pairs of underwear off the top of the laundry pile. He put the basket down and crouched to pick them up.

When he got back up, the landlord was standing before him.

Alex jumped, startled. Underwear fell back onto the floor. "You scared me," Alex said, crouching again nervously to collect the dirty clothes. "I didn't hear you come down the hall."

"Soft-soled shoes," the landlord said, smiling.

"I see." Alex was back on his feet.

There was an awkward moment of silence as Alex waited for the old man to move aside to let him pass. But the old man didn't move.

"Mr. Williams," he said finally. "I thought I heard some children in the building last night. Did you happen to hear them too?" The old man's face suddenly darkened as his bushy snow-white eyebrows knitted together and his lips pulled back slightly to expose his teeth.

Alex's eyes glanced away from the landlord's face. For a moment he considered telling the truth about the twins, but the look on the old man's face had grown even darker, almost terrifying. "No," he said, his voice wavering slightly. "I didn't hear any children." He steadied himself. "I thought I heard a dog at my door early this morning, but it was gone by the time I could check it out."

The landlord nodded. "I don't mind dogs in my building. It's children I can't stand. I don't take well to tenants deceiving me and I'd hate to have to throw somebody out because they were hiding some filthy little troublemakers from me. It's getting cold out, you know. There'll be snow on the ground before long."

Alex nodded and gave a polite smile. "I'll keep my eyes out for the . . . ratty little kids."

"I'm sure you will," the old man said, his face almost cracking a smile. He moved aside to let Alex pass.

Later, in the laundry room, Alex stripped off his t-shirt and tossed it into the washer.

It was soaked with sweat.

#

Mary and the twins came back just after four. Alex had been asleep on the couch, but got up when he heard the key slide into the lock. He tried to look busy when his wife came inside, but sleep still hung over him like a shroud.

"What took you so long?" he said. Then, seeing Mary had shopping bags hanging from both arms, asked, "And how many pairs of shoes did you end up buying?"

"We did some window shopping. We looked at girl stuff. We had a nice time," Mary said, hanging up her coat in the closet by the door. "Are you hungry?"

Alex hadn't bothered to prepare anything to eat all day and had managed with a few cups of coffee and a couple of apples. "Just a bit," he lied.

"Well, I hope you're hungrier than *just a bit*," she said, opening the door as wide as it would go. "Because we brought something special home to eat."

The twins came through the door carrying a large flat, red and white box. "Kowabunga Dude!" they shouted.

Alex could smell the pizza from where he sat on the couch and his stomach immediately went into slow growling spasms. "Is it still warm?"

Later in the kitchen, with three-quarters of the pizza gone and the twins in the living room watching professional wrestling, Alex told Mary about his morning meeting with the landlord.

"He actually insinuated that he'd throw a family out on the streets at this time of the year?" Mary said. "Just because of some kids."

Alex took the last few bites from his pizza slice and tossed the crust back into the box. "Oh, he didn't insinuate anything, Mary. He just came right out and told me."

"Not only is that insane, it's cruel and probably highly illegal." She paused to take a sip of Coke. "What did you say to him when he told you?"

Alex took a sip of Coke, too. He wasn't thirsty, but it was the only thing he could think of to put off answering the question.

"Well?"

"I didn't say anything," Alex said meekly.

"Good."

Alex was both stunned and relieved.

"I wouldn't give that old bastard the satisfaction of throwing us out. He's obviously crazy. What landlord with any kind of head on his shoulders would approve of having dogs in his building, but not children?"

"One that rents a two-bedroom apartment to us for one-fifty less per month than everyone else."

Mary was silent a moment. "I suppose so," she said. "But, still. That doesn't make it right."

#

The old man lay awake on his bed, his eyes wide and fixed on the ceiling.

He sensed the presence of purity. It was an overpowering sensation, one that sent electric fireflies skittering through his nervous system.

His body slowly writhed and twisted in the darkness. His muscles tensed and rippled as he fought back the urge to tear through the building in search of the *children*.

The hunger had grown severe, almost painful. He could almost taste it now, the intoxicatingly sweet life-giving flesh of innocence.

#

Alex was in the kitchen pouring himself a drink when the phone rang. "I'll get it" he said, sipping his bloody Caesar and adding a shake of salt to it before the third ring.

"Hello?"

"Hey, Alex. It's John."

"Hi John. How are you?" Alex said into the receiver. "Mary, it's John," he shouted into the living room. "Mary says hi." A pause. "Of course the kids are fine, why wouldn't they be . . ."

The brothers talked for half an hour. Alex welcomed the time away from his wife and the twins; he'd seen *The Wizard of Oz* before—plenty of times—and didn't share the same fascination with it as the girls did.

"Right. See you tomorrow around five. Bye."

By the time Alex came back into the living room *The Wizard of Oz* was over and they were watching film clips that were tacked on to the end of the tape.

"John and Cynthia will be coming over around five tomorrow. I told them we'd like Chinese."

Mary smiled. "Good thinking."

At that moment the tape ended and the television screen turned into a blizzard of black and white dots.

"What was that?" Mary said, slightly startled.

"What was what?"

"I heard a noise. Like there was someone at the door."

"I didn't hear anything." Alex turned to the twins. "Did you girls hear anything?"

The twins shook their heads.

It was probably the television," he said. "Something on the tape."

Mary nodded slowly.

Alex glanced at his watch. Ten o clock. "Okay you two rug rats, time for bed."

Janice and Janet moaned and groaned but eventually were up on their feet heading for the bathroom.

"I'll see them to bed if you clean up in here," Mary said, her right eyebrow arched highly and her lips curled in a sly half-smile. "Maybe we can rendezvous back here in say . . . ten minutes?"

"Sounds good to me," Alex smiled. He collected the glasses and bowls from the living room table while the twins brushed their teeth in the bathroom. A few minutes later, as he was wiping the table with a damp cloth, he heard Mary's voice in the bedroom—Probably reading the girls a bedtime story.

He also heard something at the door. It was the same muted cry that he'd heard that morning, but now there was something added to it. A scratching sound   as if the dog had returned and wanted to come inside.

Alex crept to the door. The sound grew louder as he neared until there could be no mistaking that there was indeed a dog on the other side.

Remembering that the snicking of the locks had scared the dog away the first time, Alex crouched down to look under the door, hoping to see a paw or some fur through the crack. He got down on all fours and cocked his head sideways against the carpet.

The lights of the hallway produced an unbroken band of white under the door.

There was no dog out in the hall.

Suddenly, the door exploded inward. Something heavy landed on top of Alex and was gone. He had to gasp for air as a searing, white-hot pain knifed across his midsection.

He blinked his eyes to try and see. Something warm and greasy flowed down into them. He wiped a hand across his forehead. He was bleeding. Through the red curtain of blood he could just make out a human figure turning the corner headed for the living room.

Alex struggled to free himself of the splintered wood of the door and managed to get to his feet. His head felt dizzy and he still hadn't caught his breath.

He heard another door burst open.

Screaming.

Mary, he thought. *The twins!*

He stumbled through the apartment towards the bedrooms. He saw the door to the second bedroom had been broken down. The screaming had stopped, replaced by other sounds.

Alex ran into the room. Blood was splattered over the walls and across the ceiling. Mary was slumped in the corner, sitting in a pool of blood, her face frozen in a silent scream. She'd been ripped open and body parts seemed to be bubbling out of her belly. The twins lay on the bed covered in blood, arms and legs disjointed and splayed in unnatural directions. Some*thing* was on top of them on all fours, its head was down and thrashing from side to side, tearing flesh from the leg of one of the girls.

For a moment Alex refused to accept the scene was real. Words of denial flashed across his mind until he was almost convinced it was all an elaborate joke. But the smell of blood and other body fluids sliced through the air, bringing him sharply back to reality. *This is happening!* The words roared in his ears and his heart slammed up into his throat. "Oh my God. This is happening!"

Alex fought off the shock of realization by picking up a nearby chair and bringing it crashing down onto the back of the . . . *creature*. The chair bent but did not break. The blow had no effect on the thing other than getting its attention. Alex had the chair raised for a second blow when the creature turned to face him.

The chair seemed to hover over Alex's head as if hanging by a string.

He was looking directly at the face of the creature. It was strangely recognizable to him as that of the old man, the landlord, but . . .

The chair dropped from Alex's hands and landed on the floor behind him with a loud clang.

The old man's face had changed. The silver hair had darkened and was more like fur now. His round stubby nose seemed longer and his teeth had moved forward to look like the snout of a wolf. And his eyes! His eyes were gaping black holes surrounded by empty gray pools.

"My God!" Alex screamed. "What have you done?"

The creature was upon him in a flash of blood and fur. Claw-like fingers curled around Alex's arms, tightening like iron bands. He was thrown across the room, his head and shoulder crashing into the wall. Before he fell to the floor, the creature had Alex's throat firmly in his right hand. With incredible ease, it lifted him up until he was several feet off the floor.

Alex could feel the vertebrae in his neck stretching to the breaking point. He gasped for air.

"You wouldn't let me die, would you?" the creature said in a whisper.

Alex breathed in. The thing's breath stank of flesh and blood. "What are you talking about?" he struggled to say through his collapsing windpipe.

"I had one simple rule. No children! But you liked to play games with me. Thought you could hide them from me. Idiot!" The fingers tightened around Alex's throat like a steel vice.

"All I wanted was to quietly grow old and die. But you defied me and brought children here, tempting me with the smell of their flesh." The creature shook his head. "Do you know that the pure, untainted flesh of children has kept me young for over one thousand years. Finally, I'd had enough of it. At last, I craved death over flesh."

The hold on Alex's neck loosened slightly and he managed to inhale a quick gulp of air.

"Five years I've not tasted their sweet carrion. Five years . . . Another four and I would have happily withered away into dust. But now . . ." He laughed and the stench of his breath nearly knocked Alex unconscious. ". . . Now, after giving in to the temptation of these two excellent little girls, it will be another eight before I can even begin to dream of death again."

"Bu—" Alex tried to speak.

"Don't bother," the creature sneered, its incisors shining pink in the dim light. "The time for words has long passed. Oh, I won't kill you. I'll just keep you on death's threshold a while so you can watch me feast. Be glad. My torture has lasted a millennium, yours shall be much, much briefer than that . . . just long enough for you to realize the seriousness of your error."

The creature jerked Alex's head suddenly to the right, and a flash of heat shot through his body then nothing.

The creature released its grip on his throat and Alex slumped further down onto the floor. He tried to get up, to move an arm or a leg, but couldn't.

The gash on his forehead had widened, but Alex managed to blink the blood from his eyes. He looked up at the creature. The face was even more hideous now, more lupine with sharper teeth and darker hair.

Blood ran more freely down into Alex's eyes and through the crimson haze, Alex saw the creature hop back onto the bed and sink his snout into the chest of one of the girls. He desperately tried to get up, to do something, but his body remained still. He was paralyzed from the neck down, but he could still feel pain roiling in his heart like a dark cloud. He opened his mouth to scream, but could manage no more than a muted cry.

Finally, he saw the creature hold a twitching heart in the air like a trophy. It opened its mouth wide and . . .

Everything went black.

#

The dark-haired man pulled the key from the lock and pushed the door open. The hinges protested slightly against the movement of the door before allowing it to silently swing open.

"We've done a lot of work on this place since the fire. Another couple of days, another coat of paint and it'll be like new."

"I read about that fire in the paper," the woman said, placing a hand over her heart.

Silence fell upon the room.

"How did it happen?" the husband asked.

"Well, the couple that died in the fire was babysitting their nieces when the snot-nosed brats found a book of matches. Before you know it, they set fire to the bed and the whole apartment went up in flames." He snapped his fingers. "Just like that."

"How awful," the woman said, moving her hand from her heart to the front of her mouth.

"I don't have a *No Kids Allowed* rule for nothing, you know. Which reminds me. You two don't have any children, do you?"

"No."

"That's good," the landlord said softly. "That's real good."

The husband looked at the walls, nodding his head. "I can't even tell there's been a fire here, honey. Can you?"

She shook her head.

"I can wait for you in the hall if you like," the landlord interrupted. "You know, give you a chance to talk it over."

"That would be fine."

The landlord closed the door of the apartment behind him and lit a cigarette. The smoke felt good as he inhaled it deeply into his young, healthy lungs.

This story began life entitled, "Adults Only, No Kids Allowed!" and took five years to find a home. I don't recall a lot about its beginnings, but I imagine I wanted to try my hand at one of the dark areas of the horror genre and that being when bad things happening to children. Another no-no is dogs and family pets. I remember one editor explaining to me in a rejection letter that he could allow all kinds of depravity on humans, but dogs were absolutely off limits. I always liked pushing the envelope and taking on a challenge with my writing, and it's a tricky thing to make the villain a tortured soul and the adults—who were only trying to do a good thing by baby sitting—the bad guys for not following instructions.

The Piano Player Has No Fingers

Detective Joe Williams sat stiffly on the elaborately decorated Victorian sofa in Lawrence Hayden's front room. Reynolds, the butler who'd answered the door, had told him to make himself comfortable, but the ornate sofa looked too fragile, too expensive, to relax in. He was afraid that if he leaned the wrong way the thing might fall apart.

So, he sat motionless on the sofa, looking at the paintings that were hung around the room. Each one depicted some sort of musical scene—this one a Elizabethan recital, that one a church choir, here a traveling minstrel, there a young woman playing the harp in her bed chamber.

Finally, Joe's eyes came to rest on a more contemporary painting—a group of locals playing in the back room of a barber shop after closing.

Although he didn't recognize the older paintings, he'd seen this other one plenty of times before. It was a Norman Rockwell, and for a moment Joe wondered if this painting was the original—Hayden could certainly afford it. He eased his weight forward on the sofa and got up to take a closer look . . .

"Mr. Hayden will see you now."

Joe turned to see Reynolds standing in the doorway. "This way, please," he said, his lips barely moving as he spoke.

Joe forgot about the Rockwell painting for the moment and followed Reynolds through the house. It was practically dripping with wealth and luxury, almost to the point of excess. Brass and marble were as common here as wood and plaster were in other people's homes—and dust was just about as uncommon.

Reynolds opened the right-hand side of a set of white French doors, then stepped aside to let Joe get by.

"Detective Joseph Williams to see you, sir."

Joe stepped into the room and was relieved to find Hayden sitting back in a comfortable looking wooden rocker by the window, dressed in a loose-fitting shirt and a pair of old jeans with a hole just above the right knee. He was an older man, probably in his mid-to-late fifties although he could probably pass for forty-five in a pinch. His long white hair was combed straight back in a thick shock, the hair on the sides flowing over his ears like cresting waves in a roiling sea. His face had a dark and brooding quality to it, something that virtually disappeared when he smiled and welcomed Joe into the room.

"You'll have to excuse Reynolds, he likes to announce everyone who comes to see me."

Joe nodded and sat down in an armchair next to Hayden. "Now," Hayden extended his hand, and the two men shook. "What brings you to see me, Detective Williams?"

"Please, call me Joe."

"Very well then, Joseph. What can I do for you?"

"Well, Mr. Hayden . . ." Joe paused, giving Hayden the chance to tell him he could call him by his first name. When the silence between them became awkward, Joe continued. "I'm one of the detectives investigating the Piano Player Murders."

Hayden cringed slightly and inhaled a breath through tightly clenched teeth.

"I take it you're familiar with the case, then?" Hayden nodded. "I've been following it in the papers."

"Right," said Joe, taking a deep breath of his own. "Well, last night there was another killing."

"Dear, God! No!"

"I'm afraid so. Have you ever heard of John-Allen Gardner?"

"Yes, of course. He's a jazzman, a brilliant player. Sometimes goes by the nickname *The Jagster.*"

"Not anymore. We found him this morning in a dumpster behind the El Mocambo. He'd been bludgeoned to death and like the others, all ten of his fingers had been cut off—each one neatly severed from the hand."

Hayden just shook his head.

"That makes ten victims in all," continued Joe, his stomach turning slightly at the number. "Ten of the best piano players in the city murdered, their fingers cut off   "

"It certainly is a tragedy, Joseph," Hayden interjected. "But what does this have to do with me?"

"Someone at the station told me you were a local music expert of sorts. They thought maybe you could help me out. You know, provide me with some insight into the killings."

"Well, I'm flattered, Joseph, but I'm really more of a hobbyist than an expert. I collect musical artwork, rare instruments . . . I even write a review column for *The Reporter*, but it's strictly for fun. God knows, I could never live on what that newspaper pays."

"Of course," said Joe, taking a look around the room.

"If you're wondering, my father made his fortune during Prohibition, then invested it all in real estate and oil. By the time I turned four, he'd already made sure that I'd be financially secure for the rest of my life . . . and then some."

That figured, thought Joe. Even though this room had a comfortable lived in feel to it, with a well-worn carpet and plenty of dark wood on the walls, it still looked like the playroom of a man who had far more money than he knew what to do with.

Off in one corner a violin sat in its open case inside a glass cabinet. Probably a genuine Stradavarius, thought Joe. It wouldn't belong here otherwise. There were other instruments in the room as well; a couple of strangely-twisted brass horns with complicated valve systems, and a pair of stringed instruments that bore only the slightest resemblance to modern day guitars. There was also an upright piano-like instrument made of thick grained wood and decorated in red and gold highlights.

"Is that a harpsichord?" asked Joe.

"Close, Joseph. It's a clavichord."

Joe nodded. "You have many beautiful things, Mr. Hayden," he said, more than a little dazzled by such a casual display of opulence.

"Thank you," said Hayden, taking the compliment with a gracious nod. "But enough about me and my possessions. What is it that you'd like to ask me . . . about the murders?"

"Well," said Joe, turning back around to face Hayden. "I guess I'd like to hear your take on it, you know . . . see if you've got any ideas about who might do such a thing?"

"Well, Joseph," Hayden said, clearing his throat. "I'm pretty familiar with everyone on the local music scene, from classical players to grunge bands, but I can't really say I know of anyone who'd actually be capable of such a heinous crime." He paused a moment, as if thinking. "Then again, anyone who *acted* as if they were capable of committing these murders would probably never end up killing anybody."

"What do you mean?"

"Well, it's always the brooding, silent type in these sorts of things, isn't it?"

"Quite often," Joe nodded, conceding the point.

"And the music scene is rife with those, I'm afraid."

"Uh-huh. But other than a general type," asked Joe. "Would you care to speculate on who might want to kill off piano players exclusively?"

"The only thing I can think of is that it's possibly the work of a jealous player, someone who feels they aren't getting the recognition they deserve and is killing the top players in order to move more quickly up the ladder."

"You mean sort of like in that film, *Amadeus*."

"Yes," said Hayden. "The relationship between Mozart and Salieri is a perfect example of what I'm talking about."

"What about the fingers, then?"

"Most likely for spite, I suppose," said Hayden. "That is, of course, if the fingers were taken after the victims were dead. If they were cut off while the victims were still alive I suspect the killer was trying to, uh . . . What's the phrase? Rub their noses in it."

Joe shifted uncomfortably in his chair.

"If I were you," Hayden continued. "I'd keep my eyes out for the player who emerges from the current   'second tier' of piano players in the city. If someone had gone to the trouble to kill off all the top players, then he'd already have devised a plan to capitalize on the sudden demise of his more accomplished colleagues."

"Yeah, well, up until last night, John-Allen Gardner had been one of our prime suspects."

"Oh, dear."

"Still," said Joe. "I'd appreciate it if you let me know if you think anyone's career is moving forward a little too quickly in the next little while."

"I'd be glad to," said Hayden, a touch of sincerity in his voice. "In fact, it would be my pleasure to assist you in this way."

Joe remained in the armchair for a moment, wondering if there were any other questions he needed to ask. As he glanced around the room again he noticed an antique piano directly behind him. He turned to Hayden. "Do you play?" he said, getting up out of the chair and walking over toward the piano.

Hayden let out a slight laugh. "A little. As I said, music is my hobby. I dabble in it and play a number of instruments, one of which happens to be the piano."

"That's a beautiful piece. I bet it sounds as good as it looks."

"As a matter of fact, Joseph, it does. It was made by John Broadwood and Sons of London early in the Nineteenth Century. The serial number on it suggests it was made prior to the one Broadwood sent to Beethoven in Vienna in 1816."

"Really," said Joe. Then, "How'd it end up here?"

"My father bought it on a business trip to Berlin after the war. Supposedly, it had once belonged to Hermann Goering." Hayden took a proud breath. "Needless to say, it's one of my most prized possessions."

"I can imagine," said Joe, taking a step back from the antique instrument in order to admire it better—and safely—from a distance. "Are you any good?"

"Unfortunately not, Joseph," Hayden said, his voice edged with regret. "Not as good as I'd like to be, anyway . . . but then again, who ever is?"

"I suppose," said Joe. "Still, you must play fairly well, knowing so much about music and all."

"You're very kind, Joseph," Hayden sighed. He came up and stood by Joe's side. "I can play a tune, even a classical piece or two, but . . ." A pause. "Let me put it to you this way, Joseph. I'm not in any danger of losing my fingers."

"Right." Joe smiled politely at Hayden's morbid little joke. "Well, thanks for your time, Mr. Hayden. I better be getting back to the station and see if anything new has developed since this morning."

"Very well, then," said Hayden. "It's been a pleasure, and please . . . if there's any other way I may be of assistance to you concerning this case, feel free to give me a call."

"Don't worry," said Joe. "I'll be in touch."

Hayden stood by the room's open door. "This way, detective."

#

Lawrence Hayden waved good-bye to Detective Williams one last time, then locked the front door of his home.

He turned around, and with his back to the door, muttered a few words under his breath about a meddling, two-bit detective. Then he inhaled deeply, making sure to let the air out slowly, releasing some of his body's built-up tension.

Some, but not all.

He walked down the hall and stopped at the kitchen where Reynolds sat at the table sipping a cup of tea and reading the morning paper.

"I wish not to be disturbed for the next hour," said Hayden.

"Very good, sir."

Hayden continued on down the hall, walking slowly to take in all the beauty of his home and its contents.

At the end of the hall he came upon a single door. He took a key attached to a long chain from his pocket and slid it into the lock. After opening the door, he scooped up the key and dropped it and its chain back into his pocket.

He stepped inside the room.

There was a large, high window set into in the far wall covered by a thick blackout curtain that allowed only the faintest hint of sunshine to glow out from around its edges. He switched on the light and a small chandelier hung high up against the ceiling came on. It provided some light, but still left the room quite dim—full of shadows and dark corners.

Hayden found the dim light soothing.

He closed the door to the room, making sure the lock *snicked* into place. Then he walked slowly over to the piano situated in the center of the room. It was a miniature grand piano, or "baby" grand made by the Rudolph Wurlitzer company in 1901—a practical instrument with decent tone and resonance, but nothing special about it to look at.

Still, the baby grand was his favorite instrument of all.

He had told the detective that the Broadwood in the music room was one of his most prized possessions.

One of his most prized possessions . . .

That's because this piano was *the* prize in his collection of rare and exotic instruments.

He sat down on the bench, pulled the key from his pocket once more and unlocked the hinged wooden lid protecting the piano's keys.

Then he slowly lifted the lid and looked at the keyboard . . .

Made up of eighty-eight human fingers—thirty-six black fingers and fifty-two white.

The piano was a work of art.

Absolutely priceless.

Hayden stretched his fingers once . . .

And began to play.

"The Piano Player Has No Fingers," was published in an anthology entitled *The Piano Player Has No Fingers*. As much as I'd like to say my tale was the title story of the book, I can't. That's because every story in the book was titled "The Piano Player Has No Fingers." The idea was that the editors would give a bunch of writers a title, then see what they could come up with. When I thought up the story I immediately called the editors to save the idea for myself since to me, the idea was so simple surely several others would come up with it as well. Alas, nobody did. In fact, no two stories in the book were even remotely similar, even though they all sprang from the same source.

And Injustice for Some

The air was full of the smell of death.

Although he was in one of the best hospitals in the city and people were being made well all around him, his super sensitive olfactory nerves could smell illness and decay almost to the exclusion of everything else.

Or maybe it was the smell wafting up from the wound in his shoulder, the blood and antiseptic clouding his senses and preventing him from seeing the hospital for what it was—a place of healing.

The door swung open and Doctor Sawyer trundled in, a large, plain brown envelope under his arm.

"What's the good news, doc?"

"Well, Mr. Nightshadow, sir—"

"Please," interrupted the superhero. "Just call me Nightshadow."

"All right . . . Nightshadow," the doctor said, pushing his glasses up onto the bridge of his nose. "The good news is the X-ray shows that the bullet caused no major damage."

The doctor paused, pulling his lips back in a awkwardly strained smile.

After a moment's silence, Nightshadow felt compelled to break it. "That's great, doc. These punks are getting better armed all the time. I keep telling myself to be more careful, maybe now I've learned my lesson."

Nightshadow finished speaking and the awkward silence returned.

"Uh, I don't know how to tell you this, but . . ." The doctor's eyes dropped to the floor.

"But what?"

The doctor breathed a deep sigh. "There's something else on the X-ray. It shows a mass in your chest. I'm afraid it might be cancerous."

Nightshadow's eyes opened wide and his jaw dropped, forming a perfect "O" of disbelief.

"I'm just as shocked as you are."

"Can I see the X ray?" Nightshadow's voice cracked slightly.

"Sure," the doctor said enthusiastically, as if happy to be distracted by the simple task of switching on the lightscreen set into the wall.

He slipped the X-ray into the clip at the top of the frame and let the negative fall against the light like a page.

Nightshadow slowly got up off the bed, wincing slightly from the pain in his shoulder, and made his way to the doctor's side.

The doctor remained still and silent as Nightshadow looked at the cloudy black and white image for several minutes. There was indeed something there, a fist-sized mass on the left side of his chest.

Nightshadow felt his mind go numb. His first thought was denial, that it was nothing more than a water mark on the X-ray, but he knew that was simply wishful thinking. Then, as he looked closely at the image, studying every wisp of the ghostlike ball of smoke, he thought back over the past few months.

The realization was sudden, as if another bullet had slammed into his shoulder.

He *had* been a step slower lately, sometimes even finding himself out of breath after a foot chase through the city. He'd always discounted it as age—he was, after all, on the downside of thirty-five.

And what about tonight? Sure he'd had some close calls over the years, but he'd never been so caught off-guard by a punk before. *Never.*

Suddenly growing old was something to look forward to, a goal.

For the first time in his life, Nightshadow knew fear. It coursed through his body like electricity, sending spasms of terror through his body in waves. But then the fear dissipated, giving way to anger. His body slowly became damp with sweat as fury roiled within him. In the end, all he could think was . . .

WHY ME?

The doctor must have heard him mutter the words under his breath because he felt compelled to answer.

"There is no why," he said. "There's no reason why you have cancer and someone else does not. If you were a religious man, I would tell you it was God's will, but since I don't think you're particularly devout, all I can say is it's just luck. Bad luck."

Nightshadow stepped back to the bed and lied down. All he wanted was to be alone with his thoughts. He turned his head away from the doctor so he wouldn't have to look at him.

"You know . . . Nightshadow, you're actually a very lucky man." He paused as if waiting for the superhero to say,

'Really, how so?' When he didn't, the doctor continued on as if he had.

"If this had happened to you twenty years ago, you would have been in a lot of trouble. These days cancer isn't always a fatal illness. Even though the tumor looks to be malignant, there's a good chance it could be a lymphoma, maybe even Hodgkin's disease. Both of those react very, very well to treatment. With chemotherapy and radiation, you could be back fighting crime in say sixth months to a year."

Nightshadow tried to block out the doctor's rambling. The man was talking about his cancer as if it were just another criminal he had to bring to justice, another bad guy to be put behind bars, another punk who needed his ass kicked.

"They say 'Cancer Can Be Beaten'" the doctor said. "And if anyone can beat it, Nightshadow can."

Sure, thought Nightshadow. I have *superpowers*, but I'm not *superhuman*. Stealth that made him almost invisible at night and an over-abundance of physical strength, agility and cunning had helped him stop the odd runaway train, catch countless rooftop prowlers or make city parks safe from muggers, thieves and rapists. But for all his strengths, all his deeds, it had been the newspapers that had dubbed him a *superhero*. In the end he was still human, still susceptible to human disease . . . still as helpless as the next person against the malignant cells that were growing unchecked inside his body.

Doctor Sawyer finished with his paperwork and turned to face Nightshadow. There was a gleeful smile on his face. "My son, Billy would kill me if he knew you were here, and I didn't get your autograph. Would you mind?"

"Sure," Nightshadow said in a kind of knee-jerk reaction to the question. He could never refuse a request for an autograph, especially one for a child.

The doctor handed Nightshadow a slip of hospital stationery, then took the shiny gold pen from his plastic pocket protector and gave it to the superhero.

The pen felt heavy, yet delicate in Nightshadow's hand. It was a fine writing instrument and very obviously expensive.

The doctor noticed Nightshadow admiring the pen. "My wife gave it to me when I graduated med school. She had to sell the headboard to our brass bed to buy it."

Nightshadow nodded politely.

Just then the hospital's public address system clicked on. "Code White. East 508. Code White. East 508."

The doctor hurriedly put down his paperwork and ran to the door. "Code White is for a dangerously violent person. Too bad you're hurt," he said with a sympathetic, almost pitying tilt of his head. "We could probably use your help."

"Yeah, too bad," Nightshadow muttered as the doctor rushed out the door.

Nightshadow had thought he'd wanted to be alone, but now that he was, he wanted the doctor, *anyone*, to come back and be with him.

He closed his eyes, feeling the room's walls expand outward, away from the bed in all directions, making him feel isolated, alone with his tumor.

He swore he could almost feel it growing out of control in his chest, attacking the healthy parts of his body with a malicious bent on destroying them.

His mind searched for a reason, his lifestyle perhaps, or something within his genes, but he couldn't think of any reason why he should be stricken with cancer and not someone else.

Again he came to ask the question. *WHY?* But this time it was followed by something else, a coda to the question, to his life as a superhero.

"What have I been fighting evil for all this time?" he asked aloud.

"I've resisted the temptation to use my powers for personal profit, choosing to live my life championing good. Truth, Justice, The American Way and all that crap! For what?"

He looked at the upper part of his costume hanging down from his waist. The dull black, blue, and grey that usually rippled with bulging, well-defined muscles looked flaccid and limp.

Lifeless.

Dead.

He'd lived his life helping others and what had he got for it in return? The equivalent to a knife in the back and a kick in the crotch.

"Thanks a lot," he said, staring up from his bed as if looking through the seven floors of hospital above him and into the star-bright night sky.

He was about to say something else, but the words died in his throat. He knew his voice was mute; there was no one listening. There was no God.

If there was, how could he have let this happen to *him*, Nightshadow, one of the most valiant and heroic warriors in the fight against crime, against evil itself?

It was at that moment that Nightshadow decided that things would change. If he was not long for this Earth he'd make the most out of what little time he had left.

He uncapped the pen and autographed the slip of paper for the doctor's son.

Billy,
Go To Hell.
Nightshadow.

He smiled.

He'd always wondered how a life of crime differed from one that fought against it. Perhaps he would find out.

He looked at the doctor's pen closely. It couldn't be worth more than a hundred dollars, but its sentimental value to the doctor was much, much higher. In fact, it was practically priceless.

Without a moment's hesitation, Nightshadow slipped into his costume, clipped the pen to his collar and left the hospital . . . under cover of the night.

THE END

On the Writing of "And Injustice for Some"

"And Injustice for Some" was the sixty-sixth short story I had written. By the time it found a home, it was the sixty-third short story of mine to be accepted for publication.

As short stories go it's admittedly not one of my best, but neither is it one of my worst. Trying to be as objective about the story's merits as possible—and writers can never be truly objective about their own work—I'd say it falls somewhere right in the middle, better than "War Cry" (*Deathport*) but perhaps not as good as "Scream String" (*Shock Rock 2*).

But regardless of the perceived qualities or shortcomings the story might have, I can easily say that no other story I've yet written has ever meant more to me, or come straighter from my heart.

What? you say.

A story about a superhero?

"And Injustice For Some" was written in February of 1993 in a hospital room on a borrowed portable computer. In January of that year, January 11, to be precise, (This date burned into my memory for obvious reasons) a routine x-ray revealed a fist-sized cancerous tumor in the chest of my wife, Roberta.

As I write this, I can remember everything about that night as if it were yesterday. It was a Monday night, I had been called to the hospital from an Ontario Hydra meeting, (Ontario Hydra being the group of science fiction professionals in and around Toronto) and had expected to find my wife there and everything to be fine. Instead, the emergency department looked empty, the faces of the staff solemn. The doctor who showed us the x-ray revealing the tumor seemed nervous, almost apologetic over the fact that he had discovered something terribly wrong. (The x-ray had been taken merely as a precaution as Roberta had been complaining of minor bronchitis.)

The scene in the story in which Nightshadow looks at the x-ray is exactly the way I had looked at the x-ray. His feelings were my feelings at the time.

We left the hospital and somehow, I drove us to my in-laws where our year-old son Luke was already asleep. We did our best to try and function normally—talking, watching some television—but nothing we did felt right.

How could it?

The news had been a devastating blow. Here was a woman just over thirty with a one-year-old child, a woman who had never smoked, never drank, never done an unhealthy thing in her life . . . with cancer. It didn't seem right. It didn't seem fair.

Neither of us slept well that night, but Roberta did eventually manage to get some rest. Ironically, it was the same night Mario Lemieux (the Pittsburgh Penguins hockey star) made public his ongoing bout with cancer. Roberta watched the news reports and heard how Lemieux would be back on the ice in six to eight weeks. This lifted her spirits considerably.

The next day began with the first of seemingly endless visits with all manner of doctors—from our family physician to several different oncologists, from surgeons to internalists. At this point we didn't know what the tumor was, though looking back on it, I'm sure the doctors already had an opinion they weren't inclined to share with us for fear of raising false hopes.

Things continued to move quickly and less than ten days later Roberta checked into St. Joseph's Health Center in Toronto for a routine biopsy of the tumor.

And that's when the real trouble began.

What started out as a simple biopsy to extract a small portion of the tumor for analysis quickly turned into a nightmare. Because the tumor was so large it had pushed several vital parts within the chest cavity out of place. When the doctors went looking for the tumor they accidentally cut into an artery and Roberta had to be rushed by ambulance to Toronto General Hospital where a thoracic team is on standby twenty-four hours a day. They opened up her chest, repaired the artery and took more than enough biopsy samples.

Open heart biopsy is what I like to call it.

After that operation Roberta spent two days in intensive care and the next two weeks recovering in hospital, while the rest of us spent fearful days awaiting the results of the biopsy. In the interim the doctors speculated that the tumor was possibly one of three types of cancer: Hodgkin's Disease, Lymphoma or Thymoma—the first being the most desirable, the third being the least.

(Imagine that! A most desirable form of cancer.)

It was during this time, this period of waiting, that the story "And Injustice For Some" was written.

When people talk about writing or being a writer they often say things like, "I'd like to write, but I haven't got the time." Of course, as corny as it might sound, people who truly have the desire to write, have it in their blood. Instead of wishing for the time to write, they make time for it.

They simply *have to* write.

Here I was, spending my days tending to my wife, tubes running in and out of her body and an annoying suction machine running day and night, and still I needed to write something . . . anything.

Perhaps it was a way to occupy my mind during the few moments each day when Roberta would fall asleep, or maybe I was telling myself that for her life to continue everything about our lives had to continue on unhindered.

Whatever the reason, I kept working.

My good friend, science fiction writer Robert J. Sawyer, borrowed a portable computer from his mother and in turn loaned it to me so I could work by my wife's bedside. The first story I worked on was the revisions to "Scream String" which was published in *Shock Rock 2*, edited by Jeff Gelb.

Shortly after completing "Scream String," I learned of a superhero anthology being edited by Nathan Archer and Kurt Busiek called *Behind the Mask*.

After spending a few days thinking about story ideas, I came up with a story about a superhero who discovers he has cancer. It seemed a natural considering the environment I was living in at the time. So, I sent Nathan Archer an outline for "And Injustice for Some."

He didn't like the outline for various reasons and told me the chances of him buying the story after it was written were slim.

Still, this was a story I wanted to write, if for nothing else than to capture some of the emotions I'd been feeling during that hellish month.

Now, after re-reading the story in preparation for writing this essay, I'm amazed to find that it's all there, all of my fears, all of my anger, everything I was feeling at the time. The story reminded me how devastating a blow the event had been in our lives and I'm glad now that I wrote it. Admittedly, someone else reading the story might only feel some of the emotions that were running through me at the time, while some others might not feel anything at all. No matter, it's all there for me, and as Dean Koontz so often says, writers should write the stories that are important to them.

This one was important to me.

So, I wrote the story on the borrowed portable computer set up on a food table in Roberta's hospital room and made sure as many aspects of my surroundings as possible found their way into the story. For example, my wife's room number was East 508, the same room number as in the story, and Code White is Northwestern General Hospital's code for a dangerously violent person.

When I finished the story, I sent it to Nathan Archer with little hope that he would buy it. No surprise, he quickly rejected it. After that I sent it to a few other magazines with similar results. Then I put the story away, which is very unlike me (I rarely give up on stories—my reject champion having amassed a total of twenty-four rejection slips before finding a home). To tell the truth, I really didn't care if the story was ever published in a magazine or not. I wrote the story for myself and it would always be there for me to read whenever I wanted to. So, I put it away and forgot about it— the proverbial trunk story.

Meanwhile back at the hospital . . .

After three weeks of waiting, the biopsy results came in and the doctors decided the tumor was Hodgkin's Disease— a curable form of cancer. But the relief over that diagnosis was short-lived as Roberta still had to undergo six months of intensive chemotherapy and another month of radiation treatment.

It was a difficult time, a veritable roller-coaster ride of physical and emotional pain. Roberta underwent twelve chemotherapy sessions every other Thursday. The treatment was aggressive, the combination of drugs literally toxic to the human body, and Roberta was physically incapacitated for up to five days after each treatment. Her hair fell out, she gained some weight, and every other weekend she wondered if it was all worth going through.

I guess I can best sum up that time by saying that when you count slowly, twelve is a very big number.

But, the tumor shrank throughout the chemotherapy and continued to shrink during radiation treatments. When it was all over, tests showed that the tumor was gone and all of the cancer cells had been destroyed.

Simply put, the treatment was a complete success.

Which brings me back to the story and this little essay.

The success of my wife's treatment made me think about the story again, this time with an eye to seeing it in print along with an essay about its creation. I think I just wanted these events to be on record somewhere and I'm grateful to *Iguana Informer* editor Davi Dee and *Alouette* editor Robert J. Sawyer, who allowed me this opportunity to be more than a little self-indulgent.

I also think that, in a small way, I wanted to provide the ultimate answer to that timeless question: "Where do you get your ideas?"

Life.

One final note: Today, as I write this, it is May 31, 1994. Tomorrow, June 1, Roberta will be returning to work for the first time since January 11, 1993, almost eighteen months after the cancer was first diagnosed.

And, today as I write this, April 28, 2023, 25 years since the original publication of this book, 28 years since the story's first publication, and 29 years the cancer was diagnosed. I'm happy to say that Roberta is still alive and well and as vibrant as ever. She's still working (now as a by-law enforcement officer) and looking forward to a well-deserved retirement in a few short years.

Roadkill

"Gimme another brew," Marty Slipchuck said, rolling down the window of the Cuda and lighting an unfiltered Export A.

Cal Jonas turned around in the passenger seat, got onto his knees and opened the cooler in the back seat. "Bud or Sleeman?" he said.

"They both cold?"

"Zomboid."

"Gimme a Sleeman, then."

"You got it."

Cal pulled a clear bottle from the ice for Marty and grabbed a can of Bud for himself. When he was righted in his seat he straightened his glasses on the bridge of his nose and handed the bottle of Sleeman to Marty.

"Thanks," Marty said. He opened the bottle with his teeth, spit the cap out the open window and laughed. "Who'da thought I'd ever be sucking back the good stuff regular."

Cal popped his Bud and snickered. "Yeah, you got real class now, Marty. Real class."

Marty put the bottle to his lips, upended it and emptied half its contents before stopping to breathe.

Before everything got all fucked up, Marty had worked at dozens of jobs, none of them for very long. The virus had been little more than a bump in the road of his life. While the rest of the world had gone apeshit over zombies, Marty had merely shifted gears—into overdrive.

"There's one!" Cal said, beer spluttering out of his mouth along with the words.

About half a mile away, the hunched figure of a zombie wandered out from the row of trees lining the edge of the highway. Although it stumbled aimlessly along the road, the zombie was making definite progress in their direction, no doubt attracted by their scent. Neither of them had bathed in over a week.

Marty took a final pull on the Sleeman and tossed the bottle into the back seat. He took a last drag on his cigarette, flicked the butt out the window and reached for the ignition.

Cal snickered, threw his still full can of beer out the window and put on his seat belt.

Marty had found Cal in the back of a 7- Eleven with his pud in one hand and a copy of *Hustler* in the other. He'd taken Cal with him, not only to have someone to kick around, but to have someone to talk to as well. Cal wasn't much, but he was still better than the dead stations of the Cuda's radio.

"What you gonna do this time, Marty?" Cal said. "You gonna roadkill it? Are you?"

"Not tellin'," Marty said evenly. He turned to Cal and smiled, baring all four of his teeth. "You'll just hafta wait and see."

He turned the ignition and the Cuda's headered 340 thrummed to life like some animal rudely awakened from a deep sleep. He revved the engine a few times, shifted into first and let go the clutch.

The car's rear wheels screeched against the pavement as the slicks tried to grab hold. The smell of burning rubber grew thick, then suddenly they were off, hurtling down the interstate on what felt like a rocket sled.

Marty's lips drew back into a thin white line, his fingers curled tightly around the wheel and his eyes turned ghostly white as they stared blankly out at the highway.

Cal looked over, saw the roadkilling look of the reaper in Marty's face and began bouncing in his seat. "You're gonna get it, you dead motherfucker!" he screamed.

The needle of the Cuda's speedometer began its arch across the dash.

. . . twenty . . . twenty-five . . .

Roadkilling zombies had become the one of the nation's favorite pastimes.

. . . thirty . . . thirty-five . . .

Marty and Cal had done over fifty of them in the last month alone, but they never grew tired of it.

. . . forty . . . forty-five . . .

There was a rush connected with the crunch of bone and the splat of dead meat that drugs alone just couldn't match.

. . . fifty . . . fifty-five . . .

And there was no shortage of zombies. The government—or what was left of it—had estimated there were still half a million of them roaming the streets of the city.

. . . fifty-eight . . . sixty . . .

Marty eased off the gas. Any faster and they'd totally destroy the zombie on impact, not to mention wreck the Cuda. Besides, anybody could run the fuckers over, the real fun of roadkilling was playing with them, seeing how dead you could make them before they stopped living.

With less than fifty yards to go, they could see the zombie in some detail. It was, or at least had been, a woman. She was wearing what looked to be the shredded remains of a dark gray business suit, but it hard to tell where the suit ended and the mottled flesh began.

"It's a bitch, Marty!" Cal cried. "A fuckin' bitch. I bet she liked to take it up the ass."

Marty's right hand whipped out and smacked Cal hard in the mouth. "Shut the fuck up while I'm trying to drive!"

Cal looked hurt for a moment, but quickly resumed his giggling once he looked ahead and saw that they were seconds from impact.

"Holy Shit!" Cal said.

The Cuda slammed into the zombie—

WHAM!

—breaking the dead thing in two.

The bottom half of its torso and legs stuck to the front of the car while the upper body and head slid over the hood, bounced off the windshield and flew twenty feet in the air before landing on the highway behind them.

Marty slammed on the brakes and brought the Cuda to a screeching halt.

"Fuckin' A, man!" Cal said, closing his eyes and shaking his head, giddy. "Broke the fuckin' bitch in two."

Marty smiled for the first time since starting up the Cuda. "Did you like that?"

"You re the fuckin best, Marty. Chopped her down like Paul Fuckin' Bunyan."

Marty's face turned grave. He looked in the rearview mirror. The top half of the zombie's body was still intact. It was also moving, clawing its way toward the Cuda with its arms.

"It's still alive," Marty said, calmly but with obvious pleasure as he shifted the car into reverse.

"What? No fuckin' way, man." Cal stopped giggling for a moment and turned around. "I don't believe it."

Marty eased the Cuda back, peering out the open window so he could line up the car's left rear tire with the zombie's head.

"You gonna do her slow?" Cal said.

"Yeah."

"Nice and slow." Cal was hyperventilating. "The same way she liked to take it up the ass. Nice and slow."

The Cuda came to a stop when the rear tire rolled up against the zombie. Marty eased out the clutch and the tire slowly began turning, climbing up onto the thing's head.

A loud crack ripped through the air as the zombie's skull collapsed under the weight of the Cuda, followed by a steady crunching sound as larger pieces of bone were ground into pulp.

Jets of zombie splat and dead brain matter spurted across the pavement onto the other lanes of the highway as if a rotten tomato had been roadappled by a semi.

"You're the best, man," Cal howled with delight.

Even Marty gave a chuckle. "I ain't finished yet."

With the rear tire sitting squarely on the gray pulp of the zombie's head, Marty revved the engine and popped the clutch.

Without a posi-track rear end, the Cuda's right rear wheel wouldn't move as long as the left rear kept spinning. And with nothing but slimy rotten meat beneath it, the left rear tire spun as easily as if it were on a patch of ice.

Marty put the gas pedal to the floor.

Bits of dead flesh and roadkill juice flew out in front of the car as Marty brought the V8 close to its red line.

Cal had his arms across his chest, twisting and turning in an uncontrollable fit of laughter. "Stop it, Marty," he shouted over the motor's roar. "I swear I'm gonna piss my pants."

Marty laughed then, too, pressing his foot down further on the gas.

"Oh, shit!" Cal managed to say as a wet stain began to appear in the crotch of his jeans.

Marty pointed to the piss stain and screamed with laughter.

Just then the spinning tire made solid contact with the highway.

The Cuda jolted backward, and stalled.

Marty and Cal stopped laughing.

The air was thick with the stench of charred flesh and burning rubber. The inside of the Cuda was deathly silent.

"What the fuck happened?" Cal said, finally.

"Just stalled." Marty said, turning the ignition.

Click! Nothing.

"Uh-oh," Cal said. "We're fucked."

"We're not fucked," Marty snapped, his voice a little unsteady. "Nothing I can't fix." He pulled on the lever beneath the dash to pop the hood.

They got out and went around to the front of the car. And stood there, staring.

Half of the zombie was stuck to the front of the car, the worn-down stumps of its legs were bent backward, trailing away beneath the front of the car.

"Well go ahead," Marty said. "Get it off."

"You want me to touch it?"

"No, I don't want you to touch it, stupid. There's a tire-iron in the trunk." He gave him the key.

Cal walked around to the back of the car and returned with the tire iron. Then, being careful not to touch the thing with his hands, he scraped the zombie's hips and thighs from the Cuda's grill and bumper. When the car was clean, he opened the hood.

Again they were left staring, unable to speak.

When the car jolted backward the rear wheels had thrown one of the zombie's arms up into the motor. It had gotten tangled up in the belts, stalling the car.

But that wasn't the funny part.

The funny part was that the thing's fingers were all curled up except for the middle one—the zombie was giving them the bird.

Cal giggled.

Marty's left hand flew out and clipped Cal in the back of the head. "What the fuck are you laughing at?"

Cal turned to Marty, a hurt look on his face. "Nothing."

"Good. Now climb under there and get that thing out. We gotta get the fuck out of here."

It was dangerous to be out in the open for any length of time. If one zombie had smelled them out on the highway you could bet there were more on the way. Best thing to do was to get the hell out and call it a day.

Cal got down on the ground, crawled under the car and got to work trying to loosen the zombie's arm with the tire iron. He smacked it a few times, but it was wedged in pretty tight. He changed his position and tried again.

While Cal worked under the car, Marty walked around back to see if there was any damage to the car's rear end. Except for a half inch thick coating of zombie slime in the wheel well and on the shocks everything looked okay.

"I'm going to need your help, Marty. It's really jammed in there," came Cal's voice from beneath the car.

It was followed by a scream.

Marty rushed around to the front of the Cuda, but stopped abruptly when he saw another zombie, this one dressed a little like a short order cook, down on all fours biting into Cal's neck.

Marty wanted to help, but knew it was already too late.

As the zombie prepared to take another bite, Cal looked up at Marty, his eyes wet, wide, and full of terror. "Help me," he cried.

Marty watched helplessly as the zombie's teeth crunched through Cal's skull and dug into his brain. Cal's face lit up in pain, then went limp, lifeless. His eyes remained open, but there was nothing behind them.

Marty managed to turn away. He clapped his hands over his ears, but he could still hear the ripping and slurping sounds as the zombie tore into Cal's flesh like a hungry dog with a steak.

In the distance Marty could see another zombie wandering out from the trees. Further down the highway in the direction of the city, two more figures appeared on the horizon. In minutes there'd be dozens of dead things surrounding him.

Marty slammed a fist down into the Cuda . . . And felt a hand grope for his neck. He shook himself free of the thing's grasp and slammed its head against the roof of the car.

There was the familiar sound of cracking bone as the zombie's head turned soft and pulpy in his hands. Marty let go of it and it fell onto the highway in a heap.

The other zombies were getting closer.

Marty started to run, back up the hill, back in the direction from which he and Cal had come.

#

Jackson James cupped his girlfriend's right tit in his hand and squeezed the nipple between his thumb and forefinger.

"I already told you I'm not in the mood," she said, pulling his hand away from her breast and putting it firmly back onto the seat behind her. "Besides, you said we were going roadkilling."

"We are, babe," Jackson said. "But these things take their time coming out on the road. I thought we'd do a little boffing while we waited."

"I don't feel like it, all right," she said.

"How 'bout a blow, then?"

She shook her head in mild disgust, then suddenly perked up in her seat. "There's one of those things now."

Jackson gazed at the zombie approaching them on the highway. It moved a little faster than most and was waving its arms around a bit—but that was good.

"This should be fun," he said, starting up the Chevy pick up. "This one looks like it's still got some life left in it."

A zombie story along the same lines of "But Somebody's Got to Do It," this story stemmed from the idea that in a zombie apocalypse, taking zombies out in outlandish ways might easily become a form of recreation, especially among the young. And so, roadkilling becomes a thing. However, no matter how much of an upper-hand one might have, situations change, and things break down. Meanwhile, the only constant is a continuous and relentless zombie onslaught that is absolutely unforgiving. I have to admit the ending is somewhat derivative of Night of the Living Dead, but it's such a perfect way to end a Just-Deserts kind of story, that I couldn't resist.

Lip-O-Suction

"Please have a seat, Mr. Calhoun," the receptionist said to the man towering over her desk. "Doctor Vadim will be with you in a moment."

Fred Calhoun nodded, compressing all four of his chins together tightly. He turned and made his way to a chair on the far side of the waiting room, his shoes squeaking as the wooden floorboards creaked and cracked beneath him. When he reached the chairs, he turned around with several tiny steps and slowly eased his tremendous bulk down onto a seat. The oversized chair accepted his weight with a slight groan, but did not give way under the strain.

He took a deep breath and let out a sigh. It wasn't easy to move five hundred pounds from Point A to Point B at the best of times; the mid-summer's heat was making it almost impossible.

"I'm sorry, our air conditioner is broken," the receptionist said, peering over the top of her desk. "I've called the repairman a couple of times, but you know how busy those guys get whenever there's a heat wave."

"Oh, I don't mind the heat," Fred lied, smiling. He took a handkerchief from his shirt pocket and dabbed it over his face and across his neck. "It opens up the pores, lets the skin breathe."

"Yeah," the receptionist said politely, then quickly busied herself with paperwork.

Fred pocketed his handkerchief and thumbed through a pile of magazines on the table beside him. He found none of the magazines particularly interesting and decided to read one of the Lip-O-Suction weight reduction center's advertising pamphlets instead. When he'd first heard them on the radio, the company's claims had seemed too good to be true. From experience, he knew that when something sounded too good to be true, it was usually just another scheme to lighten nothing more than a person's bank account.

But here, once again, were the words, promising so much that they could only have been spoken by an angel of God. Who else could deliver on such a promise?

Lose as much or as little as you want. No special diets, no need to exercise. Your desired weight achieved in three sessions or less or your money cheerfully and unconditionally refunded.

That's the Lip-O-Suction money back guarantee!

It was the promise of his money back that had persuaded Fred to give Lip-O-Suction a try. He'd spent close to $25,000 on diets, fitness clubs and home exercise machines in the last five years and had vowed not to borrow money for another program until he'd finished paying off all of his current loans. Besides, if he wound up getting ripped off, he'd sue the bastards. What jury would decide against him after watching him trundle his five-hundred pounds of flesh into a crowded courtroom? The way Fred figured it, the only thing he had to lose was weight.

"Mr. Calhoun?" the receptionist called from behind her desk. "The doctor will see you now."

Fred nodded. He began leaning forward until the bulk of his upper body weight was positioned over his knees. That done, he carefully continued moving forward until his rear-end began to lift up off the seat. A second later he was on his feet, bent at the waist in a crouch, rising smoothly to a standing position. He breathed a sigh when he was finally upright and walked across the waiting room towards the doctor's office.

"It's the second door on the left," the receptionist said, pointing down the hall with her pen.

Fred went down the hall, shoes and floorboards squeaking all the way. He paused for a moment at the door, took a breath and opened it. The first thing he noticed was the colorful banner on the far wall that read: *Diet is a four-letter word*. He smiled, then looked over the rest of the room. Apart from the sign, the white walled room had little character. There was a single set of cupboards over a sink and counter along the same wall as the door. Spread across the countertop were several plants set in glass pots, their thick networks of roots looking like worms in the rich black soil. An examination table was positioned against the wall on the other side of the room, beneath the banner. There was, Fred noted, no weigh scale anywhere. The overhead lights were on and the one small window on the outside wall was fully covered by a blind. Fred turned around, backed up to the examination table and set himself down.

Less than a minute later the doctor squeezed through the doorway and lumbered into the room.

Fred was shocked by the incredible girth of the man. The doctor, draped in a tent-sized knee-length whitecoat, had to be seven-hundred pounds if he was one. For the first time since childhood, Fred experienced the odd sensation of feeling dwarfed by another human being. He was overcome by a mixture of emotions, primarily relief in knowing that there was someone on the planet bigger than he was, and disbelief that such a big man could be placed in charge of a so-called weight reduction center.

"Mr. Calhoun, I presume," the doctor said with a chuckle, pronouncing the name cal-hoo-en.

"Yes," Fred said, arching his eyebrows and turning his head slightly to the right. "And you are Doctor Vadim?"

"Augustine Vadim," the doctor said, his voice possessing a distinctly eastern European accent that seemed to suit his raven black hair and deeply set coal black eyes. "My secretary calls me *Doctor* Vadim." A smile. "But you may call me Gus if you like." Another laugh. "So, I see you have a problem with your weight."

Fred fought off the urge to make a sarcastic comment about the doctor's powers of perception, took the handkerchief from his pocket and wiped the sweat from his face. "I don't mean to sound abrupt, doctor . . . uh, Gus. But you don't look like you should be running a weight reduction place. You're fatter than I am."

"Yah, I am probably a few hundred pounds heavier," the doctor said, rubbing his hands over his belly like a summertime Santa Claus. "But does that mean I don't know what I am doing?"

"I suppose not," Fred admitted; and it was true. He'd been to plenty of slim staff clinics that hadn't been able to help him lose a thing.

"Let me assure you, Mr. Calhoun, that you have absolutely nothing to worry about. We have a success rate of one hundred per cent and we have never had a single client ask for his or her money back. It is amazing, I know, but it is true."

Fred felt at ease with the doctor. He was, after all, heavier than Fred and knew what it was like to be a fat man in a thin society. Finally, here was someone who understood what it was like to walk down the street and hear children and adults alike making fun of you as you passed. Here was someone who knew what it was like to be unable to find clothes that fit, who knew how humiliating it was to get leers from supermarket cashiers when you bought a bag of potato chips, who knew how embarrassing it was to be unable to fit into theater seats, who knew how lonely it was to spend evenings home alone, and finally how terrifying it was to lie awake at night in the darkness forever asking, "Why me?"

"I'm willing to give it a try," Fred said.

"Excellent, Mr. Calhoun. That is all that we ask of our clients." The doctor paused to fold his massive arms across his equally massive chest. "Now, how much is it that you would like to lose."

Fred had thought about this question at length. He didn't want to sound greedy by asking for too much, but he also didn't want to ask for too little and risk not getting his money's worth. "One-hundred-and-fifty pounds."

"Come, come, Mr. Calhoun," the doctor said, shaking his head.

Fred's heart sunk deep into his huge belly.

"We can do much better than that. I would guess that you weigh four-hundred-and . . . ninety-two pounds. Correct?"

"Ninety-three."

"I'm off by one. Ah, it's late in the day," the doctor said with obvious pride. "I think we can manage between two-hundred-and-fifty to three-hundred pounds in three visits. Sounds good, yah?"

"Sounds *too* good," Fred said.

"Don't forget the guarantee, Mr. Calhoun."

"I haven't forgotten," Fred said, looking down to the floor and shaking his head. He hadn't weighed less than two-hundred pounds for years—even in his dreams.

"Good. Then we will put your weight-loss goal at three hundred pounds in three visits."

"Does that include today's visit?"

"No. Today is not a visit. I couldn't help you now even if I wanted to. Today, we just get to know each other and say hello.

We will begin the weight reduction process the next time you visit."

"How soon will that be?" Fred started getting up, slowly. "My secretary will call you when we are ready to see you again. You will only have a day or two's notice, so don't make any plans you can't break."

"No problem," Fred said, getting to his feet. "I don't do much. I'll be ready."

"Excellent," said the doctor. "I will see you next time then." He turned, squeezed through the doorway and waddled off down the hall.

Fred followed the doctor out of the room and stopped to say goodbye to the receptionist. After taking a signed check, she assured him he would be notified for an appointment within the next four weeks.

Outside the center, Fred's head was spinning. On the one hand, he wanted with all his heart to believe that what the doctor was saying was true. On the other hand, the whole thing sounded too good to be true, and that made it feel too much like a scam for comfort.

As his clothes began sticking to his sweat-soaked body, Fred decided on a compromise. He'd give the doctor a month to make a second appointment, but he'd keep his lawyer's number handy just in case.

#

As it turned out, Fred was back at the Lip-O-Suction center less than three weeks later.

Once the appointment had been made, the days between visits seemed to drag on like months. Meanwhile, all of Fred's skepticism concerning the company's incredible claims was washed away in a tidal wave of optimism and hope.

Even the unbearable mid-summer's heat—which caused huge dark sweat stains to appear randomly on his shirt and pants as he sat in the center's waiting room—didn't seem to bother him.

His mind and tremendous body were just too tightly focused on the prospect of weighing less, of being . . . thin, to be concerned about anything else.

"Mr. Calhoun," the receptionist said, "the doctor will see you now."

Fred slowly rose to his feet and made his way across the waiting room. If such a thing was possible for a five-hundred-pound man, there was a bit of a spring in his step.

"Second door on your left."

Fred smiled as he passed the woman and went on down the hall. The room was the same as it had been on his first visit, except this time the window blind was open wide to the clear night sky.

Fred had just eased himself down on the examination table when the doctor came through the door.

Once again, the doctor's appearance was a shock to Fred's system. On his first visit, the doctor had been a huge man of upwards of seven hundred pounds, but now he was a sleek, athletic looking man of no more than two-hundred.

"Ah, Mr. Calhoun, how are you today? Ready to begin our program, I hope."

Fred looked at the doctor in silence. The doctor's face was much thinner than it had been on the previous visit, but there could be no doubt that it was the same man—the haunting darkness of his deeply set eyes was unmistakable. But how? A loss of five-hundred pounds in less than a month wasn't just impossible, it was downright unnatural.

"I told you, Mr. Calhoun that just because I was fat didn't mean I knew nothing about losing weight," the doctor said, spinning around to show off his lithe figure.

"It's incredible," Fred said, spellbound by the doctor's miraculous weight loss. "But—"

"Never mind, Mr. Calhoun," the doctor said, busily preparing a tray of utensils. "Please get out of your clothes and lie down on your stomach."

Fred followed the doctor's orders and slowly began to disrobe, keeping a close eye on the doctor's preparations all the while. In the center of the stainless-steel tray were several medical instruments including a scalpel, needles and sutures of various sizes, a bottle of rubbing alcohol and several cotton balls.

"I've been meaning to ask you, doctor," Fred said as he lifted his belly onto the examination table, "How will you be doing the actual liposuction? I don't see any equipment in this room."

"Don't you worry, Mr. Calhoun," the doctor said, dismissing Fred's question with a wave of his hand and moving across the room until he was standing directly in front of him.

Fred, lying stomach down on the examination table, glanced up at the doctor. He was about to protest, demand a proper answer, when his attention was caught by the doctor's face. The expression on it was hypnotic. *And his eyes* . . . Fred suddenly felt himself drifting away into something like a dream. . . . *his eyes* . . . His body was being overcome by a sense of calm, of trust. . . . *were black and bottomless and mesmerizing* . . .

Fred felt the ice-coldness of rubbing alcohol on the skin of his left buttock. A second later he felt the penetration of a needle, followed by the slight spreading of numbness to the entire cheek.

And then he felt a strange sensation in his buttock, as if something was tugging at him from inside. It wasn't an altogether unpleasant sensation, especially since Fred knew that what he was feeling were fat cells being sucked from his body.

He was on the road to thinness. He closed his eyes and felt himself dozing off in a dream-filled and contented sleep.

Sometime later, he awoke to the gentle rocking of the doctor's hand on his shoulder. "Wake up, Mr. Calhoun," the doctor whispered into his ear. "Time for you to go home."

"All done?" Fred asked, slowly rising to a sitting position on the examination table. He blinked the drowsiness from his eyes and looked the doctor over curiously. The man looked heavier, as if his body had filled out slightly in the last little while. His face too was rounded on the edges, pudgier.

"Yah," the doctor said, passing a beefy hand over his mouth as if to clear away something sticking to his lips. "I should be ready to see you again in about . . . thirty days."

"I'm looking forward to it already."

"Yah," the doctor said as he was leaving the room. "I'm sure you are."

For a moment in the empty room, Fred tried to recall what had happened to him, but found he couldn't—the last few hours were nothing more than a hazy and dreamlike blur in his mind. He thought the doctor had looked fatter than he remembered, but he couldn't be sure. All he could be sure of was that his body was covered with numerous pairs of pin prick scars and that he felt lighter . . . *thinner*.

A few seconds later, his clothes confirmed it. His pants were several sizes too big and there was room for four of his fingers between his buttoned shirt collar and the flaccid skin of his neck.

He couldn't wait to get home.

#

"Three. Hundred. And. Fifty. Two. Pounds," said Fred's electronic bathroom scale. He'd gotten the scale years ago through some diet center's special offer and had always despised the hollow and impersonal monotone of the thing's voice. But today, the words were as soft and as soothing as music to his ears.

He stepped off the scale and thought about it. One-hundred-and-forty-one pounds. Gone. Just like that. At this rate the goal of three-hundred pounds in three visits would easily be met. He'd be thin and normal by the end of the year.

He went from the bathroom to the bedroom where he looked through his closet and drawers for some old clothes that might fit him better. As he went through the racks of pants hanging in the closet, he again tried to recall just what had happened in the doctor's office. He even stopped his search for clothes as he thought about it, but his mind was almost a blank on the subject. His recollections were vague at best and rapidly fading. An hour later, all he could remember was that he'd had one Lip-O-Suction session and was eagerly looking forward to a second.

He also found he was famished. He ordered a pizza. There was no special diet to follow on the Lip-O-Suction program and Fred found himself in the almost euphoric position of being able to indulge himself without feeling even the slightest pangs of guilt. That, he decided, was the best part of the program.

He was called in for his second session four-and-a-half weeks later. The session went much like the first, although Fred hadn't found it to be quite so relaxing. Although he remained semi-conscious throughout the session, he found he could remember almost nothing about it when it was over. The only way he knew he'd actually had a session was that his bathroom scale told him so.

"Two. Hundred. And. Fifty. Seven. Pounds," the scale said after the second session. He was still overweight, but after losing almost half of his body weight in two months Fred couldn't think of himself as being anything but thin.

Fred celebrated his new thinness by taking out what little money he had left in his bank account and heading for the mall. After a stop for dinner at the Mandarin's all-you-can-eat Chinese Food buffet, he walked through the mall, trying on all sorts of different brightly colored shorts, tank-tops and t-shirts, and snacking on a variety of treats from ice cream cones to cinnamon buns and coffee.

While he tried on all kinds of clothes, he decided to buy just two outfits. Although he had one more session to go and it looked as if Doctor Vadim would be keeping good on his promise of three-hundred pounds in three visits, somewhere in the back of his mind Fred knew it wouldn't last. He was eating like a team of horses and there was no way he could continue to eat so much and keep his weight down under three-hundred pounds. He knew it, but he couldn't stop himself from doing it—he just had to eat, as if his body needed calories and was by-passing his brain to get them. He didn't even like some of the foods he was eating; they were just bits of fat and protein that slid down his throat and were lost in the bottomless pit of his stomach.

But as the weeks passed, the bathroom scale never wavered from "Two. Hundred. And. Thirty. Five. Pounds."

He wondered how it could be that he still weighed the same considering he was eating the equivalent of five to six dinners per day and his bowel movements had remained twice-a-day normal. He thought about it, but after years of obesity, Fred knew a good thing when he saw it and accepted it for what it was—his dream come true. Somehow, his body was allowing him to eat as much as he wanted but never, ever making him pay for it in flab.

And once he'd convinced himself that he wouldn't be gaining back the weight he'd lost, his life began to change. He gave his fat wardrobe to charity and replaced it with a sharp and stylish new thin one. He changed jobs too, taking full advantage of the newfound acceptance society was giving him as a slim, middle-aged man. He quit his job as an injection molding machine maintenance mechanic and took another job as a quality control inspector at a rival plastics factory. The extra money that came with the new position came in handy in paying off outstanding bills and in keeping food in good supply at home.

He was eating more and more, spending close to half his weekly pay on food, but still weighing in at under two-hundred-and-fifty-seven pounds. But while his body never got any bigger, his name did. He went from calling himself Fred Calhoun to Alfred H. Calhoun. The name, he hoped, sounded impressive without being pretentious.

One person who was impressed by the name and overall demeanor of Alfred H. Calhoun was Wendy Weismayer, a full-figured, thirtyish, red-headed secretary in the factory's office. Alfred spoke to her occasionally, steadily growing more comfortable around her until he gathered up enough courage to ask her out on a date.

"Sure, why not?" she'd said.

Alfred spent the next few nights cleaning his apartment and allowing his food stocks to deplete down to a minimum. He fully expected, or at least hoped, that the two of them would end up coming back to his apartment and didn't want his floor-to-ceiling stockpiles to arouse unwanted suspicion.

They went out on a Saturday night, ate dinner at the Swiss Chalet and saw a romantic comedy starring Ted Danson. Although he'd eaten at home before picking up Wendy, Alfred found himself wanting more food at the restaurant than he'd ordered. But in the interest of keeping up appearances, he'd eaten his half-chicken dinner and gone on to the movies hungry. Once at the theater, however, he made numerous excuses to get up from his seat so he could sneak candy bars and licorice whips at the snack bar.

When the movie ended, Alfred suggested they go back to his place for drinks. To his surprise, Wendy quickly accepted the invitation.

One drink turned into several and before Alfred knew it, he and Wendy were naked on the bed. The prospect of sex—

although anxiously anticipated in his dreams prior to the date—had Alfred both terrified and awed. And when it was over, Alfred was disappointed to find it hadn't been as good as he'd imagined; but at least now he wasn't a virgin.

And as Wendy slept, seemingly contented, Alfred sat on the edge of the bed thinking about what had become of his life after his dramatic weight loss on the Lip-O-Suction program. He was thin, his self confidence level had been dramatically increased, his sex life was—well, he had one now—people didn't laugh at him behind his back anymore, he had a better job and his finances were in order. Compared to his old life, his new thin life was an unqualified success. By rights he should have been a very happy man, but the truth was, he was miserable.

The insatiable hunger had the most to do with it. Trying to keep his body's hunger satisfied was exacting too great a toll on him. Although he still weighed two-fifty-seven, he felt incredibly weak, almost hollow inside. He was eating massive amounts of food, but his body didn't seem to be benefiting from the intake, or for that matter, didn't even seem to be acknowledging the fact that he was eating anything at all.

He sat on the bed a moment, scratching his rumbling, grumbling stomach.

And then suddenly the thought flashed across his mind like a lightning bolt: *tapeworm!* He began to sweat, to tremble in the fear of imagining a parasite slithering through his intestines and sucking the life out of him from within. He got up from the bed and went to the living room where he gulped thirstily from a bottle of whisky to try and calm his nerves. With his fear deadened slightly by the alcohol, he vowed to visit his doctor first thing in the morning.

Then he went to the kitchen to fix himself a little snack.

#

"As far as the tests go, you're a perfectly healthy man, Fred," Doctor Sheldon Katz said, giving his long time patient a buddy-buddy slap on the shoulder.

"No tapeworm?"

"No tapeworm."

"But how could I eat so much and not gain any weight."

The doctor sat behind his desk, shrugged his shoulders and smiled. "I don't know," he said. "All I know is that I can't find anything wrong with you."

"Aha," Alfred said, the index finger of his right hand pointed to the ceiling. "That doesn't necessarily mean there is nothing wrong with me."

The doctor stared at his patient a moment before slowly removing his glasses and rubbing the bridge of his nose between his fingers. "I don't understand you. You weighed five hundred pounds most of your adult life and used to spend most of your time complaining to me about how fat you were. Now, you've lost the weight and are perfectly healthy, but you feel guilty because you're eating a lot and not gaining any weight. Think for a moment, Fred. Do you sound like a rational man?"

Alfred slumped back in his chair.

"You've been given a second life," the doctor said, replacing his glasses. "You should be running with it, enjoying yourself."

"I suppose you're right," Alfred said.

"Would you like me to recommend you to a good psychiatrist?" The doctor's voice was once again full of concern. "Your problem just might be a reaction to your sudden weight loss."

The thought of seeing a shrink made Alfred jump from his chair and look toward the door. "Thanks, but no thanks. I guess it's just a phase I'm going through. I'll probably be over it in a week or two."

He was out of the office before he'd even finished talking. Outside, Alfred felt weaker and more afraid than ever before. Maybe what was wrong wasn't a physical thing that could be detected by medical tests; but that didn't mean there wasn't anything wrong with him. What if the thing being eaten away was his soul? What then?

Whatever it was, Alfred was sure it was something very real, something slowly killing him from within.

He considered the few options open to him at length. He could go on living as he had been, eating massive amounts of food for the rest of his life and perhaps getting a job in the food services industry to cut expenses. Or he could go to another doctor for a second opinion. But he didn't put much faith in that idea; Doctor Katz had been Alfred's doctor all his life and if he said there was nothing physically wrong with him, Alfred was inclined to believe him. Finally, he decided the only real alternative he had was to make another visit to the Lip-O-Suction center for a talk with Doctor Vadim. If anyone knew what was happening, he would.

It was late in the evening, but Alfred went straight to the Lip-O-Suction center from Doctor Katz's office. There was no one in the waiting room when he arrived. Although his third session wasn't until later in the week, the secretary told him he'd be able to see the doctor after a short wait.

"I see you haven't gained your weight back," the doctor said when he met Alfred in the examination room.

This time the doctor was fat—Alfred guessed close to three-hundred-and-fifty pounds—and extremely cheerful. The sight of the overweight doctor calmed Alfred somewhat, but he was still determined to get some answers.

"Most of our clients find they have to make repeat visits every eight to ten months to keep their weight down. You should consider yourself lucky."

"I don't consider myself lucky at all, doctor," Alfred said. "It's more like I've been cursed."

"Oh?" the doctor said, his eyebrows arching inquisitively.

Alfred looked into the doctor's eyes . . . and suddenly felt his resolve fading into the back of his mind. The doctor took Alfred's hand and led him over to the examination table.

Alfred undressed methodically, as if in a daze, and crawled up onto the table. Seconds later he felt himself falling into a light and pleasant sleep.

He awoke a short time later, his eyes opening to the view of the beautiful star filled night sky through the window before him.

But there was a disturbing sound, a slurping kind of a sound that people sometimes make when they eat Popsicles or watermelons on hot summer days. Alfred looked at the window for several long moments, waiting for the focus of his eyes to move from the view of the night sky to the dim, thin reflection of the inside of the room in the bottom left-hand corner of the windowpane.

And then he saw . . . the doctor's face firmly planted on his right buttock, lips pressed hard against the skin and ringed by a milky white seal of effluvium.

At first Alfred denied that what he was seeing was actually happening. He blinked a few times in the hopes that the disturbing image in the window would right itself in his mind and turn out to be nothing more than an optical illusion. But the image in the glass did not change.

Still disbelieving, he arched his back and twisted his head around until he was able to see over his shoulder. What was happening was unmistakable now, and becoming more disgusting with each passing second. Alfred suddenly jumped off the table and scrambled across the room with a speed and agility he never knew he had.

With his back to the wall, Alfred picked up a nearby stool and held it over his head with both hands, fully prepared to bring it crashing down on the doctor's head at any moment.

"What kind of freak are you?" Alfred cried, tightening his grip on the stool. "Just stay where you are! I don't want to have to hurt you."

The doctor stood in the middle of the room, looking just as startled as Alfred. His lips and cheeks glistened with oil. Globules of fat oozed out from the corners of his mouth and streaked down his neck in greasy white rivulets. "Wha—" The doctor tried to speak, but that only succeeded in causing a spurt of fatty liquid to dribble down his chin onto the floor. He swallowed. "What happened, Mr. Calhoun? Why aren't you asleep."

Alfred remained frozen in place, his back firmly pressed against the wall. He looked the doctor over curiously. His body was even heavier now, bloated almost to the bursting point.

"You must allow me to apologize," the doctor said, wiping a sleeve across his mouth. "This has never happened before. Never."

"What's never happened before? What were you doing to me?"

The doctor's surprise seemed to have abated as he pulled a second stool into the center of the room and sat down on it so that he was sitting directly opposite Alfred. He took a deep breath and began. "Mr. Calhoun, you are no doubt familiar with vampires and the legend of Count Dracula?"

"From what I've seen in the movies."

"Hmm. Then, perhaps I should explain. Count Dracula was one kind of vampire, one who required fresh blood to survive. A vampire in a broader sense, however, is a parasitic creature who must feed off another living thing to survive." The doctor paused a moment, perhaps hoping he wouldn't have to go on.

"Are you saying that you're a vampire?"

"Yes, I am. But I'm also saying you are one too."

The room was filled with a long, awkward silence. What the doctor had said didn't make sense to Alfred.

"I am a lipophilic vampire, Mr. Calhoun. It means I prefer human fat over blood. I can eat regular food, but my body can't extract nearly enough fats from even the fattest foods to keep me healthy. Only human body fat is rich enough, I'm afraid."

Alfred listened silently, his mind and body reeling in shock and unable to move.

"It is a rare disease among vampires and, despite what has happened to you, was for centuries believed to be non-communicable. That is why I felt secure in opening this business. I feed easily and well, and I help people, make them happy. It is a good life."

Alfred saw a spurt of fat . . . his fat . . . oozing from the corner of the doctor's mouth and thought about being consigned to the same fate for the rest of his life. "You bastard," Alfred cried, raising the stool higher over his head.

He tensed his muscles, readying himself to bring the stool crashing down upon the doctor.

"Let me assure you, Mr. Calhoun. There is nothing in this room, or even in this building, that you could use to hurt me."

The doctor's words were said with such assurance that Alfred knew he was powerless to do anything. He also realized that it was true—he was one of them.

His grip on the stool loosened until it fell to the floor behind him. His body trembled and he slowly fell forward onto his knees, sobbing.

The doctor moved across the room and crouched down on the floor next to him. Alfred felt the doctor's comforting hand come to rest on his head, and heard a few softly-spoken words.

"Don't worry, Mr. Calhoun. Everything will be all right." And for some strange reason, he believed him.

#

The big black woman came into the office with slow, plodding steps. She eased herself into a chair and smiled.

"Good afternoon, Mrs. Langlois," Doctor Vadim said. "And how are you today?"

"Fine," she answered, the skin of her cheeks and neck rippling outward in a wave as she spoke.

"Good," the doctor said, smiling. "Allow me to introduce you to my partner, Alfred H. Calhoun."

Alfred reached out and shook the woman's hand. He'd never imagined such hunger was possible before, but as he closed his hand around the woman's beefy fingers and allowed his eyes to stare hypnotically into hers, he consoled himself with the knowledge that he would soon be allowed to feed.

This story is a favorite of mine. Throughout my writing career I have rejected the notion of the vampire being a noble and revered character. By definition they are parasites, gaining sustenance from a living host. That would put them at the bottom of the food chain, not the top. I explored this notion in my novel *Blood Road* about a vampire truck driver having to live off the blood of hitchhikers, and being constantly on the move just to remain alive. I remember trying to promote that novel with the tagline, "Not all vampires are tall, dark and handsome. Some are old, fat and ugly." Well, not too many people wanted to pick up that book, even though I think it's one of my best novels. But I digress... this story came about when I realized that fat and blood have many of the same properties. And since that were true, what if there were such things as fat-sucking vampires? And if there were such creatures, how would they go about indulging in their special thirst while living amongst humans?

Afterlife

"**D**addy," Lisa cried. "Daddy, please slow down. You re scaring me!"

Daddy took a gulp of Comfort. "Shut up!" he shouted.

He stomped his foot down on the accelerator. The Ford raced forward. The needle on the speedometer arced past sixty, sixty-five, seventy . . .

He leaned to his right, looked his daughter in the eye. "You just keep quiet til we get where we re going. If you re a good girl, daddy's got *something special* for you."

She wiped away a tear and nodded.

The car skidded slightly on the rain slicked road. He jerked upright, put the Comfort between his legs and grabbed the wheel with both hands.

Lisa wanted to cry out again, but dared not. Daddy had the look in his eye and she already knew what the *something special* was. If she said anything more he might stop the car and give it to her now. If she kept quiet he might get drunk and forget all about it.

She curled herself up into a tight little ball, leaned against the door and pretended to fall asleep. With her eyes closed she listened to the rain on the roof, the tires on the road, the faint song on the radio, the slosh of Comfort in the bottle and her own frightened breath . . . She tried not to cry.

He shook his head. "God damn bitch woman," he screamed.

He pulled the bottle from between his legs, capped it with his lips and upended it. The Comfort splashed down the bottle's neck and into his throat.

Fifteen minutes ago Lisa had been lying in bed, listening to mommy and daddy having another fight. A bad one.

Mommy had told daddy to get out of the house. She said she wasn't going to let him do it anymore, not to her and not to her baby. She said she was going to move away and tell the police so he could never come near them again. That's when daddy hit mommy. Mommy had been strong. She'd hardly cried at all.

Then Lisa was in the car with daddy, driving too fast, too fast.

She peeked open an eye. Shadows moved across daddy's face, making him not look like daddy anymore.

The bottle of Comfort was empty. He pulled it from his lips and tossed it onto the floor.

Another curve. The Ford skidded left.

The inside of the car was suddenly bright with light. The sound of a gas horn blared.

His feet moved for the brake, but found nothing but Comfort.

Lisa closed her eyes.

And died.

#

The front door squeaked shut, followed by the heavy clomp of boots in the hall.

Lisa closed her eyes tight and pulled the covers over her head. The boots came to a stop at her bedroom door.

One, two, three . . . she counted inside her head. . . . *six, seven, eight* . . . The floorboards groaned uncertainly. . . *nine. Ten.*

The boots moved on, fading in the direction of mommy's room.

A door squeaked open down the hall, the door to mommy's room. "About time you came home," mommy said. Her voice was hoarse. She'd been crying. "Run out of money?"

"Shut up," daddy said.

"No," mommy said. "I won't. I can't take any more of this."

Mommy's bed creaked.

"Get out!" she said.

"You don't tell me to get out," daddy screamed. "This is my fuckin' house."

Mommy's bed creaked louder. There was the sound of a slap. Then mommy cried.

Lisa put the pillow over her head, but she could still hear slapping sounds. She hummed a little song, but she could still hear mommy crying.

This won't happen when I'm older, Lisa thought. Mommy said we'll run away when I'm older. Things will be better, then. Mommy said.

"You're hurting me," mommy cried. "Please don't . . . hurt me . . . "

Lisa wanted to cry, too, but tears would not come. All she felt was anger. Daddy was supposed to love mommy. He said he did, but he didn't. Mommy said she loved daddy, too, but Lisa knew she didn't. Daddy made her cry too much.

Lisa hated daddy.

She got up from her bed and ran down the hall past mommy's bedroom.

In the kitchen she pulled a knife from the butcher's block. She reached it easily, not needing a chair to reach the counter. It was almost as if she were bigger . . . *older.*

The knife felt good in her hand, not too big like it did whenever she cut tomatoes for salad.

She could still hear mommy crying. Softly now.

She went back down the hall to mommy's room and pushed the door open.

The room was dark, but Lisa could see daddy lying on top of mommy. There were tears all over mommy's face. Bruises, too.

"Go back to your room, honey," mommy said.

Daddy turned his head. "Don't you ever knock?" he said. He got up off mommy. He had no clothes on. "Get the hell back to your room before I make you," he said.

"No," Lisa said. "I won t."

"Are you defying me, you little cocksucker?"

Lisa hated that word. Daddy always called her that when he was mad. Lisa had asked the boys at school what it meant. When they told her, she hated the word. Hated daddy.

She raised her arm. The knife blade flashed in the darkness.

She brought it down in one swift motion.

The tip of the knife disappeared inside daddy's belly. It came back dripping red.

"What the fuck," daddy said, holding his hands over the leaking red hole in his stomach.

Lisa waved her arm again. This time the knife went into daddy's leg. She pushed the knife deeper, twisting it so it scraped and crunched against his bones.

"Lisa, honey," daddy said, his face looking warm and friendly, the way a daddy's faces are supposed to look. "You're hurting daddy, now. Why don't you stop and give daddy the knife?"

"No, I won't," she said.

Daddy swung his fists, but he couldn't touch her.

She pulled the knife from his leg and stabbed it into the other.

Daddy screamed. Blood was beginning to leak out of the holes in his body like tears. He fell to his knees.

Lisa continued stabbing the knife into daddy. Into his heart, into his arms, into his neck, into his mouth, into his eyes.

Daddy hurt. He screamed now, screamed loud, begging her to stop.

But Lisa wouldn't listen. And she wouldn't stop. It felt too good to stop.

At last, daddy stopped screaming. He put his hands over his face and cried.

With daddy's hands out of the way, Lisa saw a part of him that she'd missed.

She looked at his *something special*, remembering the feel of it on her chest, on her belly, in her mouth and between her legs, down there . . . *in* there.

But instead of stabbing at it, she ran the serrated edge of the knife against it, until the blade was buried deep into the skin. Then she drew the knife back and forth several times, sawing at daddy's *something special* until it came off and landed on the floor.

"That's mommy's little girl," mommy said. Mommy hadn't moved from the bed, but she was watching, smiling.

Daddy stopped crying, then. He fell forward onto the floor.

Daddy's back was clean. Lisa raised the knife above her head and stabbed it deep into daddy. The first two times she hit bones and had to try again. The third time the knife stuck. She pushed it in as deep as she could, then left it there.

"Bye mommy," she said, as happy as a little girl could be. "I'm going out to play."

"Okay, sweetheart," mommy said. "You have fun now."

Lisa ran down the stairs and onto the porch.

The sun shone brightly. It was a beautiful day.

On the front lawn, waiting for Lisa, was her best friend April. April had died the year before, chasing a ball into the street.

"Hi April," Lisa said. "I was wondering if you'd be here."

"Of course I'm here, Lisa," April said. "What kind of heaven would it be without your friends."

"But my daddy's here. My daddy didn't go to heaven."

"No, he didn't," April said. "Your daddy's here with you, but he didn't go to heaven."

Daddy's Ford pulled into the driveway. Daddy got out. He had the look in his eye. "Lisa," he said. "Get into the house, right now."

Lisa looked at April. They both smiled. "Yes, daddy," Lisa said.

She followed him inside.

She went to heaven.

And he went to hell.

Point of view is a difficult thing for a writer to learn, or at least it was for me. I'm not sure if I was the problem or no one ever explained it to me in a way I could understand. Probably, it was a combination of the two, but once I had an understanding of it, I decided to explore the possibilities. While this story isn't some ambitious multiple POV story told from the viewpoint of everal different characters, it does posit that there can be two vastly divergent viewpoints on a single tragic event.

Family Ties

He threw the covers off and sat bolt upright on the bed. "Did you hear that?" he whispered.

"Mmmmm?" his wife mumbled. "What?

"A scream. A woman's scream."

His wife rolled onto her back and looked at him. "How can you hear anything over that train?"

He strained to listen for it again, but the train was rumbling by and the roar and clang of the cars was enough to drown out any other sound.

He lay back down on the bed and pulled the covers over top of him. Their warmth was a welcome relief from the shivers that had been brought on by the scream.

There *had* been a scream, he was sure of it. A blood curdling scream, edged with terror, sharp as a knife edge. It had come with the train. As if someone had been on the tracks, in front of . . .

But if that were the case the engineer would have tried to stop, blown its horn. Something.

"It was probably two cats fighting out on the lawn, hon. Go back to bed."

He lay awake, eyes wide and staring at the ceiling. It hadn't been a cat, that he knew for sure. He had *felt* emotion in the scream. Surprise, fear, despair, anguish, horror. They had all been there. This had been a human scream.

With his wife's breath falling into a regular rhythm next to him, he got out of bed and went to the kitchen. He looked out the window at the railroad crossing not a hundred yards from the house. The tracks looked quiet and cold, rails slicing into the darkness like twin steel blades.

Maybe I was imagining things, he thought. He glanced at the clock above the stove. Who'd be out walking the tracks at this time of night, anyway? He cracked open the refrigerator and took a few gulps of orange juice straight from the jug.

He returned to bed and spent what was left of the night trying to get back to sleep.

#

Gardner Shaw worked as a features reporter at *The Brampton Times*, a daily newspaper serving the half million people who lived in the bedroom community northwest of Toronto.

He'd taken the job less than a month ago, coming from *The Cambridge Reporter* where he'd been working the police and court beats for the last three years. He'd moved into the old house at fifty-two Mill Street North, ready to settle in for the next little while. He'd started out ten years ago working at a tiny weekly in Kapuskasing and had moved closer to Toronto—closer to the big time—every couple of years. Now he was so close he could taste it. But he knew he'd have to spend at least five more years working just outside Toronto before he could expect the chance at a job at the *Star* or *Globe*.

It was a good time to start a family.

He'd been reluctant at first, but the joy on his wife Susan's face every time she mentioned having a child was too persuasive. It always won out over all the logical reasons like cost, time, responsibility . . .

So here he was a month at a new job and a child due in four.

He'd spent the last two weeks finishing up the baby's room, papering it in a neutral design of pink ponies and powder blue clowns. It was a cozy little room that would hopefully provide his child with a sense of love and warmth.

It was already full of toys and stuffed animals.

He hated to admit it, but he was looking forward to the baby's arrival. Almost to the point of being impatient. Like most men, he was hoping for a son, but knew he would love a daughter just as much. More than anything, he was looking forward to being a father. A dad.

He sat at the kitchen table, sipping his coffee while he read the morning edition of *The Brampton Times*. He was pleased to find the night editor had liked his piece on Pinkles The Clown—a city employee who spent every Saturday visiting the children's ward at Peel Memorial Hospital—enough to place the story above the fold on page one.

Just then a freight train passed, its four diesel engines roaring so loudly that it sounded for a moment as if it were chugging down the street in front of his house.

The engines passed and the noise died down slightly as the rest of the train rattled by, every fourth of fifth car sounding as if it might fall apart rounding the next curve.

"Doesn't that bother you?" people would ask when they came to visit.

He had one pat answer. "It passes so often, you don't even notice." It was a little cliche, but it was true. He hated the thought that such a noisy intrusion into his life could numb his mind so much as to fade into the background, but it had happened. Anyway, the proximity of the track made the house cheap enough for them to afford. That was a big consolation, as was the thought that his stay in the sleepy bedroom community was a temporary one. The next time he bought a house, when he moved into Toronto, he'd be patient enough to wait for just the right one. A reward to himself and his family for the long, hard work he had done to climb the journalistic ladder.

He closed the paper and folded it into quarters. As he drained the last of his coffee, another train passed by.

This time he strained to hear the scream. To his surprise it was there, muffled, faint.

He rushed over to the window to see the last car slide out of view. Nothing.

How long would he hear this . . . phantom scream?

He let the blinds roll back and readied himself for work. He was interviewing a falconer this morning about how his birds kept Pearson International Airport clear of pigeons and gulls. It would be an odd, quirky kind of story, and he was looking forward to flexing his creative muscles on it.

He stopped at the bedroom door to say goodbye to his wife. She was still sleeping and he decided not to wake her. He closed the door gently, then tiptoed down the hall to the front door.

As he stepped outside, his attention was again drawn to the tracks. He looked down that way often. To see what? He didn't know.

He knew the newspaper reporter part of him looked that way to see if the police were out searching the tracks, looking for body parts. That would be the obvious aftermath of the scream.

But another part of him wanted something to have happened on the line because it would mean he *had* heard something. Or perhaps that someone else had heard something and he wasn't going out of his mind.

But the line was clear.

Two kids on bikes crossed the tracks, their fenders rattling as they bumped over the rails.

Forget about it, he told himself.

Life goes on.

#

The interview with the falconer had gone better than expected. The man's talk had been animated and he had countless fascinating anecdotes to relate; each one was usable, so the article had practically written itself.

Gardner found himself in the newsroom at three in the afternoon with time on his hands. Normally he would have gone home early, but the company was currently undergoing contract talks with the union and wanted everyone to put in seven-and-a-half hour days, with accumulated overtime given as days off with pay. That suited him just fine. He'd been accumulating overtime for weeks and planned to take the time off when the baby came. Quality time with the family—part of being a dad.

Then, as he rifled through one of his desk drawers in a feeble attempt to look busy, he was struck by a thought. Maybe there was something to the railway line . . . and the screams. Maybe there was a story behind it, some spooky kind of mystery. Hell, October was less than two weeks away, maybe he could write something up about it for Halloween.

He got up from his desk and headed downstairs.

He'd worked at five different dailies and had yet to find a newspaper morgue that wasn't something out of a Stephen

King novel. Dark, dirty and smelling of furnace oil, newspaper morgues were places where old newspapers were kept for reference. Dead stories of long dead people. But did that mean the place had to *look* like a crypt too?

He descended the last few steps and switched on the light, fully expecting to see a rat's tail curl around the corner of the desk at the far end of the room.

To his surprise, the place wasn't as bad as he'd expected. He'd heard that the paper had hired a summer student to put the morgue in order, and judging by the looks of it, she'd done a pretty good job. Old newspapers were stacked on floor-to-ceiling shelves on the left side of the room, while a row of filing cabinets lined the wall on the right.

He checked the index cards under "T" for train stories and "M" for Mill Street North. He found nothing under the latter and only a few features on new trains and retiring engineers under the former. He decided to check "R" for railroad and found what he was looking for. There were six index cards listing railroad-related stories, one of which listed stories concerning accidental deaths, suicides and murders connected with the rail line that ran like an artery through the heart of the city.

A quick scan of the card and he'd found it, a brief reference to a story about a murder committed on the line.

At the Mill Street North crossing.

He jotted down the date of the story on a scrap of paper and noticed for the first time that his hand was shaking. He slapped his right hand over top of it and found his palms were sweating as well.

He took a deep breath and went over to the wall of newspapers. All of this should have been on microfiche, but *The Brampton Times* was a little behind on some of the most basic technological advances. The managing editor had told him that microfilming the morgue was in next year's budget, but a couple of newsroom veterans had told him not to hold his breath.

After a brief search he found the edition he needed.

The headline immediately caught his eye.

PREGNANT WOMAN PUSHED ONTO TRACKS

He remained still, reading the article where he stood.

A nineteen-year-old Brampton woman was killed early Sunday morning when she was pushed in front of an oncoming train.

Iris Higson was killed instantly when she was hit by a westbound freight train at the Mill Street North level crossing just behind the Brampton GO Station.

Higson had been returning home from a party, walking along the tracks with her boyfriend, twenty-year-old old Bill Purcell.

According to police, the two were having a heated argument after Higson had told Purcell she was pregnant with his child. Angered by the news, Purcell, who admitted to having had alcohol and illegal substances earlier in the evening, pushed Higson onto the tracks.

Higson's death scream awakened people over a block-and-a-half away.

Purcell turned himself in to police late Sunday morning and confessed to the crime.

Charged with second-degree murder is William Allen Purcell of Bramalea.

Gardner was incensed by the killing. His body was flushed with heat and the edge of the newspaper had crumpled into his angry right fist. Swirling somewhere in the midst of his rage was a heartfelt sadness for the woman and the innocent, unborn child.

He and Susan had been trying to have a child for years and had even booked an appointment with a fertility specialist to find out what the problem was. But then, she'd come home one day with the good news, and a new stage in their life had begun. One of responsibility, commitment and sacrifice.

Having a child was something they'd had to work for. And here was this punk, probably too drunk or stoned out of his mind to even remember what he'd done.

It just wasn't fair.

But Gardner had been working in newspapers long enough to know that these kinds of things happened all the time. He couldn't let it get to him too much. If he did, he'd be out of the business in a year.

He took the newspaper upstairs to the circulation department and photocopied the article. Susan would want to know about this story. She was a bit of a horror fan and would be interested in hearing about a local ghost story.

Ghost story?

Was that the scream he was hearing?

He shook his head. "Couldn't be," he said aloud, as if saying it out loud rather than merely thinking it would confirm the notion's impossibility.

"Couldn't be," he said again. "Couldn't be."

#

He came to an abrupt stop at a light on Main Street, the stuffed Pooh Bear on the seat next to him rolling forward onto the floor. There were plenty of stuffed animals in the crib in the baby's room, but the Pooh Bears were on sale with a fill-up at the Petro-Canada station and he just couldn't resist.

Buying the thing had made him feel good, like a daddy.

When the light turned green he turned left onto Church and drove along the edge of the expansive GO Station parking lot. Each morning it filled to capacity with cars left behind by commuters taking the GO Train into Toronto. By darkfall each night it was empty and barren. A good place to play road hockey with his son . . . or teach his daughter how to ride a bike.

He was just about to pass the entrance to the lot when he decided to turn in. He had tried to block all thoughts of Iris Higson from his mind, but he hadn't been able to. It was a sad story. A tragedy. Two young lives eliminated in the blink of an eye while another basically useless one was allowed to grow old and gray.

It wasn't fair.

But then life, and death, never were.

He drove to the westernmost corner of the lot and parked the car. According to the story in the newspaper, the murder had occurred just on the other side of the fence.

He got out of the car and walked around the edge of the fence and onto the tracks. He looked south and saw that the light was on in the living room of his house. Susan must be home, he thought. I should hurry this up.

Hurry what up? He wasn't even sure why he'd stopped.

Probably his newspaperman's sense of curiosity. He'd often found himself visiting crime scenes, trying to absorb some of their atmosphere, smell some of their smells. It was a little thing, but it was a little thing that had helped him win two Western Ontario Newspaper Awards for his feature writing.

But there was something different about this . . .

Something . . .

Was grabbing at his feet.

He looked down and saw nothing there. Just the pale brown suede of his desert boots against the oily wooden ties and dirty black cinders between the rails.

Still there was something there. He could feel it, clawing at him, pulling down on his feet and legs to keep him from moving, from running away.

He tried lifting his feet, but they wouldn't budge.

In the distance, he saw a pin prick of light. He turned around to look in the other direction and saw the lights over the tracks change.

From red to green.

His efforts intensified. He grabbed at his legs, pulling on them in a vain attempt to lift them off the ground.

The train was nearing, its dot of light growing larger each second.

This is crazy, he thought. This can't be happening.

But it was.

He knelt down and untied his shoes, hoping to leave them behind as he leaped to safety. But his feet were as firmly secured to his shoes as his shoes were to the ground.

The train was even closer, the light grown into a tiny white ball. He could just begin to make out the black silhouette of the hulking mass behind it.

He tried one last time to move. His legs were tired, drained. They would not move.

He raised his arms over his head and began waving them frantically at the train.

Why doesn't the engineer stop?

He could hear the train now, the rumble and clang of it sounding more like some great metal monster than a mode of transportation.

The flashing red lights of the level crossing began blinking on and off. The bell rang *ding, ding, ding.*

And then the light at the front of the train quickly transformed into a big round disk, growing ever larger until it washed out everything in Gardner's world, bathing all of it in a bright, bright white.

Blinding him.

Just before impact, Gardner felt something press against him. It felt like a body. A woman's body. Breasts full and soft against the small of his back.

And something else.

A slight pressure against his right thigh, like a child taking hold of his leg. Holding on tight.

The train was upon him.

He screamed.

And the blinding white light turned black.

#

Susan sat in the rocking chair in the living room, knitting. The chair had been a gift from Gardner's parents. It was old and worn and a bit uncomfortable, but Susan loved it. What she looked forward to most of all was rocking in it while her child suckled at her breast. A simple pleasure, like knitting booties and sweaters and mittens.

But then, everything had been wonderful so far, not the least of which had been Gardner's attitude. He'd turned out to be more enthusiastic about the baby than she could have ever imagined. He was a good man. Helpful and supportive.

She knew, intuitively, that he'd be a good father to her child. It was one less thing to worry about and made the uncertainty about how their lives would change in four short months so much easier to handle.

She glanced at the clock.

It was getting late, but Susan wasn't concerned. She'd been married to a newspaper man far too long to start worrying whenever he didn't call or came home late.

She reached down for another ball of yarn when she heard something.

The scream.

She gave a little laugh.

I've finally heard it, she thought.

I can't wait to tell Gardner when he gets home.

Looking back on this collection with the clarity and wisdom of twenty-five years, it has become apparent to me that I was very interested in examining the family dynamic early in my writing career. "The Basement," "Mother and Child," "S.P.S." "No Kids Allowed," and "Afterlife" all seem to examine some aspect of marriage or the family unit, something I never noticed back in the day. The setting in this story is similar to where Roberta and I were living at the time it was written. The house was so close to the railway tracks and passed by so often, after a while you never even noticed the noise the trains made.

Rat Food

(with David Nickle)

Mrs. Puhn awoke with the sticky sweet taste of strawberry jam on her lips. She couldn't see out of one eye and for a moment was sure she'd lost it. But as quickly as the fear came, the eye slurped open as the rubbery seal of jam gave way around its lid. Mrs. Puhn blinked as the world came back into focus.

She'd fallen into the mess. On the linoleum floor in front of her, reddened shards of the old jam jar lay scattered. A moment before, Mrs. Puhn had been cleaning the refrigerator when the rat had brushed her leg. Now, the appliance's ancient coils hummed over her head, the light from its open door casting a weak yellow glow across the kitchen floor. The rat that had startled her was nowhere in sight.

Mrs. Puhn took a moment to feel out the rest of her body — it ached, there was no getting around that. Hands, arms, ankles, legs, ribs: they always hurt after a fall. At least no bones seemed to be broken, and there were no bruises for Patty to see.

"Just a fall," she said aloud. "Just a little fall."

She rolled onto her side. The jam had streaked the floor in slashes. There were intersecting trails through them, like footprints on either side of a puddle.

"Dear, dear," said Mrs. Puhn, taking a deep breath that filled her nostrils with the sweet smell of strawberries. "Rats!"

She rolled onto her stomach, hoping she wouldn't roll onto a piece of broken glass or get her dress too dirty with jam. It was a white dress and Patty had washed it the last time she'd been by. Was that last week or earlier? Mrs. Puhn wasn't sure. *Just last week*, she decided. *Patty went to the pharmacy to refill my prescription—and there's ten pills left in the container.*

Patty was Mrs. Puhn's only child and her only companion since all of her other friends had left the neighborhood. They'd all gone to "Retirement Homes" and hospitals, where their children had convinced them they'd be better taken care of.

But Mrs. Puhn would have none of that. *This is my home*, she'd say. *I've lived here all my life. What would I do anywhere else?*

Her next-door neighbor, Mrs. Franklin, had put up the same argument. But she eventually gave in to the pressures of family and "friends," and moved out last fall. Mrs. Puhn had watched her leave from the living room window, too terrified even to step out onto the stoop and tell her old friend goodbye.

Patty hadn't been too insistent that Mrs. Puhn join Mrs. Franklin. Of course Patty hadn't seen the rats and didn't know about the fainting spells. Those were Mrs. Puhn's little secrets, and as long as they stayed secret, Mrs. Puhn could stay on Sparroway Street.

Mrs. Puhn began the long and difficult task of getting back on her feet. She began by rolling onto her stomach and moving her hands and knees toward each other in a crawl. When she was finally on all fours, she reached for the kitchen table and pulled herself up.

Mrs. Puhn began cleaning. *Patty mustn't see a mess on the floor. And she mustn't see one of the rats—not a one.*

"She'd have me in a home by the end of the week," whispered Mrs. Puhn.

An hour later the kitchen was clean. It wasn't immaculate, but it would do. There were no signs of jelly on the floor or walls, and all the broken glass had been swept away. A thick smell of strawberries lingered. Mrs. Puhn hoped Patty would think it was the scent of some new air freshener.

After washing her face, Mrs. Puhn glanced at the clock and saw that her daughter wouldn't be arriving for another fifteen minutes. If Patty was anything, she was punctual; if she said she was coming by at one in the afternoon, then there would be a knock at the door at one.

Mrs. Puhn limped slowly back to her kitchen to make sure that everything was in order and that the rat was gone.

As she flicked on the light, she saw a rat's tail curl around the far corner of the cupboard.

"Oh, stay away, please!" she said in the humbled voice of one near defeat.

"Just for a little while. My daughter is coming by, and if she sees you she'll take me away."

Mrs. Puhn took a breath; the kitchen was silent.

She gave a satisfied nod and headed for the front door. She didn't want Patty to have to knock more than once. Too long to answer the door would get her talking about "Homes" as much as would the fainting spells or the enormous rats that had found their way into Mrs. Puhn's house in recent weeks.

Just out of the kitchen, Mrs. Puhn was struck by a thought so simple and perfect she had to stop and catch her breath.

What if the rats didn't have to come into the kitchen to look for food? I don't go to the market if I don't need anything. If the rats had all the food they needed, maybe they wouldn't come looking!

Mrs. Puhn placed a hand over her mouth. She wondered why she hadn't thought of it before.

She made her way back into the kitchen and set to work. After only a brief search, Mrs. Puhn had gathered an impressive larder for her rats: on top of the refrigerator there was a mottled black banana that she had forgotten about weeks before; in the cupboard under the sink, way at the back, was a four-year-old bag of dry cat food that hadn't been thrown out after Sweetie, Mrs. Puhn's pet Calico, was run over by a low rider in front of the house; inside the refrigerator was a green-tipped half of a cantaloupe that she'd meant to eat Sunday.

It was a meal fit for a—Mrs. Puhn giggled—*a rat!*

Mrs. Puhn knew where the rats came in. She'd tried blocking the hole where the radiator pipes came through the wall many times before, but each time she closed the hole the rats re-opened it, always making it bigger.

After awhile, Mrs. Puhn stopped trying. In a strange way, she found the rats' persistence flattering. Although one had given her a fright that afternoon, Mrs. Puhn realized there was really nothing to be afraid of. The rat had looked big, but it wasn't really. Only as big as a healthy cat. As big as her Sweetie had been.

Mrs. Puhn set the cantaloupe on the floor behind the radiator. Then she dropped the banana so that it landed on top of the cantaloupe without a sound. The cat food showered down onto the floor like hailstones. Mrs. Puhn shook the bag until it was empty.

When the knock came at the door, Mrs. Puhn dropped the bag on the floor and hurried out of the kitchen. She thought she might be able to reach the door before the second knock, but by the time she arrived at the little vestibule, the door was already swinging open. Mrs. Puhn stared at Patty, aghast.

Patty smiled and pulled the shiny new key out of the door lock. She held the key up and raised her hands in surrender. "Guilty. I'd meant to tell you about the house key; I had it made when you were in hospital last month, just in case . . . "

Mrs. Puhn was speechless. For the moment, any thoughts of the rats in her kitchen were forgotten. *This is my house! If you want inside, you can knock and wait until I answer the door, just—*

"—like everyone else."

Patty's expression made Mrs. Puhn instantly regret her words.

"I beg your pardon, Mother? Are you all right?"

Mrs. Puhn straightened the folds of her dress. As she did, she was sure she could hear crunching as the rats' tiny jaws tore into Sweetie's food. "I was only saying . . ." she said, hoping it was loud enough to mask the noises coming from the kitchen, ". . . if you want to visit me, you only have to knock. I'll come to the door."

"Ah." Patty nodded.

Mrs. Puhn pursed her lips. Her heart was racing, but she daren't give any indication of that. With great effort she tried to make her breath regular and smiled.

"Well, dear, now that you're here, why don't we sit down a moment?"

Patty smiled back. "All right. You go to the sitting room and I'll make us both some tea." She started toward the kitchen.

"Wait!" Mrs. Puhn closed her eyes. *Did I sound too anxious? Oh dear!* When she opened her eyes, Patty was standing in front of her, head tilted inquisitively.

"Mother?"

Mrs. Puhn took a breath. "I won't have you making tea in my kitchen. You are my guest, after all. You sit down and I'll have some tea and biscuits ready in no time."

Patty pressed her lips into a thin white line. "All right, Mother," she said. "Mother knows best."

Mrs. Puhn hated that phrase—*Mother knows best*—almost as much as she disliked the way Patty hugged her these days. *As though I were some frail old bird who'd crumble into dust the moment she squeezed me*. Mrs. Puhn stood between Patty and the kitchen until her daughter had respectfully moved into the sitting room and sat down on the sofa.

"There, now." Mrs. Puhn turned and made her way back to the kitchen. When she arrived, the kitchen was silent. Maybe it was Mrs. Puhn's imagination, but the whole room seemed cleaner, brighter.

"Good babies," she whispered as she filled the kettle. "Sleep now. Mummy will bring more food soon."

Turning on the stove, Mrs. Puhn remembered the cat food bag she'd dropped on the floor.

She didn't recall picking it up. Mrs. Puhn looked down at the empty floor and   frowned. She wasn't forgetful about things like that. *If Patty had seen that!*

"Why the little dears," she said aloud, laughing.

"Mother?" Patty called from the sitting room. "Are you all right?"

"I'm fine, dear," said Mrs. Puhn. "You just stay right there."

#

Patty stayed for another hour, and during that time mother and daughter played out the ritual of their visit to perfection. Mrs. Puhn asked how Patty's work at the Department of Transportation was going, and Patty filled some time talking about her co-workers and their tiny shifts in the office pecking order. Then came Patty's turn. She asked how her mother's health had been, asked if she'd been taking her medication, asked if she'd been eating properly and if those "black boys" across the street were giving her any trouble. Fine, yes, of course, and no, they're really dears, Mrs. Puhn answered. And then Mrs. Puhn asked if Patty was seeing any nice men these days, and it would be Mrs. Puhn's turn to watch her daughter squirm.

"Well Mother," said Patty finally. "I think it's time." She leaned over and gave Mrs. Puhn another one of her hugs— this one so light that Mrs. Puhn was sure Patty hadn't even touched her.

"I'm glad you dropped by," said Mrs. Puhn, hoisting herself up. Patty shushed her off with her hands—*Oh don't get up*, the gesture said. Mrs. Puhn ignored it and saw Patty to the door.

"See you in a week," said Patty as she got into her battered old Dodge and backed out of the drive. Mrs. Puhn waved and, when Patty was out of sigh, shut the door and went back to the kitchen. The smell of strawberries was thick and comforting.

"Now what," she wondered aloud, "might they like tomorrow?"

Mrs. Puhn sat down at the kitchen table   with   a scratch pad and pencil. With a shaky hand, she began to compose a list.

#

When she got home from the grocery the next day, Mrs. Puhn tipped the delivery boy a dollar and made an inventory of her purchase: seven tins of sardines (they'd been on sale for forty-nine cents each!); a carton of strawberries, only just beginning to soften (ninety-nine cents); a big wedge of Italian cheese (mice were supposed to like it; maybe rats would too); another bunch of bananas (they'd just gobbled up the first one, they'd be simply thrilled by a whole bunch); a bag of dry cat food; some chicken parts; a package of hamburger meat; and a liter of skim milk to wash it all down.

She nodded approvingly. There was more in the other three bags, but this should do for now.

Mrs. Puhn got up and started work. She cut the cheese into rat-sized portions and laid them out on the table. Then she took the bananas and carefully peeled each one. She took a big mixing bowl from the cupboard and poured the milk into that. As an afterthought, she dumped the carton of strawberries in the bowl, too. The milk sloshed over the rim and onto the table, but Mrs. Puhn didn't worry about the mess—Patty wouldn't be back for a whole week.

Mrs. Puhn opened up a can of sardines and set it next to one of the bananas. Then she tore the cellophane from the package of ground beef. She opened the cat food bag and gathered up a handful; with her other hand she scooped up some beef. "Chow chow chow," she sang, rolling the greasy meat together with the hard nuggets of cat food. Sweetie had so loved ground beef with her dinner; Mrs. Puhn was sure her little friends would, too.

Piece by piece, Mrs. Puhn brought the feast to the hole by the radiator. She set the bowl down on the kitchen floor, but dropped everything else behind the radiator. Perhaps, Mrs. Puhn thought, the rats had taken some of the food she'd left yesterday away to their lair; the linoleum was spotless.

Mrs. Puhn went back to the kitchen table and sat down.

She had to wait longer than expected, and for a moment she was sure the rats had taken their fill and gone off ungratefully to some other kitchen on the street. But Mrs. Puhn dismissed the thought with a smile and a shake of her head. *No. Not my rats*, she told herself. *They need me.*

Yet they still took their sweet time in coming. The sun had crept the length of the floor before the first pair of eyes appeared behind the radiator. Mrs. Puhn had begun to doze in the afternoon heat, but she perked right up when she saw those eyes.

"Are you the big fellow?" she asked aloud. "Did you give me that awful fright yesterday?"

The rat's eyes flashed orange, reflecting the sunlight back through the spaces between the radiator's fins. Mrs. Puhn took the gesture to mean *yes*.

There was a squishing sound as the rat sloshed through the food. She had to lean forward and squint to see, but Mrs. Puhn could just make out the black, hunched over back of the rat as it set hungrily to the cheese. Its tiny forepaws worked like hands, lifting the morsels up to its jaws, which gnawed at the food relentlessly. Mrs. Puhn nearly clapped with joy, but stopped herself—*Mustn't frighten the little fellow*—and placed her hands stoically across her lap.

Before long, a second pair of eyes appeared at the hole, then a third, and a fourth. *Wonderful.* Mrs. Puhn thought, *simply wonderful!*

She counted nine pairs of eyes before the first rat came out from behind the radiator to investigate the milk bowl. This rat wasn't as big as the first—it was more the size of a pet store rat, but its pelt was the matted grey of the wild.

The wild little rat didn't spare Mrs. Puhn a glance as it sniffed up to the bowl. After a second's consideration, it reared up on its hind legs, and—forepaws holding the bowl's rim for balance—touched it snout to the surface. It seemed to like the mixture, because it stayed there for almost a minute, lapping at the strawberry-flavored milk. The rat seemed to be having a hard time staying upright though, and Mrs. Puhn resisted the urge to pick it up and hold it over the bowl.

Other rats finally joined their little brother at the milk bowl. They flowed out from either side of the radiator and converged on the bowl in lines of twitching fur. The level of milk sank visibly lower, and Mrs. Puhn finally counted a total of six rats around the bowl's rim. That seemed to be as many as the bowl could handle, so others moved out across the floor, their tails flickering mischievously as they sniffed the corners and crannies of Mrs. Puhn's kitchen floor.

Mrs. Puhn couldn't contain her joy any longer. As Sweetie and her friends feasted, she clapped her hands and laughed. "Wonderful!" she squealed. "Simply wonderful!"

#

That night, Mrs. Puhn undressed and put on her favorite nightgown. Unlike the other gowns in her closet, she had bought this one for *herself* nearly ten years ago. Everything else in there Patty had picked out for her in a one-sided shopping spree last summer. "You can't go on wearing the same old things, you know," Patty had said.

Mrs. Puhn liked her same old things. This gown was long and soft, with adorable little frills trimming the collar—and most importantly *I bought it myself.*

She pulled back the bedspread and carefully lowered herself onto the mattress.

She settled back onto her pillow and turned out the lamp. The day had been *good*, and she felt warm inside. It was good to have Sweetie back again; she had been gone for far too long.

And as for Patty . . . If Mrs. Puhn were to be honest, it wouldn't be such a bad thing if Patty went away for good. After all, Mrs. Puhn reflected around a yawn, now that Sweetie was back it wasn't as though she didn't have friends.

#

A cool midnight breeze drifted in through Mrs. Puhn's bedroom window. It jostled the curtains, made a rattle over the bottles on her vanity, and whispered over Mrs. Puhn's sleeping lips. Her eyes fluttered open, and those lips flickered into a smile.

Something tumbled over her feet. *Sweetie*. She could feel the cat's agile little paws as they moved up her leg. Mrs. Puhn made a clucking sound. "Come here, Sweetie. I'll give baby a scratch."

Sweetie crawled onto Mrs. Puhn's stomach. "There," she murmured into the dark. "There's my little Sweetie." Mrs. Puhn reached down and found the cat's tiny ears. Sweetie had always loved to be scratched behind the ears; she'd sit still for hours if Mrs. Puhn could scratch that long.

Mrs. Puhn frowned. Sweetie had been into something. Her fur was slick with oil and the ends were matted. "Naughty girl," Mrs. Puhn said. With difficulty, she raised her head to see what Sweetie had done to herself.

The glittery pink eyes of a rat stared back from Mrs. Puhn's stomach. Its whiskers twitched twice, then stilled.

As she moved, it reared up, its thick body completely blocking the dim light from the window.

Mrs. Puhn screamed.

Not Sweetie, she whimpered inside. *Not cats, not friends!*

"Beastly, filthy rat!" Mrs. Puhn kicked and the rat jumped from her lap to the floor. Mrs. Puhn sat up—much too quickly.

A needle of pain moved up the left side of her body. Mrs. Puhn's eyes popped wide and she fell back into the bed.

Been foolish, been stupid. Ice flowed along her nerves. *They're rats! Carry disease!*

"Wicka," she sputtered, trying to move her lips to say *wicked*. But her mouth wouldn't work anymore. She fell back onto her side. Nothing worked anymore.

Something smart and knowledgeable in the back of her head whispered the word:

Stroke.

Mrs. Puhn watched as a string of saliva pooled on her pillow. The sharp stink of urine filled her nostrils.

She prayed the voice in her head was wrong.

#

Try as she might, Mrs. Puhn couldn't faint. She wanted to; she almost wanted to die rather than face time in her new prison. But it seemed as though her fainting reflex had been burned away as surely as had control over her arms, legs and head. Mrs. Puhn could swallow, she could nearly blink, and she could breath, but that was all her body could do.

Her mind, however, was another matter. If the stroke had muddled everything else while traveling its course, it had cleared and straightened her old woman's mind. And as the morning sunlight grew brighter, Mrs. Puhn had plenty of time to think.

Many of her thoughts came in the form of regrets. Why hadn't she paid attention to the fall in the kitchen? She remembered the loss of feeling then, and if she'd been smart she would have called Doctor Poulous and gone to the hospital. Older regrets came, too. Patty, whom Mrs. Puhn remembered having some affection for, had somehow become a woman to be lied to.

Other thoughts came too, though; and they were driven less by regret than by outright fear. Chief among them was the recurring picture of Mrs. Franklin and her long, sad march to the end of her driveway and the waiting taxi. Compared to Mrs. Puhn now, Mrs. Franklin's departure had been dignified. How would it be for Mrs. Puhn? She would be carried out of her home strapped to a stretcher—that's how. She could see herself as if looking out from her own living room window: her head cricked back, eyes twitching madly at the attendants, and a big sodden diaper wrapped around her middle to hold the stink inside.

And that would be the extent of the rest of her days.

Holding the stink inside.

And then there were the rats . . .

Mrs. Puhn let loose a broken, untapered moan. *The rats*. Her thoughts pointed to this as her greatest folly. These were creatures that scurried the sewers, that dined on refuse. Mrs. Puhn had granted them elixir, a taste of real food—kitchen food. How many of them had feasted in her kitchen last night?

At least one of them had stayed the night. What did her kitchen look like this morning? She hadn't even put away the rest of the groceries, she realized. The rats would fill their stomachs on those well enough, but what would they eat when they were gone? The old rat food? Rats weren't friends; they were animals, with animal hungers. Mrs. Puhn tried to shut her eyes, but the best she could do was squint. She couldn't cry, either, no matter how hard she tried.

As the day progressed, the sunlight shone directly through the window. It grew warm and sticky in the bedroom, as it always did during the summer.

Mrs. Puhn's thought kept coming back to the rats. What were they doing now? Had they gone back under the radiator? Was it too much to hope that they had left when their meal was finished, as they had the first time? Mrs. Puhn thought it unlikely.

There was a scurrying at Mrs. Puhn's feet. She caught her breath and tried to look down, but her eyes wouldn't move, at least not enough to do any good. *Have they finished the larder already? Are they tasting me now?*

A rat appeared in Mrs. Puhn's field of vision. It might have been the little fellow who'd first licked the milk bowl the night before. He seemed large from Mrs. Puhn's perspective, but he was nowhere near the size of the others.

The rat squeaked as it sniffed its way up to Mrs. Puhn's nose. She could feel the pinprick clutch of claws on the skin of her face, the scratch of whiskers against her eyeballs.

Mrs. Puhn moaned.

Then the rat moved down her face, and she felt its claws pulling against her slack lips. Something brushed against her teeth, tiny feet padded on her tongue. She tasted the musty salt-sulfur of rat-fur for an instant before the animal re-emerged. There was a soft thud as the rat landed on the carpet by her bed, and a diminishing scurry as if fled the room.

Mrs. Puhn tried to spit the taste from her mouth, but she couldn't. After trying for what seemed like hours, she finally swallowed, over and over until the rat taste went away.

#

In the heat of late afternoon, hope came to Mrs. Puhn. There was tingling in the third finger of her right hand, a tingle that built up to a sharp pain like a needle from Doctor Poulous and then vanished just as quickly. Mrs. Puhn's heart raced within her paralyzed chest. *Feeling!*

Gingerly, almost afraid to attempt it in case she failed, Mrs. Puhn lifted her finger. She couldn't see it, but she felt the movement against her nightgown.

The finger had definitely moved. Recovery was a possibility. But, Mrs. Puhn realized, not an imminent one. This was just a finger. It might take days, even weeks for her to regain the use of the rest of her body. How could she survive?

Hunger flared in Mrs. Puhn's belly, but died again at the recollection of the rat in her mouth.

She wouldn't be the only one who would be getting hungry.

#

The room grew dark.

Tears had finally come to Mrs. Puhn's eyes. How hungry would the rats be now? She'd been tasted; and once the kitchen food was gone, the rats would come to the bedroom, for a different kind of meal.

In the dim orange of twilight, the rats returned. Mrs. Puhn could hear them climbing the stairs in thumps and scurries, squeaking hungrily as they came. How many could there be? It sounded like a hundred, maybe a thousand—all the rats that had ever lived in the sewers beneath her home. Tears streamed down Mrs. Puhn's cheek and dampened her pillow. She didn't dare whimper.

The sounds grew louder. As they did, Mrs. Puhn was assaulted by a strong new stench. It came in a terrible wave. She squinted her eyes and wrung out the last tear.

A rat, heavy and clumsy, leaped onto the bed. Its long tail brushed against her leg, but it didn't stop there. It moved up along her torso, crawled over her arm and finally entered her field of vision.

The rat was holding something in its forepaws. *Oh sweet Lord*, Mrs. Puhn said to herself.

It was a rudely-rolled ball of ground beef, now darkened at the edges from the quickening warmth of the day.

The rat lumbered closer to Mrs. Puhn. It rolled the meatball against Mrs. Puhn's lips. It was nudged inside with the help of the rat's huge, tangy snout. Then it pulled back and looked at Mrs. Puhn expectantly.

The meat sat in Mrs. Puhn's mouth as she tried to spit. It tasted black and felt like mud on her tongue. Mrs. Puhn should have retched then, but she couldn't retch any more than she could spit. Instead, she smoothed the meat carefully with the back of her tongue. She swallowed. The mass clotted in her throat for an instant, then slid down her gullet. Mrs. Puhn gasped.

Satisfied, the rat turned and—tail whipping across Mrs. Puhn's face—humped off the bed. As fast as it was gone, another rat took its place. This one held a mass of pulp that had once been a strawberry. It went easily into Mrs. Puhn's mouth, and the rat didn't have to push it far before she swallowed.

More rats came, one after another, bringing all manner of feast. Strips of well-aged chicken; rat-sized pieces of cheese; nuggets of dried cat food (Sweetie's favorite); candle wax; a wad of cellophane; string from behind the stove; sardines, small and slick and easily swallowed; milk, kindly regurgitated by a huge pink fellow; and a banana, turned brown and soft in the heat.

The little dears, Mrs. Puhn thought. She would have to think of a way to thank Sweetie and her friends. It was a finer meal than Mrs. Franklin had likely eaten today; and as she ate, Mrs. Puhn was sure she was feeling better.

A rat brushed her hand and she felt a tickling on her palm.

Her finger moved. With all her strength, Mrs. Puhn lifted it, and oh so gently ran the tip along her Sweetie's snout.

This is the only piece of fiction I've ever done in collaboration with another writer. It happened while I was filling in at the *North York Mirror* newspaper for a woman who had gone on maternity leave. Dave Nickle, a reporter at the paper, who was also a fellow member of our writer's group (The Cecil Street Irregulars), had gotten me the job on an emergency fill-in basis. So, while at work, Dave and I would talk about the stories we were working on and I mentioned this idea I had for a story about an old woman who would feed the rats in her apartment so they wouldn't come around at the wrong times, like when people were visiting. I told him how I thought the story would end when he said words to the effect of, "You know what would be cool? If it went like this..." and the story immediately took flight. Now, this was at a time when computer word-processing programs weren't very good at talking to each other, so while we tried to email the story back and forth, we ended up having to meet in person to discuss changes to the story and implement them. Our first submission of the story was to *Borderlands 2* in 1990, where it was rejected. Then it went to four other markets before we submitted it to *Masques 5,* the next installment of the series of anthologies edited by J.N. (Jerry) Williamson. He didn't take the story -- and I'm not sure if there ever was a *Masques 5* -- but he did give us several pages of notes on how to make the story better. We took him up on almost all of his suggestions and then saw the story rejected six more times (including another submission to *Borderlands 5*). After a full six years of trying to sell the story to a horror market, we were out of ideas. And so, we sent it to the Canadian magazine *On Spec.* This proved to be a shrewd move as it gave us a legitimate reason to mail a hard copy of the story to every member of the Horror Writers Association so they might consider it for the Bram Stoker Award. It won the award in the short story category in 1997.

Baseball Memories

There was nothing wrong with Samuel Goldman's memory.

Not really.

Sam had a memory like most people when it came to regular things. He forgot the odd birthday or anniversary now and then, but no one ever thought him to be anything more than slightly absent-minded.

Sam remembered what he wanted to remember. His wife Bea could tell him a hundred times to take out the garbage, but he never took notice of her, especially when he was doing something important—like watching a baseball game on television.

Sam liked baseball, not just watching it, but everything about the game. He was a fan in the truest sense of the word—he was a fanatic. He was also a student of the game and, as a student, he studied it with a peculiar passion that made everything else in his life sometimes seem secondary. Sam was never absent-minded when it came to baseball. Where baseball was concerned, Sam's memory was an informational steel-trap, a vault containing all sorts of trivial information. Inside Sam's head were the numbers for hitting averages, home runs, stolen bases, RBIs, and ERAs for just about anybody who was or had been anything in the sport.

Sam's head for figures made him a great conversationalist at parties, and as long as the talk centered around his favorite subject he was a fine. Once he got his hands on someone who was willing to quiz him or be quizzed on baseball trivia, he never let them out of his sight. The only way to get rid of Sam at a party was to ask him how much he knew about hockey—which was nothing at all.

Some of Sam's friends began calling him "Pschyclo" because he was a walking, talking Encyclopedia of Baseball to which they could refer to at any time to clear up some finer point of the game. His friends would be sitting in a circle on the deck in Sam's back yard talking baseball over a few beers when some statistic would come under question and the discussion's decibel level would get turned up a few notches. It was up to Sam to turn the volume back down and restore order with the right answer.

"Sammy, what did George Bell hit on the road in 1986?"

".293," Sam would say without hesitation.

"And how many homers?"

"Sixteen of his thirty-one were hit on the road."

"See I told you . . ." one friend would say to another, proved correct by the circle's supreme authority.

Sam considered himself gifted. He thought that what he had was a natural talent for numbers, something that might, at the very least, get him on the cover of a magazine or onto some local talk show.

It had begun as a hobby, something he liked to do with a cup of coffee and a book late at night after the rest of the family had gone to bed. Lately, however, it had become something more, something abnormal if you asked Bea.

But even though Bea wasn't crazy about baseball or her husband's love affair with the game, she put up with it as most wives do with their husband's vices. She thought it was better for their marriage if Sam spent his nights at home with his nose buried in a baseball fact book instead of in a bar flirting with some woman with an "x" in her first name.

"As long as he sticks to baseball it's pretty harmless," she always said.

And then one day she began to wonder.

The two were sitting at the breakfast table one Saturday morning when Sam said something that put doubt in her mind about her husband's mental well-being.

"Why don't we take a drive up north today and visit your cousin Ralph?" he said.

Bea was shocked. She looked at Sam for several seconds as if trying to find some visible proof that he was losing his mind.

"Ralph died last winter, don't you remember? We went to the funeral; there was six inches of snow on the ground and you bumped into my mother's car in the church parking lot. She still hasn't forgiven you for it."

Sam was shocked, too. He could remember how many triples Dave Winfield hit the last three seasons but the death of his wife's cousin had somehow slipped his mind.

"Oh yeah, that's right. What the hell am I thinking about?" he said and then added after a brief silence. "I better go out and wash the car."

#

Things were fairly normal the next few weeks. Sam was still able to wow his friends with his lightning-fast answers and astounding memory. As long as baseball was in season Sam was one of the most popular guys around.

A co-worker of Sam's even figured out a way to make money with his head for figures. Armed with *The Sports Encyclopedia of Baseball*, they'd go out to some bar where nobody knew about Sam and bet some sucker he couldn't stump Sam with a question.

"Who led the Cleveland Indians in on-base percentage in 1952?" the sucker would ask, placing a ten-dollar bill on top of the bar.

"Larry Doby, .541, good enough to lead the American League that year," Sam would answer. After a quick check in the encyclopedia, the two had a little pocket change for the week.

Sam was astonished at the financial rewards his talent had brought him. He had always thought himself something of an oddball, but if he could make some money at it—tax free to boot—then why the hell not. The prospect of riches made him study the stats even harder, always looking to increasingly older baseball publications to make sure he knew even the most trivial statistic.

"Well would you look at that," he would say as his eyes bore down on the page and his brain went through the almost computerlike process of defining, processing and filing another little known fact. It took less than ten seconds for him to remember forever that a guy by the name of Noodles Hahn led the Cincinnati Reds pitching staff in 1901 with a 22-19 record. Hahn pitched 41 complete games that year and had two-hundred-and-thirty-nine strikeouts to lead the league in both categories. No mean feat considering the Reds finished last that season with a 52-87 record.

The information was stored in a little cubby hole deep within Sam's brain and could be recalled anytime, like a book shelved in a library picked up for the first time in fifty years. The book, a little dusty perhaps, would always tell the same story.

#

Bea went to see Manny Doubleday, their family physician, the morning after Sam did another all-nighter with his books.

While it was true Sam had bought her some fine things since he'd been making money in bars, Bea felt the items were bought with tainted money. The fur coat had been hanging in the hall closet since the day Sam had bought it for her—not because it was the middle of summer, but because she was ashamed of it. She never showed it to guests, even those who might have thought Bea the luckiest girl in the world—and Sam the greatest husband.

Bea sat quietly in Doctor Doubleday's private office, waiting. The office was decorated like a tiny corner of Cooperstown. On the walls hung various team photos and framed press clippings about Manny Doubleday in his heyday. On the desk were baseballs signed by Mickey Mantle and Hank Aaron, even one signed by Babe Ruth, although the authenticity of it came under suspicion since the "Bambino" had signed his name in crayon.

From down the hall the doctor's melodic whistling of "Take me out to the ball game" pierced through the space made by the slightly ajar door. Moments later the door burst open and in strode the portly doctor. Doctor Doubleday had been the Goldman's family physician for what seemed like forever. He delivered both Sam and Bea into the world and always looked upon the couple's marriage as a match made by his own hands. He was also a former minor league pitcher and big baseball fan, something that had cemented a friendship between the doctor and Sam since Sam was a teenager. The doctor knew of Sam's ability to remember statistics and thought it was simply wonderful.

"What seems to be the problem, Bea?" he asked, picking up a dormant baseball from his desk and wrapping his fingers around it as if to throw a split-fingered fastball right over the plate.

"It's Sam, I think he's—"

"How is the old dodger?" the doctor interrupted as he took a batter's stance and pretended to swing through on a tape measure home run. "You know I've never seen anyone with a memory like his. It's uncanny the way he can tell you anything you want to know at the drop of a hat."

"Yes, that's what I mean. I think he's overdoing it a bit," Bea said, sitting up on the edge of her chair anxious to hear some words of support.

"Nonsense," replied the doctor.

Bea slumped back in her chair.

"What your husband has is a gift. He has a photographic memory that he's chosen to use for recording baseball statistics. It's harmless."

"It used to be harmless. He used to do it in his spare time, but now he's obsessed with it. He lets other things slide just so he can cram his head with more numbers. He's beginning to forget things."

"Bea," the doctor said, putting down his invisible bat. "Forget for a minute that I'm your doctor and consider this a discussion between two friends. Most people are able to use about ten percent of the brain's full capacity. Your husband has somehow been able to tap in and exceed that ten percent. Maybe he's using twelve or thirteen percent, I don't know, but it happens. He could be making millions at the blackjack tables in Atlantic City, but he chose to use his gift for baseball. Just be happy it's occupying him instead of something more dangerous. I'll talk to him the next time he's in. How are the kids?"

Bea was brought sharply out of her lull and answered in knee-jerk fashion. "Fine, and yours?"

#

She was satisfied, but marginally. It was one thing for the doctor to talk about Sam's mind in the comfort of the office, it was another thing entirely to sit at the dinner table and watch Sam try to eat his soup with a fork.

"Honey," she'd say. "Why don't you try using your spoon? You'll finish the soup before it gets cold."

"Yeah, I guess your *right-handed batters versus lefties*," Sam would reply and then sit silently for a few moments. "Did I say that? Sorry Bea, I don't know where my head is."

Sam knew he was spending a little too much time with his baseball books. He was weary of the numbers and after a couple hours study some nights the inside of his skull pounded incessantly and felt as if it might explode under the growing pressure. But he loved the game too much to give it up.

Besides, the money he earned on the bar circuit was too good to give up. It was so good in fact that he could probably put the kids through college with his winnings — something he could never do just working at his regular job.

Sam worked as an airplane mechanic in the machine shop at the local airport. He was good at his job and always took the time to make sure it was done right.

One day he was drilling holes in a piece of aluminum to cover a wing section they had been working on. The work was monotonous, so Sam occupied his time thinking about the previous night's study.

Pete Rose hit .273 his rookie year, .269 his second, .312 his third . . .

The drill bit broke and Sam was brought back into the machine shop. He stopped the press, replaced the bit, tightening it with the key.

Lou Gehrig hit .423 in thirteen games for New York in 1923, .500 in ten games in 1924, .312 in his first full season in 1925 . . .

Sam started the drill press and the key broke free of its chain, flew across the shop and hit another mechanic squarely on the back of the head.

He was once again brought into reality. He shut the drill off and rushed over to see if his co-worker was still alive. A crowd had gathered around the prone man and all eyes were on Sam as he neared the scene.

"What the hell were you thinking of?"

"You gotta be more careful."

"That was pretty stupid."

The other mechanics were crowing at him in unison and Sam felt like a baseball that had been used too long after its prime. His insides felt chopped up and unraveled as he looked at the man lying on the floor.

A groan escaped the downed man's lips. "What the hell was that?" he asked. The crowd around him let out a collective sigh. Sam felt better, too, but just slightly. The shop foreman walked up to him, placed a comforting hand on his shoulder and told him to go home.

"Why don't you take the rest of the day off, before he gets up off the floor and these guys turn into a lynch mob."

"Sure boss. I'll go *home run leaders for the past twenty years.*"

"What?"

"Nothing, nothing. I don't know what I was thinking of."

#

On the way home, Sam stopped by The Last Resort, a local sports bar with big screen TV and two-dollar draughts. He needed a drink.

After what happened at the shop, Sam thought he might be going crazy. Baseball trivia was fun, but if it turned him into an accident waiting to happen he might as well forget all about his baseball memory.

He sat on a stool in front of the bartender and eased his feet onto the brass foot-rail. Comfortable, he ordered the biggest draught they had.

As he sipped the foam off the top of the frosted glass, he overheard a conversation going on down at the other end of the bar.

"Willie Mays was the best player ever to play the game, and believe me, I know . . . I know everything there is to know about the greatest game ever invented."

Sam watched the man speak for a long time. He stared at him, trying to see right through his skull and into the folds of his brain. Sam wanted to know just how much this blow-hard really knew.

"Go ahead, ask me anything about the game of baseball, anything at all. I'll tell you the answer. Heck, I'll even put ten dollars on the bar here—if you stump me it's yours."

"How many home runs did Hank Aaron hit in his first major league season?" asked Sam as he carried his beer down the bar toward the man.

"Awe, that's easy, thirteen, Milwaukee, 1954. I want some kind of challenge."

"All right, then. In what year did Nolan Ryan pitch two no hitters and who did he pitch them against?"

"Another easy one. Nolan Ryan was pitching for the California Angels and beat Kansas City 3-0, May 15, and Detroit 6-0, July 15, 1973."

Sam was startled. No hitters were something he'd studied just the night before. This guy was talking about them like they were old news.

"Okay, now it's my turn," the man said, massaging his cheeks between his thumb and forefinger. "But first, would you care to put a little money on the table?"

"Take your best shot," Sam answered, slamming a fifty-dollar bill down on the bar.

"Well, fifty bucks," the man said, impressed. "That deserves a fifty-buck question!"

The man looked into Sam's eyes. A little sweat began to bead on Sam's forehead but he was still confident the bozo had nothing on him.

"Okay, then. Who was the Toronto Blue Jays' winning pitcher in their opening game 1977, and what was the score?"

Sam smiled, he knew that one. But suddenly something about the way the other man looked into his eyes made his mind draw a blank. It was as if the man had reached inside and pulled the information out of Sam's head before Sam had gotten to it. The beads of sweat on Sam's forehead grew bigger.

"I'm waiting," said the man, enjoying the tension. "Awe, c'mon, you know that one. I only asked it so you'd give me a chance to win my money back."

Sam closed his eyes and concentrated. Inside his brain, pulses of electricity scrambled through the files searching for the information, but all pulses came back with the same answer.

"I don't know," said Sam finally.

"Too bad. It was Bill Singer, April 7, 1977, 9-5 over Chicago. Fifty bucks riding on it, too. Better luck next time, pal."

The man picked up the money and walked out of the bar. Sam stood in silence. He'd never missed a question like that before—never! He finished his draught in one big gulp and ordered another.

#

Sam said nothing about the incident to Bea over dinner. He ate in silence, helped his wife with the dishes and told her to enjoy herself bowling with the girls.

When she was safely out of the driveway, Sam dove into his books. He vowed never to be made fool of again and intensified his study. He looked up Bill Singer and put the information about him back on file in his head. He studied hundreds of pitchers and after a few hours their names became a blur.

Noodles Hahn, Cy Young, Ambrose Putnam, Three Finger Brown, Brickyard Kennedy, Kaiser Willhelm, Smokey Joe Wood, Wild Bill Donovan, Twink Twining, Mule Watson, Homer Blankenship, Chief Youngblood, Clyde Barfoot, Buckshot May, Dazzy Vance, Garland Buckeye, Bullet Joe Bush, Boom Boom Beck, Bots Nickola, Jumbo Jim Elliot, George Pipgrass, Schoolboy Rowe, Pretzels Puzzullo, General Crowder, Marshall Bridges, Van Lingle Mungo, Boots Poffenberger, Johnny Gee, Dizzy Dean, Prince Oana, Cookie Cuccurullo, Blackie Schwamb, Stubby Overmire, Webbo Clarke, Lynn Lovenguth, Hal Woodeshick, Whammy Douglas, Vinegar Bend Mizell, Riverboat Smith, Mudcat Grant, John Boozer, Tug McGraw, Blue Moon Odom, Rollie Fingers, Billy McCool, Woody Fryman, Catfish Hunter, Vida Blue, Goose Gossage, Rich Folkers, Gary Wheelock.

Sam slammed the book shut. His head was spinning.

He felt like he couldn't remember another thing, not even if the survival of baseball itself depended on it.

But then a strange thing happened.

Sam swore he heard a clicking sound inside his head. His brain felt as if it buzzed and whirred and was suddenly lighter.

He reopened the book and looked at a few more numbers. He took them in, closed the book once more and recited what he had learned.

"We're back in business," Sam said out loud and returned, strangely refreshed, to the world of statistical baseball.

Bea came home around eleven o'clock and found Sam in the den asleep with his face resting on a stack of books.

"Doesn't he ever get enough?" she muttered under her breath and poked a finger into his shoulder, trying to wake him.

"Huh, what . . . Phil Niekro, Atlanta Braves 1979, 21-20 at the age of 40. Gaylord Perry, San Diego Padres 1979, also 40, 12-11 . . . "

"Sam, wake up! Isn't it time you gave it a rest and went to bed?" Bea said, pulling on his sleeve, hoping to get him out of his chair.

"Who are you?" asked Sam, looking at Bea as if they were meeting in a long narrow alleyway somewhere late at night.

"Well, I'll say one thing for you, Sam, you still have your sense of humor. C'mon, time for bed."

"Which way is the bedroom?" Sam asked. He thought his surroundings familiar but wasn't too clear about their details.

"Into the dugout with you," Bea said, caught up in the spirit of the moment. "Eight innings is more than we can ask from a man your age!"

After the two were finally under the covers, Sam lay awake for a few minutes looking the bedroom over. The pictures on the wall looked familiar to him and he thought he might be in some of them.

Comfortable and exhausted, he finally dozed off.

#

Sam's brain was hard at work while the rest of his body rested in sleep.

It had started with a faint click but now his brain hummed and buzzed with activity. After being bombarded with information over the past months, every available cubby-hole in Sam's brain had been filled. There wasn't room for one more ERA, one more home run, not even one more measly single.

But like an animal that has adapted to its environment over the course of generations, Sam's brain was evolving, too, and decided it was time to clean house.

The torrent of information it had been receiving must be essential to the survival of the species, the brain reasoned. Why else would so many names and numbers be needed to be filed away? So the brain began a systematic search of every piece of information previously stored, from birth to present, and if it did not resemble the bits of information the brain was receiving on a daily basis, out the window it would go.

Sam's brain decided it wasn't essential that he remember how to use the blow-torch at work, so the information was erased to open up new space for those supremely important numbers.

By the time Sam awoke, a billion cubby holes had been swept clean.

Sam walked sleepily toward the kitchen where Bea already had breakfast on the table.

"What's that?" Sam asked, pointing at a yellow semi sphere sitting on a perfect white disk.

"Are you still goofing around," Bea answered. "Hurry up and eat your grapefruit or you'll be late for work."

Sam watched Bea closely, copying her movements exactly. He decided he liked the yellow semi-sphere called grapefruit and every bite provided a brand new taste sensation on his tongue. Sam's brain couldn't be bothered to remember what grapefruit tasted like, not even for a second.

Bea helped Sam get dressed for work because he said he couldn't remember which items on the bed were the ones called pants and which were the ones called shirts.

Bea decided she'd speak to Dr. Doubleday the moment she got Sam out of the house and insist he come by and give Sam a check-up. She nearly threw Sam out the door in her rush to call the doctor.

As the door of the house closed behind him, Sam tried to remember just exactly where he worked and what it was he did for a living.

He also wanted to go back to The Last Resort and show that joker at the bar that Sam Goldman was no fool.

If only he could remember how to get there.

"Baseball Memories," was the fourth story I wrote and the first story accepted for publication. It was written on the computers of *The Brampton Times* newspaper (where I had been a sports reporter) in what has become my hometown of Brampton, Ontario. Anyway, after writing the story I searched the *Short Story Writer's Market* that was published annually by Writer's Digest and found a literary magazine called *Aethlon: The Journal of Sports Literature* published out of East Tennessee State University. Luckily, after its publication I sent a copy of the story to Karl Edward Wagner and he selected it for reprint in *Year's Best Horror Stories XX*. A great honor and one I compare to a ball player hitting a homerun in his first major league at bat.

To Be More Like Them

She got onto the school bus, took her usual spot directly behind the driver, then sunk down in the seat until she knew she couldn't be seen by the kids at the back.

Those were the popular kids.

The cool kids.

And although they were as far away from her as the bus would allow, they were never far from her thoughts. In fact, they were always on her mind, gnawing at it like rats on cheese.

Her name was Sherry Lace. A decidedly beautiful name, one that she'd been proud of as a little girl.

"What's your name, honey?'

"Sherry Lace."

"My but isn't that pretty?"

"Uh-huh."

"Aren't you going to knock them dead when you get older?'

"Uh-huh."

A pretty name, except that it just happened to rhyme with Scary Face, which is what all the kids called her now. Although the nickname rhymed with her own, they weren't being clever. It didn't take much thought or imagination to turn Sherry Lace into Scary Face when she had a scar that started just under her right eye, went across the tip of her nose, and curved around her cheek all the way to her left ear.

In addition to the skin, several muscles had been cut and nerve endings damaged, and although the scar had already had six months to heal, it still looked red and fresh. It was sore too, making it painful for her to talk and agony for her to laugh. It hurt even to smile.

It also made it hard for her to out in public. She would have dropped out of school if they'd let her, but all the adults had convinced her to tough it out, saying it wouldn't be that bad.

But it was that bad. Worse than bad. Every day was a nightmare.

"It's getting better every day, hon."

"A little bit of make-up and you can hardly tell."

"The kids will understand."

Yeah, right.

The kids understood. They understood that she was a freak, a monster, a walking wound.

Scary Face, they called her, to her face and behind her back. They understood just fine, and they wanted nothing to do with her.

She was on the outside, looking in.

She had always been there too, even before the scar.

She'd never been pretty enough to be part of the cool group. She'd never been smart enough to be one of the brainers. And she'd never had the physical strength or coordination to be an athlete. She'd dressed in black, thinking she might be able to join the goths, but they didn't want her either, which hurt most of all, since most of them were rejects from other cliques themselves.

Even the geeks teased her, as if they knew that by teasing her, they would deflect some of the ridicule from themselves, be part of a group, no membership required. All you had to be able to do was laugh at your classmate and sleep soundly through the night.

Everyone was part of that group—everyone but her.

The bus came to a stop and four more kids got on. The bus was filling up now, and space was getting tight. One of the boys getting on—Bill, she thought his name was—searched the length of the bus for an empty seat.

She moved over to make room for him, but he just kept standing there, looking for an empty seat with the others farther down the bus.

"Sit down," said the driver.

"But I—"

"Sit down!" the driver repeated, this time with even more authority.

With a sigh, Bill sat down next to her, not looking too pleased about having to sit next to Scary Face.

Maybe he thinks he'll catch something, she mused, like a scar. Or maybe he'll be contaminated by the loser bug and suddenly find himself with her, on the outside looking in.

"Billy," whispered a voice behind her.

She wanted to turn around to see who was talking, but she knew that if she did, one of the kids at the back would greet her with an angry look and the words, "What are you looking at, ugly?' It was so much easier to do nothing.

When the bus came to a stop at the next light, Bill was gone, hurrying down the aisle before the bus started moving or the driver noticed he was out of his seat.

And so she was alone again. It was actually better this way. After the brief moment of hope was gone—the one in which she thought that maybe, just maybe, he was sitting next to her because he wanted to, or because, hey, it was no big deal – when that moment was gone it had become painful to have him sitting next to her, knowing that he'd rather be somewhere else, anywhere else, even under the wheels, instead of sitting up at the front of the bus, behind the driver and next to Scary Face.

"God, how could you stand it, being next to *her*," they would say when he finally reached the others. "How could you stand it?"

It made her laugh as much as it made her cry.

If they couldn't handle being in the seat next to her, then what would they do if they found themselves not in the seat next to her but in *her* seat, in her shoes . . .

In her face.

#

The school day began much like every other—alone and in silence. She made a trip to her locker, put her lunch away and grabbed the books she'd need for the morning's classes.

Her locker was close to the door, so it was easy for her to slip into the school unnoticed, but her homeroom was at the other end of the building and getting there was like running a gauntlet each morning. Most of the kids would just whisper "Scary Face," bark like dogs, or make noises like they were about to throw up. They did it so often that she hardly heard them anymore. Sometimes, however, they could be even more cruel.

She was halfway to homeroom when it happened.

"Hey, Scary Face," someone called out. "What happened? Cut yourself shaving?"

Roars of laughter.

Her face turned red. Her scar began to throb.

The first impulse was always to run away, but she refused to do it. She'd never run from anything in her life, and she wasn't about to start now. She wanted to scream out, confront whoever it was who'd said that, but she'd done that only once before.

"Who said that?"
Whispers and giggles
"Who was it?'
Silence.
"Like I thought. To chicken-hearted to say it to my face."
"Better to have a chicken heart than a hamburger face."
More laughter.
"Scary Face. Scary Face. Scary Face."

Her lesson learned, she remained still and silent, taking it all in.

There were whispers up and down the hallway, and the words "Scary Face" seemed to linger in the air like smoke.

How could they be so cruel? How could they be so relentless in their abuse? She'd often asked herself these questions while she lay awake at night, staring at the ceiling.

The hallway slowly came back to life, with the giggles and laughter bubbling up from the bottom of the whispers until someone, maybe the one with the big mouth, began howling with laughter.

The scar throbbed in pain, felt as if it had opened up and was dripping blood down her cheek. She moved forward through the crowd, heading for her homeroom, but was happy just to make it to the bathroom and a stall before she broke down and cried.

Imagine, she thought. I'd wanted to be more like them.

And that's when something happened inside.

The ached in her heart turned itself off, like a light switch that illuminates a room one minute then leaves it in total darkness the next.

Suddenly, there was no more pain. No more tears.

She felt as if a weight had been lifted from her shoulders. The heat was gone and the scar no longer throbbed. She went back out into the hall, and for a moment, she imagined herself walking not though a hallway full of students, but through a forest of dead trees and barren soil.

It brought a smile to her face.

Even though it pained her, she smiled broadly at them all, baring her teeth in a sort of sneer.

And the noise in the hallway slowly died down until it was deathly silent, as if everyone knew that...

Something had gone drastically wrong with the routine.

#

She hadn't always had the scar.

And while she'd never really been pretty, she had looked good enough to hope that puberty might somehow transform her into a beautiful woman.

After all, her mother had been a beauty.

But her looks had been lost too, the same night she'd got the scar.

That night, her father had come home drunk. He'd done something stupid like lose his job, gamble away his paycheck, or total the car. Who knew what the problem was -- it didn't matter anyway. The important thing was that he'd come home drunk, and that things would go one of two ways. He would either head upstairs, fall onto the bed, and sleep it off, or he would come into the living room looking for a fight.

Turned out to be the latter.

He'd stumbled to the doorway, leaned shakily against the frame, and said, "What the hell are you looking at?"

"Nothing."

Whether her mother had meant it sarcastically or not, Sherry was never certain. Her father had sure taken it to be a jab, however, and in minutes her parents were screaming at each other at the top of their voices, using words and calling each other names that Sherry had been told never to say herself.

While the two went at it, she had tried to sink into the couch, hoping that this fight wouldn't last too long. But the row wasn't showing any signs of ending. Instead, it was getting worse. They'd moved into the kitchen, and things were getting broken. They were pushing each other, and if it didn't stop soon, someone was going to get hurt... worse than usual.

And then her mother had screamed. "Put that down!"

There was fear in her voice.

Real terror.

Sherry had jumped off the couch and run into the kitchen in time to see her father standing there with a six-inch knife in his hand. He was slashing it wildly back and forth in front of her mother, getting closer to her throat with each swing.

"No. Dad. Stop!" she'd cried.

And then her father had turned to look at her. The knife had flashed across her field of vision. There was intense heat across her face, and then wet warmth running down her cheeks.

And the fight was over.

Her mother had ridden with her in the ambulance.

She'd never seen her father again.

She'd heard that he'd been roughed up pretty bad in prison. Apparently, inmates didn't relate all that well to guys who cut up their own kids.

So maybe some good had come of it.

The doctors who had sewn up her face had said that in another year, they'd be able to do some work on the scar to make it less noticeable. They'd also sent her to visit a woman who specialized in makeup for people with skin conditions and facial deformities.

Sherry had gone to see her once, but the makeup had felt heavy on her skin, had cracked when she smiled and had left the scar red and raw the next day.

She'd cried for a long time after that.

Even the lady who fixed up freaks couldn't help her.

#

That night Sherry slept like a baby, the smile still lingering on her face.

In the morning, she got onto the bus refreshed and looking forward to the day. She took her usual spot directly behind the driver, but now she sat so that her head and shoulders rose up over the seat and would be in full view of the kids at the back of the bus.

If they teased her today, that would be fine with her. It might as well be today, in fact, seeing as it would be one of their last chances to do it.

After today, things were going to be different.

"Hey, Scary Face!" someone called from the back of the bus.

Sherry ignored the comment, wondering why no one could think of something better. Maybe she could come up with something, mention it to a few kids, and see if it spread through the school. Something catchy like Slice Girl, or Scarlet.

Very cool.

"Scary Face," somebody whispered behind her.

Sherry turned around and smiled.

The kid behind her looked surprised at the move, his eyes growing wide with just a hint of fear.

Good, thought Sherry. Get used to it, kid. There'll be plenty more where that came from.

The kid looked away, unable to stare into Sherry's eyes for more than a few seconds. Sherry's smile widened, and she turned back around in her seat. As the bus pulled away from the stop, she slipped her hands into her knapsack and ran her fingers along the handle, then traced a finger down to the plastic cover sheathing the blade.

The police had taken the knife as evidence, then had given it back to her and mother other a few months later when the trial was over and they didn't need it anymore. At the time, Sherry had wondered why the police thought they'd want the knife back, but now she was glad they'd returned it.

She had tried to be more like them, like the kids on the bus and the kids in her school, but none of them could look past the scar and see the girl behind it. They wouldn't let her into their world because of the way she looked.

She closed the fingers of her right hand around the knife's rough wooden handle and slid the plastic cover off the blade with her left.

The bus pulled into the school and stopped.

The doors opened up to the schoolyard.

She had wanted to be more like them, but that had been wrong. She knew that now.

She tightened her grip on the knife and got off the bus.

She could never be like *them,* but maybe she could make them a little more like *her.*

This was one of my first attempts at writing for young adults, which would eventually lead down the path of me writing the novel Wolf Pack, which almost 20 years after publication became the basis for a television series on Paramount Plus. But I digress... The idea for this story sprung from my time working as a School Bus driver (a job I did for three years and was a terrific compliment to my work as a full-time fiction writer) where I would see young adults be absolutely cruel to one another, especially those that they decided were weak and wouldn't push back when bullied. It plays on the idea that we all want to be accepted, liked, and to fit in, which is not always possible no matter how much someone wants it. I'm particularly proud of the ending and always enjoyed the reaction I got when reading it to school-aged children, a seemingly slow realization that the shit was about to hit the fan.

About the Author

Edo van Belkom is the author and editor of some 35 books and over 300 short stories of horror, science fiction, fantasy, and mystery. His short fiction has been published in countless anthologies such as Year's Best Horror Stories, Year's Best Erotica, Robert Bloch's Psychos, the Hot Blood and Shock Rock series, as well as several anthologies based on RPGs. His story "Rat Food" (with David Nickle) won the Bram Stoker Award from the Horror Writers Association, and "Hockey's Night In Canada" won the Aurora Award, Canada's top prize for speculative fiction.

Most recently, his Silver Birch and Aurora Award-winning young adult series Wolf Pack has served as the inspiration for the Jeff Davis supernatural TV show Wolf Pack, starring Sarah Michelle Gellar, which premiered worldwide on Paramount Plus in January 2023.

Books by Edo van Belkom

The *Wolf Pack* Series*
Wolf Pack
Lone Wolf
Cry Wolf
Wolf Man

* This series has served as the inspiration for the Jeff Davis supernatural TV series Wolf Pack on Paramount Plus

Other Novels
Wyrm Wolf
Lord Soth
Mister Magick
Army of the Dead
Teeth
Martyrs
Scream Queen
Blood Road
Battle Dragon
Kilgore and Co.

Mark Dalton, Owner Operator
SmartDriver
Trouble Load
On Ice
Highway Robbery and Other Stories
Reefer Madness and Other Stories

Collections
Death Drives a Semi
Six Inch Spikes

Non-Fiction
Northern Dreamers
Writing Horror
Writing Erotica

Anthologies
Be Afraid!
Be Very Afraid!
Aurora Awards
Northern Horror
Tesseracts 10*
(with Robert Charles Wilson)

Milton Keynes UK
Ingram Content Group UK Ltd.
UKHW011308180224
438033UK00001B/4